KU-524-887

The Swap

Also by Fiona Mitchell

The Maid's Room

9510000230723

FIONA MITCHELL

The Swap

HODDER &
STOUGHTON

First published in Great Britain in 2019 by Hodder & Stoughton
An Hachette UK company

1

Copyright © Fiona Mitchell 2019

The right of Fiona Mitchell to be identified as the Author
of the Work has been asserted by her in accordance with the
Copyright, Designs and Patents Act 1988.

All rights reserved. No part of this publication may be
reproduced, stored in a retrieval system, or transmitted, in any form
or by any means without the prior written permission of the publisher,
nor be otherwise circulated in any form of binding or cover other
than that in which it is published and without a similar condition
being imposed on the subsequent purchaser.

All characters in this publication are fictitious and any resemblance
to real persons, living or dead, is purely coincidental.

A CIP catalogue record for this title is
available from the British Library

Hardback ISBN 978 1 473 65966 7
Trade Paperback ISBN 978 1 473 65967 4
eBook ISBN 978 1 473 65964 3

Typeset in Plantin by Palimpsest Book Production Limited,
Falkirk, Stirlingshire

Printed and bound in Great Britain by Clays Ltd, Elcograf S.p.A.

Hodder & Stoughton policy is to use papers that are natural,
renewable and recyclable products and made from wood grown in
sustainable forests. The logging and manufacturing processes
are expected to conform to the environmental regulations
of the country of origin.

Hodder & Stoughton Ltd
Carmelite House
50 Victoria Embankment
London EC4Y 0DZ

www.hodder.co.uk

For my mum and dad, with love

Prologue

The woman is lying on the trolley, her legs stirruped, fingers laced together on top of her clinic gown.

'Annie Perry, date of birth, 5.6.1984?' Doctor Michael, beside her, asks.

As Mark tightens his grip on his clipboard – he heard that surname earlier – the door opens a notch.

'Doctor Michael, could you come down to treatment room 3 please?' a female voice calls.

A crease forms in Doctor Michael's forehead, as though someone has nicked it with a knife. He turns towards the door.

'We're about to do a transfer here.'

'It's a matter of urgency.'

He climbs to his feet with a sigh. 'Okay. Mark, would you prepare the embryos for Ms Perry's transfer?'

It's the third time today that Doctor Michael has asked him to get the embryos from an incubator alone, even though clinic guidelines state that doctors should do everything in tandem, one watching over the other as they manipulate sperm and eggs and move embryos from one part of the lab to another. Work has already begun to install videocams in each lab to watch out for mistakes, but this lab doesn't have one yet.

Mark's ears are ringing as he goes into the lab; his headache is getting worse. *Hamilton. Elliott. Perry* – here's the incubator belonging to the woman in her forties who underwent a transfer earlier. He looks at his clipboard; she was Tess Perry. Doctor Michael had mumbled his way through her name and date of birth, and the woman had tried so hard to hold herself still that she'd been shaking with tension.

Mark scrutinises the label on the incubator door. *A. Perry.* Scrawls and loops and squiggles; it's not easy to read, but it's definitely an A not a T, he can see that only now. He opens Annie Perry's incubator: it's empty.

He checks the front of all the incubators again. There on the bottom right, he finds an incubator labelled with the name, *T. Perry.* He opens the door. Two petri dishes sit on the middle shelf. Two petri dishes that shouldn't be there.

He'll have to go out there and tell Annie, the other Ms Perry, that her embryos have been transferred into another woman.

But back in the treatment room Annie's eyes widen at the sight of the petri dishes in his trembling hands, as if he is holding live twins.

He tries to ignore his pounding heart, the sour, dry taste on his tongue, but already the guilt is a stone in his chest and it's getting heavier.

Part One

Chapter 1

He's the kind of child you want to give back. The thought floats uninvited to the surface of Tess' head. She clenches the steering wheel tighter, the burnt skin stretched pink over the knuckles of her hand.

Freddie, in the back seat behind her, slams his foot into the base of her spine. 'Are we there yet?'

'Almost.'

No one would be able to tell from the tone of her voice that she doesn't like her two-year-old son. The thought makes her feel ashamed. She can't see him in the rearview mirror, only Ruby beside him, cuddling her toy rabbit, her curls the colour of butter.

Freddie thrums his fingers against the glass, and Tess' breath follows suit. Any second now, there'll be a burp, a roar, another question. The diamond pendant tucked beneath her silk blouse bangs her chest like a nervous tic.

A snatch of Lady Gaga booms from the rolled-down window of a passing car. Tess switches on the heating and turns it up to full. The oranges on the passenger seat wobble, releasing their fresh scent. A large bottle of water sloshes in the footwell.

She stops at the traffic lights and snatches up her mobile phone, scrolling through the social media campaign she's running for one of her clients.

Beep! The lights have turned green. She eyes the driver behind, his knotted mouth declaring a silent 'for fuck's sake.' She raises her nail-varnished hand in a gesture of apology and pulls away.

'Are we there yet?' asks Freddie.

'Soon.'

'When?'

She doesn't reply.

The driver overtakes her, his middle finger vertical behind the glass.

'When?'

'Ten minutes,' she blurts, though she knows it's more like twenty.

The roadside ferns flicker in the breeze and wizened trees whizz by. She passes a shop with mirrored windows and her personalised number plate stares back at her. TES5 DPE. Matteo bought it for her birthday five years back. Ridiculously middle-class. But this is just another badge that she wears, like driving a four-by-four and shopping at Waitrose. It's not who she really is.

She spots a headless mannequin in a shop window, a poster stuck to the glass, proclaiming *Not Your Daughter's Jeans*. She looks down at her trousers, navy blue like her blouse. Then a splash of yellow drops into her thoughts – Freddie's scooter; she's left it back at the park. It's too close to lunch time to go back; Freddie's behaviour gets worse when he's hungry. She'll just have to phone when she's home, hope that someone's handed it in.

She slows and tries to see Freddie in the mirror. He didn't sleep well again last night. Perhaps that explains the way he squished those cyclamen flowers in his hands, the way he'd climbed that tree, felling a branch, bark exploding. 'Down, boy!' the park keeper had hissed as if her son were a dog. She rushed out an apology.

There is something off with Freddie, and not just today, but she can't face going back to the GP, not after that last time. Freddie had been running a temperature; he'd been lethargic and manageable, so she'd let her guard down. He'd broken away from her, charged down the corridor and burst through an unlocked door. Tess had raced after him. The face of the woman lying on the trolley was mangled with shock, the cave of the plastic speculum between her legs yawning. 'Fanny, fanny, fanny!' Freddie kept shouting as Tess dragged him out of the room by his wrist and back into the waiting area where people tried to hide their sniggers, faces behind hands. He'd picked the word up from Jenna who'd been talking about waxing. Why do people give the female genitalia girls' names anyway? *Fanny. Lily. Minnie*, when Vagina is a perfectly good name. She pictures it in *The Baby Name Wizard* book. That would shut up those playground mothers with their Phoebes and Palomas. *Oh, look, here comes my little Vagina.*

Freddie's foot dents the back of her seat and presses. He sniffs, the sound of his snot bubbling through her. She grips the wheel tighter still.

'Mine!' snaps Ruby.

In the rearview mirror, Tess sees Freddie dragging Ruby's toy rabbit towards him. Ruby snatches it back with a rip.

'I want!' shouts Freddie, his hand clamped on the rabbit's ear.

'No!' says Ruby.

'Let go of it, please,' says Tess, attempting a patient tone.

The boy grasps harder, the toy ripping more.

'Stop!' says Ruby.

Tess passes a lane with a sign that says *Private*.

'Mine!' shouts Freddie.

Ruby starts to scream.

'Freddie, let go of Ruby's toy!' The authority in her voice is strident, but Freddie's hand stays locked on the rabbit.

She can hear the drag of the seatbelt, a *clickety-click*. The electronic seatbelt alarm starts to ping through the din.

'For goodness' sake, Freddie, I'm not going to put up with this kind of behaviour anymore.'

Yet another hot flush is heating Tess up from the inside. There's the rustle of clothes.

'No!' shouts Ruby, Freddie now on top of her.

Tess watches the back of his head, the raggedy tufts of his shoulder-length strawberry blond hair, and Ruby's legs pumping; her sobs come loud and fast.

'Get back into your seat immediately!' says Tess, as near as she ever gets to shouting.

The road is four lanes wide and there's nowhere to stop. She glances in her rearview mirror again. There's a thick queue of cars behind her and a red line seams the tarmac. Ruby continues to sob. Sweat is pumping out of Tess' torso now, her shirt sticking to her skin like cling film. So much for black cohosh.

Ping-ping-ping. A sign flashes past. *40mph.*

'Freddie, stop being a nuisance and get back into your seat!'

Freddie plants his face on Ruby's. Ruby screams.

Tess takes a bend too quickly, catapulting Freddie into the footwell. She looks away from the road, turning round to make sure Ruby is alright. The little girl's eyelashes are beaded with tears, and there, above her right eyebrow, the skin is gaping like a button hole – Freddie has bitten her open.

The pressure starts to build in Tess' head; her hands crush the wheel. Ruby struggles against the seatbelt, but where can Tess pull in?

'I want my mummy!' Ruby screams.

'I'll be able to stop in a minute, darling,' says Tess.

She pushes her foot harder on the accelerator and the car in front draws speedily closer, too close, large and looming and silver. She slams on the brake, but her car continues to hurtle forwards. Her handbag topples onto the floor, tossing out the little wooden memory box. The oranges bullet downwards.

There's an almighty crash of metal, which rodeos Tess, her head jerking forwards and back, her shoulders and torso following suit. Tyres screech; silver paint fountains out like sparks.

The airbag is a sudden rubbery swell around Tess' head. And still the car is screeching sideways, the stench of burn filling her nose, her throat. A car alarm is shrilling. Tess bites her tongue and tastes blood. The car careers onto the pavement, felling a lamppost, then grinding to a stop.

The cap fizzes off the sparkling water bottle in the footwell. A child is mewing gently.

'Ruby?' says Tess. She tries to turn her neck, but the airbag is boxing her in.

'Freddie?'

The child continues to moan and someone burps.

'Freddie?'

Tess runs through a checklist of her own body. There's pain in her neck, down her spine, but it barely registers.

'Ruby?' Still nothing. 'Freddie, are you okay?'

'My leg hurts, really huuuuuurts!' Freddie wails.

'Can you move it?'

'No.'

Oh, God. 'Can you wiggle your toes?'

'Yes.' His voice quavers.

The reek of burning is getting stronger, muffled voices outside the car. Someone shouts, 'Now!' Someone else says, 'Holy fuck, there's two kids in the back.'

Tess can smell petrol.

'Freddie, can you see Ruby?' She tries to twist her head, but agony stabs into her shoulder blades and up her neck. Her heart is speeding, but she needs to stay calm. She breathes deeply, but still the panic burgeons.

Someone taps on the driver's window. 'Emergency services are on their way, love.' It's a man's voice. 'They'll get you out of there, just hang tight.'

She lifts the palm of her burnt hand and presses it to the glass. His thick fingers meet hers, the window warm between them.

'Freddie, I need you to tell me, is Ruby moving?' asks Tess, her hand still on the glass. 'Is she breathing?'

'No.' Freddie starts to cry.

The hard ball of tension in her throat makes it difficult to swallow and when she does, her ears crackle.

A siren rises in the distance. Tess closes her eyes and in the amber-grey darkness of her head, she sees a teenage girl, her long brown hair flowing down her back, the red of her dress. She is walking and getting further away.

'Wait,' says Tess, though her mouth stays closed.

'Can you tell me your name, love?' The man calls from outside the car, but Tess is drifting.

She follows the girl deeper into the shadows behind her eyelids, then everything goes black.

Chapter 2

▌

Tess stares up at the strip lighting, her fingers crinkling the cold cotton sheet. People in scrubs are blurry around her. She tries to sit up, but pain spears the back of her shoulders and forces her down again.

A nurse moves in front of her then, mousy hair so sparse her scalp shows through. 'You blacked out after the collision. Nothing broken though.'

'What about the children?' Tess' chest is buzzing with panic.

'Your son has severe lacerations to his leg. He's lost a lot of blood. We've had to give him a transfusion.'

Tess searches her own arms for a puncture wound, but can't see one. 'You didn't give him my blood?'

'We always take blood from stock.'

'Where is he?'

'In paediatrics. Your daughter's there too.'

Daughter?

Tess grasps for clarity, the past spooling through her head. The orange lick of the flames; the word *Why* dredged up from somewhere deep inside of her, phlegmy and desolate.

She closes her eyes and tries to find the girl in the darkness again, but this time there's nobody there.

▌

A voice wakes Tess. Matteo's voice.

'I only know because I gave blood a couple of months ago.' His Italian inflection carries through the curtain pulled around her bed.

'Perhaps they gave you the wrong information,' says a woman, the nurse from earlier possibly, though Tess can't remember the cadence of her voice.

'Well, it's very worrying if they did,' says Matteo.

'Your wife is definitely an O, and Freddie a B, so you being blood group A, well, it's just . . .'

'What?'

'Genetically impossible.'

Tess hears nails scratching skin.

'If you don't mind me asking, did you have assisted fertility, a sperm donor or a donated—'

'He's my son.' The word 'son' comes out on a spit. Tess pictures the muscles flexing in Matteo's cheek the way they do when he's angry, his set jaw.

'I didn't mean to . . . It's just that, well, IVF can sometimes drift to the back of people's minds.'

Matteo continues speaking, his voice too low to hear. Why are they talking about blood types? Has something gone wrong with the transfusion? A strand of her black hair comes loose from her head and settles like a pen mark on the white sheet.

A face peeps through the curtain then, topped with a Brillo-pad fringe. Luca's smile reveals his overlapping incisors. 'Hello.' He bounds in, folds himself across her, a plump cheek cushioning her face, her ten-year-old son.

'Have you seen Freddie and Ruby?' she asks.

'No, but Daddy has. Freddie's had loads of stitches in his leg.'

'Is Phoenix with Freddie?'

'Dunno,' Luca shrugs.

She should go to Freddie right now; he's there alone, her here, and Matteo out there still deep in a conversation she can't make out. She tries to sit up, but the pain flattens her again.

'Poor Mummy.'

Phoenix comes in then, keeping space between him and Tess,

and towering over her, his hair gelled into a quiff, which makes him taller still.

'You smell funny,' he says.

'Thank you!' she says. It's too late, he's heard the clip in her voice. She doesn't understand why she can't gauge the moods of her twelve-year-old and edit herself accordingly. It's become a reflex to snap at him.

'Silly, Mum,' he says and flops into the easy chair, draping one of his gangly legs over the arm.

'Why did you crash?' asks Luca.

'Because she's a rubbish driver,' says Phoenix.

'Freddie was . . .' Her head aches and swims.

'Being naughty,' says Luca.

'You don't like Fred, do you?' says Phoenix, glaring at Tess.

'Of course I do,' she snaps. She can't seem to regulate her voice, her mind is so hazy.

Phoenix looks away. Luca sits on the bed and squeezes her toes through the blanket, the fluorescent lighting picking out the leftover shimmery shadow on his eyelids.

There's a big gap between Freddie and her older boys – perhaps that's why she doesn't have much patience with him; perhaps she's grown out of looking after tots. At 45, perhaps she's too old. Not that she planned it this way.

Her navy leather handbag is there on the bedside cabinet and she thinks of the memory box falling out of it, onto the floor of the car. Will she get the box back? Her hand jerks towards the bag, shooting pain into the side of her neck.

Luca places the bag beside her, and she searches inside it. The curtain whips back, rings scraping the pole, and there is Matteo, a fug of aftershave preceding him. He bends and kisses her hard on the lips.

'How are you feeling?' he asks.

'Freddie's on his own,' she says.

'He's sleeping. They want to keep him in for a couple of days.'

'And what about Ruby?'

'Jenna's with her now,' he says. 'She's got the all clear to take her home.'

Guilt burrows into Tess. Perhaps Jenna will come to say goodbye, then again, maybe she won't; maybe she'll keep her distance from now on and who can blame her? Tess might have killed her daughter, and that bite is bound to leave a scar.

Matteo taps Phoenix's hand and flicks his head sideways.

'But *I'm* sitting here,' says Phoenix.

'Come on,' says Matteo, exasperation in the edges of his voice.

Tess reaches for Phoenix's hand as he stands; it slips away. 'Darling, I'd love something to drink. Will you take Luca and go and get me a glass of water, please?'

Phoenix rolls his eyes. Luca walks out of the cubicle, but Phoenix stays put. Tess lays her hand on the small of his back. 'Please, I want to talk to Daddy.'

Matteo shuts the curtain behind Phoenix and sits. 'How did this happen?'

'Freddie bit Ruby's face. She started screaming; he launched himself at her. I lost control of the car.'

He digs his thumb into a dent in the arm of the chair. 'At least it'll fade,' he says.

'What will?'

'Ruby's cut.'

'It's a bite mark, not a cut.'

Matteo looks away, shakes his head, the muscle in his cheek rippling. 'We need to take a firmer hand with him.'

'I treat him the same as the others.'

His chest fills with air. 'Maybe we need to try something different.'

'There's something not right with him, Matt.'

'Lots of children bite. Lots of children play up.'

'I don't just mean the biting; it's the tantrums; he hardly sleeps. I heard someone – was it one of the nurses? – saying something about blood groups. What was that about?'

'She was talking about the transfusion.'

She balls her hand in the hammock of the sheet covering her thighs. 'I don't know what to do with him anymore,' she says.

'He knows how to push your buttons, that's all; he doesn't act like that when I'm around.'

The veiled criticism bores through her skull. 'Well, I'm all out of ideas. I've tried reward charts, the naughty step – I've even begged him to behave, but he won't listen.'

'We just have to keep going. He'll get the message eventually; he'll calm down.'

'I don't have time for it.'

'You need to make time.'

'I'm already tearing myself in two, balancing my business and Freddie's needs.'

'So wind things down a bit.'

'Why can't *you*?' she asks.

He slams his mouth shut like he's trapping a retort, and looks about the cubicle. 'Maybe we need some outside help.'

'We've got Jenna.' She gives a pretend laugh. 'Mind you, I'd be astonished if she wants to let Ruby anywhere near Freddie after this.'

'I don't mean childcare, I mean a doctor, a child psychologist, some kind of professional.'

Noisy air shoots from her mouth.

'Come on, Tess, you don't eat meat, but you aren't imposing that on the kids. The same should go for counselling.'

She bites the side of her gum. An image of a beige lady in a winged chair drops into her head. 'And how did it make you feel, reading those condolence cards?' the woman had asked. It hadn't worked for Tess, so why would it work for Freddie? And besides, delving deeper into Freddie's behaviour might involve examining her own. Don't counsellors always blame the mother? She doesn't want to confront that possibility.

'No one wants to play with him,' she says. 'And now, what

he's done to Ruby . . .' She shuts her eyes for a moment. 'What did Jenna say anyway?'

'She's relieved everyone's alright. Don't worry about Jenna. She knows Freddie can be challenging, but she's always been understanding about it.'

'I crashed the car though. I could have killed Ruby for God's sake.'

'But you didn't, Tess, Ruby's okay.'

'It's one thing hurting your own child, quite another hurting somebody else's.'

She realises what she's just said and can't bring herself to look at him. What happened all those years ago gnaws at her, and the cubicle bloats with silence.

Using the flap of the bag as a shield, she digs in, and feels for the memory box. She removes the lid carved with the outline of a castle, and there inside it is a small bag of ash. Relieved, she closes the lid. She's boxed the whole thing up into this small, tidy package, and still she clings to it like a crutch.

▌

Wearing the pyjamas that Matteo brought in for her, Tess walks along the corridor in her pumps.

A nurse peers at her through a pair of smudged glasses. 'Are you okay there?'

'I'm looking for my son, Freddie Rossi,' says Tess.

'Little poppet,' says the nurse. 'You'll find him in the first room on the right. He's been ever so good. Hasn't complained once.'

Tess watches Freddie through a window scarred with old Sellotape marks. He's asleep in the nearest bed, his cheeks with colour in them for once. She goes in and sits on the edge of the bed, the line attached to the drip curling into the back of his hand. She looks at the sachet of blood, *Type B* printed on a sticker, the name Freddie Rossi scribbled on in black marker pen. That nurse was right about his blood type. The crumpled sachet makes her think of the night he was born. That doctor with his suede shoe wedged against the end of the bed for leverage. The pulling, the tearing.

A child fidgets in one of the beds and coughs.

'Freddie,' she whispers.

He opens his small blue eyes, the skin clinging too close to his skull. When he sees her, he turns his head away then tucks a hand beneath the sheet.

'I want Daddy.'

'Daddy's gone home now. It's late. He'll be back tomorrow.'

Freddie's swallow makes a clicking sound. Tess bends over and kisses his cheek. His nostrils are red-rimmed, his breath putrid as if he's been sleeping with his mouth open. He wipes her kiss away.

'Where's Phoenix?' he asks.

'He's at home too. You'll be going home soon, but you have to rest for now. Are you sore?'

He doesn't answer, just stares at the curtain pulled halfway around his bed. She rises, and stands two foot away from him.

Nothing about Freddie makes any sense. His short, skinny frame, the hair that everyone calls red even though it's the colour of copper. A thought starts to beat through her. She tries to push it down, but it plays on repeat anyway. *He's not mine. He's not mine. He's not mine.*

Chapter 3

Florida, USA

Annie gets up off the floor, the screwdriver hanging from her hand. She hasn't been able to fish out her wedding ring from between the stripped wooden floorboards where she dropped it. Her padded knees are sugared with dust like a couple of Dunkin' Donuts. She puts the screwdriver on the lip of the sink then pulls her paint palette earrings out of her earlobes and throws them into the mess of her jewellery box. Undoing the top button of her flamingo print pyjama top, she douses her cleavage with perfume.

The bathroom door scrapes across the floor as she opens it and bounds into their cluttered bedroom. Carl is marooned on the futon, with a photograph album on his lap, his feet pointing ten to two.

The thick tube of the free-standing air-conditioning unit has been shoved through the open window, and the room thunders with noise.

'I've lost my ring,' she says. He doesn't hear her through the clanking. 'Carl?'

She stands there watching him, the skin above his eyebrows crimping into a frown as he scans the photographs, the dim light casting shadows over his face. Spiky reddish beard, red cheeks and nose, an old T-shirt too loose around the neck. He spends most of the day outside fixing swimming pools, but never bothers with an SPF (he should be spreading it double with his colouring). He drinks in air then blows out abruptly.

'What's wrong?' she asks, but still he doesn't hear. He tips his head back and looks at the ceiling.

She moves towards him then, and he turns and flinches when he sees her. She tilts her head coquettishly and gives him a little smile then lowers herself to the bed, her chubby foot upending a glass of water she hadn't noticed was there on the coir-carpeted floor.

She rubs the puddle in with her foot – at least it'll give a patch of the carpet a wash. Taking the photograph album, she flings it to one side, pushing him backwards.

'Whoah!' He puts his hands into the air as she smacks her lips over his. His mouth goes on lockdown; his rigid shoulders rise to his ears, the pillow of his loose belly beneath hers.

'Wer yer doing?' his muffled voice fights its way through.

She pulls away. 'What does it look like I'm doing?'

The whites of his eyes expand like he's afraid of the answer.

'Just relax,' she says.

'But, I don't really feel like—'

'What's going on, Carl?'

'Nothing.'

'You've got something on your mind.'

'I haven't.'

He pulls her towards him, presses her head into his man boobs and sighs. She stays there, defeated.

A sex life in three acts. Act one: The can't-keep-your-hands-off-each-other. Act two: The having-sex-to-try-to-get-pregnant. (Even after she'd found out that they wouldn't be able to have a baby naturally, she'd continued poking her hopeful legs into the air after they'd done it). Act three: Once every two months.

Pat-pat-pat goes his meaty hand on the back of her head as if he's petting a pug. But then maybe it's her who's brought this on. The way she'd railed at him all those years ago, saying things that couldn't be unsaid. The way her body had filled out – not fat exactly, but not slim either, a bag stuffed a bit too full. She and Carl are a matching pair.

'I love you, you know,' he says in a languorous voice, still patting.

She pushes herself away and stares at him. 'What's happening to us then?'

'Nothing's happening.'

'Exactly!' She chews the inside of her cheek. 'You're so distant all the time, faraway.'

'I'm right here, aren't I?' he says.

'I mean, we don't talk, we just . . .' She blows air into her flustered face.

'What do you want to talk about?'

She folds her arms. 'You keep drifting off like you're thinking about things, things you won't talk to me about.'

'I don't.' He stretches out the words.

'I mean, you're not ill or anything? You would tell me, right?'

He tries to smother his smile, but his eyes light up with laughter.

'Stop it,' she shoves his arm.

'What ails you today, Mrs Amstel?'

'Shit, don't call me that. I feel like your mother.'

'Oh, pardon me, Mzzzzzz Perry.'

She laughs, leans across and picks up the photograph album – Willow showing her chocolatey fingers to the camera in one picture.

'Look at her, such a beauty,' she says.

'Not like us at all,' he says, and rubs at his beard.

'Goddamn cheek!'

Carl's not smiling though. 'I just mean that hair, that skin,' he says.

The fact that Willow doesn't look like either of them has given Annie a licence to be immodest, to agree with people when they say, 'Your daughter's so pretty,' but Carl's words have made her heart plummet.

The air-conditioning starts quaking even more. It strikes her then that she won't be able to hear Willow if she shouts out. She gets up and switches it off.

'I dropped my ring between the floorboards in the bathroom.'

'Not again.' He drags himself off the bed, his pyjamas bottoms riding down, revealing his butt crack.

He lumbers out, and she swoops towards Willow's bedroom.

The fairy that Annie made with tissue-paper wings and concertinaed gold legs billows on the partially open door. The bed is empty, a depression in the pillow. Blood starts to burble through Annie's ears.

'Willow!' she calls.

She drops to her knees, but there is nothing but clods of dust under the bed, a screwed-up tissue and a facedown book against the wall. She hears Carl say something in the bathroom, the plod of his feet.

'Willow, honey!' she calls, pins and needles of fear in her chest.

The doors to the wardrobe are partially closed and when Annie opens them, Willow is there, curled at the bottom, her fingers plunged into her rosebud mouth. Relief pours through Annie.

'What's going on?' asks Carl, the screwdriver vertical in his hand.

He comes to Annie's side, gazes at his daughter in her floral pink nightie, her teddy bear locked in her arms.

'Oh, kiddo,' he whispers, and shakes his head, a smile on his face.

'Full of surprises, isn't she?' says Annie as Carl lifts Willow, the girl's eyes flickering open then closed, her body floppy.

The teddy bear falls to the floor. Carl puts Willow back into bed and Annie tucks in the teddy bear beside her.

'She gave me such a scare,' she says.

He pulls her ring off the screwdriver and tries to push it onto her pudgy finger. It gets jammed, but he perseveres, ramming it into place. He loops his arm around her shoulder, and they stand there watching Willow, her long, conker-brown hair strewn across her olive-skinned face, two moles under her eye like a semi-colon.

They head back to bed. Carl snaps on his eye mask patterned

with slices of cucumber, and she switches off the side light. She holds his hand under the sheet, lying in the congested heat, ears alert to every creak and settle of the dilapidated apartment.

As the time passes, still she feels wired. She can tell by the pace of Carl's breathing that he isn't asleep either.

'You would tell me if there's something wrong?' she asks.

'Go to sleep, honey,' he says and swallows.

She turns onto her side, and her foot strikes something, the photograph album still on the bed. She prods it and it falls to the floor with a clonk.

Chapter 4

Surrey, England

Tess is at home, lying in bed beside Luca as he reads his book. The house is quiet, just the mimosa swishing beyond the window, Freddie asleep in the next room along.

Since the accident four weeks ago, he's been less fraught, content to dig at the garden mud with a spade while she pulls weeds beside him. He even laid his head in her lap while she sat on the sofa one day, updating her clients' social media accounts. She cupped her fingers around his face and typed one-handed. He hasn't been needling her for attention. He's been easier to like, to love, because it must be a kind of love that she feels for him, not the same as what she feels for Phoenix or Luca, but love nonetheless. The knowledge of his blood type is an undertow though. She knows she should let it go, enjoy his new equilibrium, but she can't.

'It's time to turn off,' says Tess. Luca flings his book to the side and pulls the duvet up to his chin. She closes her own novel.

'Try and kiss me,' he says, his bare foot in the air poised to defend himself, a game they play every night.

She laughs, puckers exaggerated lips and leans into him, his arms crisscrossed over his face. He bats her back with a hand and she upends the glittery L on the bedside cabinet along with a photograph frame dotted with footballs, a hopeful Christmas present from Matteo.

'This is so easy,' he says.

She holds up surrendered hands. 'Oh, Lulu, I give up.'

'I win.'

She cuddles into him, his arms tight around her.

'Danny's lucky.'

'Why?' She tries to pull away, but he holds her there, speaking warmth into her ear.

'Because he doesn't have brothers.'

'You love your brothers.'

'Do I?'

'Of course you do.' She thinks of her own sister, Angela – her report card decorated with As; the photograph of her in her mortar board on top of their parents' mantel. The only picture of Tess that graces that carved wooden shelf is one of her and Matteo on their wedding day, Tess caught mid-blink, so that her eyes are permanently shut.

'Freddie's weird,' he says.

'What do you mean?'

'Bites like a dog.'

'Not since he came home from hospital.'

She sits up, combs Luca's thick hair away from his face; it springs back, covering the top part of his eyes. She's hoping that the accident was such a shock to Freddie's system that he won't bite anyone again, that he won't misbehave, that he'll be more like Ruby – content to sit on his own and play, using a spoon to eat instead of his hands. Since the accident, she's had nothing more than a text from Jenna. Tess had left a garbled message gushing apologies, and asking how Ruby's face was healing. She'd held her hand to her throat as she spoke in a bid to stop her voice breaking, but still Jenna hasn't called her back.

'Freddie's okay when he's sleeping, I suppose,' says Luca.

'And what about Phoenix?'

'Ugh,' says Luca. She tweaks his nose, takes his toy monkey off the floor and presses it under the duvet.

'Sleep tight,' she says, and kisses him.

She goes downstairs into her office, the darkness a black sheet over the VELUX windows, the air scented with rosemary, the lit candle flickering in a draught.

Something moves across the parquet flooring, a spider with a body as big as a marble. She empties a jar full of pens, clambers to her knees and presses the glass over the spider. It scuttles away so fast that she shears off two of its legs. It stutters forward. She pushes on a shoe, rams her foot down then grabs a tissue and wipes up the black jam of it, dropping it into the bin.

She opens a blank page on her iMac and makes a start on a blog post for her interior designer client. An hour goes past, then she allows herself a look at her own Facebook page. She uploads a picture of Phoenix standing in front of the Chinese characters on the white board at his after-school Mandarin lesson, Luca beside him crossing his eyes. *Friday fun,* she types and adds a smiley face emoji.

She pushes her shoulders back, scans the neat rows of books on the shelves above the desk, arranged according to the colour of their spines – Man Booker Prize nominees and Penguin Classics, a bumper thesaurus and a Chambers Dictionary. All those words she knows the meaning of, yet so many she doesn't know how to pronounce. How long was it before she knew that 'banal' did not in fact rhyme with 'anal'? And how many times had she said it the wrong way? She feels the inner heat of shame.

Five likes on that photograph of Phoenix and Luca already, though that's nothing unusual for a collector of online friends like her. Her eyes brush over some of the names, people she knew at university and colleagues from the marketing team she worked in before she had Phoenix. The front door slams, the Victorian stained glass window in it rattling.

'Daddy!' Freddie's voice crackles through the baby monitor – he's not asleep after all. She keeps it switched on, so she can hear him when he wakes. Feet pad up the stairs; Matteo's been working late again at the hotel.

His voice echoes through the monitor. 'How's your leg, my boy?'

There's the suck and pucker of Matteo's affection, Freddie's laughter lighting up the monitor's arch of red beads. The cuts on Freddie's thigh are angry hashtags, even though the stitches have come out.

She looks at her emails. There's one from a mother of a boy in Freddie's Montessori class. Another refusal to the invitation to Freddie's birthday party – that's five refusals so far.

She switches off the iMac, takes a padded envelope from the desk drawer and slides the contents out – three plastic bags with cotton buds and folded instruction leaflets inside.

She didn't want him. The jagged thought scythes her head. She wanted a girl, needed a girl, to try to erase what had happened to her first born, Ava. She'd be fifteen now.

Pregnancy didn't agree with Tess. She'd battled through diabetes with Phoenix, osteoporosis with Luca, then there'd been the three miscarriages, but still they went on trying for a third child. Matteo hadn't wanted to do IVF at first, but she'd worked on him. 'What if it's twins?' he'd asked. But she didn't care if it was twins, triplets even, just so long as one of them was a girl, a girl to fill up the gaping space inside of her.

It was Tess who'd found the clinic in America that offered gender selection IVF. If she was going to pump herself full of drugs, she wanted to make sure she'd have the girl she so desperately wanted. 'We can only work with what we have, and you have a low number of follicles in line with being 41,' the doctor had said. 'But there's still a chance,' Tess had replied, and he'd tilted his head and given her an unconvincing, stretched-out 'yes.'

So they'd stayed in a hotel, the boys in an adjoining room. And she'd had her eggs harvested, four of them – only two of them had fertilised. The doctor phoned, said he had carried out a test that showed that one of the embryos was female.

'I don't want the boy,' she'd said to Matteo after the appointment.

But over the next two days, her heart had filled with trepidation. The odds of giving birth to a live baby at her age were low, and this would be her last pregnancy. Then another thought took hold and wouldn't let go. If she didn't transfer the male embryo, it would get thrown into the bin because she certainly couldn't contemplate donating it to another woman, wondering whether it had turned into a child she'd never get to see. She thought about how she rarely put food in the freezer, and the times that she had, she'd taken out a lasagne and a container of soup and watched them thaw, coagulated. It was a waste, but she usually threw that food away.

She reached her decision on the morning of the transfer. 'I want both the embryos put back inside me,' she'd said.

'Are you sure?' Matteo had asked. There'd already been one little death in the family, she couldn't bring herself to be the cause of another.

'I am,' she said.

When she took the pregnancy test, she stared at it in astonishment. A girl, she convinced herself, or twins. For those first few weeks, she carried herself around like glass, then her sense of smell heightened. She'd felt sicker than she had done with her other pregnancies, a pervading nausea that lasted all day and sent her throwing up into the toilets at work. An early scan showed a single baby and hope swept through her, her little girl had made it; the delusion was persuasive. At least she'd given the boy a chance, she had no reason to feel guilt on that account. At the next scan she was buried by the realisation it was a boy she was having. A fluttering kind of sob leapt out of her mouth, which the nurse must have mistaken for laughter.

'Look, he's waving at you there,' she'd said, gesturing towards the scanner.

Matteo had smoothed his thumb over the burn mark on Tess'

hand. She let him examine it, the patch she so often sat on, or covered up with long-sleeves, the rivulets of waxy skin, the drip marks through it.

After Freddie was born, it was as if her head was stuffed with lard, and it was siphoning into her arms, her legs, her heart. She'd only been able to shake the feeling off when she'd launched her business two months later, her vagina still smarting, her breasts aching with the milk he wouldn't take.

She and Jenna had shared the childcare between them, and having Ruby around diluted what Tess felt about her son: something lukewarm and not enough.

She hears footsteps on the stairs and pokes everything back into the envelope. The office door slides open, and there is Matteo, a patch of stubble the size of an eye on his jaw, his collar with a grey smudge on it. There's something haggard about his face, his cheeks caved in shadow, one of them dissected by pink scratches.

'I thought you were in bed,' he says.

He sits in the Balzac chair, the tartan blanket slithering off the back to the floor.

'Why are you so late?' she asks.

'We're going to have to cancel the bathroom refurb.'

'But why?'

'Why do you think, Tess? It's going to cost a fortune.'

'But the hotel's doing well.'

His Adam's apple dips as he swallows. 'Bookings are down on this time last year.'

'Oh. Should we be worried?'

Matteo shrugs. Something falls upstairs and the chandelier, which resembles a ring of icicles, chinks and shakes. Tess stares at the ceiling and presses her bare foot over the webbed toes of the other one. She's considered surgery to separate them, but she avoids hospitals if she can.

'I can't believe he's still awake at this time,' says Matteo.

She slides her tongue over her suddenly dry gums and forces herself to speak. 'I've been thinking more about what that nurse said to you.'

'Which was . . .?'

'About Freddie having a completely different blood type to us.' She cradles her hands under each of her elbows.

He regards her with disgust. 'He's our son, Tess.'

'She said that it was genetically impossible.'

He shakes his head, looks away from her.

'I know what I heard,' she says.

'I'm not doing this.'

She bites her teeth together; she'll stick that cotton bud into Matteo's mouth when he's sleeping if she has to.

'Just because you find him difficult, just because you can't cope. Christ, Tess, he's our son – I don't give a damn about what that nurse said.'

'If there's a chance Freddie might not be ours, I want to know.'

'This is about Ava, but Ava's gone. You should concentrate on what you do have; you should concentrate on Freddie.'

His words crawl in through her ears and hook inside her chest. She lifts the envelope, slapping it onto the table. 'I want us to do a DNA test.'

She tries to hold herself still, her rigid neck aching with tension.

'Oh, come on!'

'What if they mixed up the embryos at the IVF clinic?'

'Don't.'

'If he isn't ours, who does he belong to?'

Matteo puts both his hands to his head like a crash helmet. She leans further forward in the chair, planting her feet flat on the floor.

'And if he isn't ours, what happened to our embryos?' she asks.

'Oh, Tess, this is fantasy.'

'You heard what that nurse said.'

She takes his dry hand; the eczema on his fingers sandpapers her skin.

'I always thought the worst thing that could happen to anyone was if their child went missing,' she says. 'Having to live not knowing what had happened to them, but that could be what's happening to us.'

'If we do this, they could try to take Freddie away from us,' he says.

She squeezes his fingers. 'I need to know if my children are out there somewhere.'

'If this turns out to be true, it'll be harrowing. We can't even begin to imagine how hard it'll be.'

'I need to know.'

'We can't do this, think of the consequences,' he says.

But there's something surrendered about his voice, and he owes her this. He owes her this because of what he did to her all those years ago. The livid burn stares up at her as she opens the instruction leaflet and starts to read it for the fifth time this evening.

Chapter 5

The dining table is buried beneath paper cloths, *3 Today* a hundred times over. Tess slices through Freddie's name on the cake and, with a pinned-on smile, hands Lucinda Lacey a portion that says *die*.

There are six children in the kitchen-diner playing pass the parcel, the sweaty Papa Smurf entertainer pulling the elasticated beard off his chin and dabbing himself down with a screwed-up tissue. Matteo taps his mobile phone, stopping the nursery-rhyme music sailing from the Sonos. Ruby is holding the stuffed package.

'Rip off the paper then pass it on,' says the entertainer.

Ruby's cheeks are two pink discs – even from here, Tess can see the scar over her eye. Her baby sister Frannie is sitting in a rubber ring further into the room, shoving a rattle into her mouth, a spit bubble forming. The paper crown on Freddie's head slips down, hiding the tops of his eyes. Jenna is watching him, her stare as sharp as a drawing pin, but at least she's here. The children's laughter is hollow in the half empty L-shaped room. There are demolished hors d'oeuvres on the steel-topped island unit, crumbled breadsticks and bowls smudged with leftover dips.

'So how's work?' asks Lucinda, a chocolate sponge crumb specking the side of her nose.

Tess towers over her. 'Busy. I've got quite a few projects on the go. I can't seem to turn anyone down.'

'I wouldn't know,' says Lucinda.

'At least you get to do one job properly,' says Tess. 'I'm splitting myself apart trying to do too many things at once.'

'If only you could clone yourself,' says Lucinda.

'Two of me? Matteo would have a nervous breakdown.'

Lucinda laughs. Tess flicks through her phone and uploads the best pictures to Facebook – the dog-shaped chocolate birthday cake, the goofy pressed-together smiles of Ruby and Luca. *Another year older – 3 today*, she types. A savage hot flush closes in on her then, turning her breasts into a sweat sandwich, dampening her black dress.

Lucinda's son, Charles, is buck-toothed in a T-shirt, the word *Batman* stretched across his rotund chest. He is watching the parcel intently just like the twins Callum and Clare with their matching golden curls.

'How are you after the accident anyway?' asks Lucinda.

'It was Freddie who came off worse.'

Lucinda sips her drink and stares at Freddie, her forehead folding. Anticipating more questions, Tess moves away and slots crockery into the dishwasher. She catches her reflection in the polished steel cooker hood – the thick slick of foundation, the middle parting in her black hair so straight it could have been drawn with a ruler. The children toss the parcel between them, a net bulging with balloons overhead.

Luca comes into the room, dressed in a pink tutu, and sits beside baby Frannie, pushing a finger into her fist. She smiles at him, and blows more bubbles.

Tess walks up to Jenna, and to her relief Jenna bumps her hip against Tess' on purpose. 'You're going to be devastated if that boy turns out to be straight.'

Tess smiles. 'Look at him with Frannie. She's so cute.'

Jenna checks the fly of her jeans, which are torn artfully across the knees, her silk-backed cardigan slipping off a bare shoulder. The look of someone who doesn't try all that hard with their appearance, but probably does.

'Yeah, she is, but take it from me, you don't ever want to go back there. Make me go to another baby jingles class and I might have to shove the barrel of a gun into my mouth.'

'Or a bottle of vodka,' says Tess.

Matteo is beside Lucinda then, engaging her in conversation, his shirt collar open, the waistband of his pressed black trousers so high he looks like a professional from *Strictly Come Dancing*. All that pouting and gyration, the mouthing of silent words to the music. 'Come and get me,' and 'Ooh baby.' It was no wonder so many dance partners ended up in a relationship.

'Thanks for coming to this,' says Tess.

'I couldn't miss my own nephew's birthday.'

They're family, so it's not as if Jenna can cut Freddie out of Ruby's life completely. Maybe that's why they're here, maybe they have to be. Even so, Jenna has only started texting Tess again in the past week.

'Freddie's been a lot better lately,' says Tess. 'Fewer tantrums.'

'He's always been good for me. He never hurt Ruby before.'

'Her face.' Tess shakes her head.

'I'm hoping it'll fade.'

'I'm so sorry, Jenna.'

'Matteo says you're looking into a child psychologist.'

Tess' neck goes rigid. 'Maybe it was a phase, maybe he's come through it.'

'Maybe, but shit, T, not many three year olds write off cars.'

'It was me who did that.'

'It wasn't your fault, and God knows you don't need any more guilt to contend with.'

Tess scans Jenna's face, her blonde hair escaping her ponytail. Does she know about what really happened all those years ago with Ava? What Matteo did; what she did? Tess had begged Matteo not to confide all the details to Jenna. Tess had wanted to shrug off Jenna's pity back then; she didn't want her blame too. But surely Jenna didn't know; she would have said something to Tess by now.

'What do you mean – guilt?' asks Tess.

'Three kids, your business . . . It's not easy doing both.' Jenna swallows. 'Speaking of which, I'm not going to be able to look after Freddie for a few more weeks – Rach is off on her holidays, so I'll need to be at the gallery every day.'

'I'll look after the girls for you then.'

'But you've got your marketing stuff.' She folds her arms. 'No, look, a friend of mine has offered to help me out; it'll be easier that way. Give you time to focus on Freddie.'

'I need to do a wee-wee,' says Charles, gazing up at Tess and yanking the crotch of his trousers.

Tess points the way to the loo, and Charles heads out, Lucinda scurrying after him. Jenna touches a gentle hand to Charles' head as he passes. *To be like that . . .* Tess has to fight her way through arthritic stiffness when it comes to being tactile.

The children are throwing the gift to each other now, a pile of tangled wrapping paper in the centre of their circle. The music cuts out.

'*Fanculo!*' says Matteo, shaking his mobile phone. 'What's wrong with this thing?'

The Papa Smurf entertainer pulls off his red cap and scratches his tousled head.

'We want songs!' says Freddie.

Another child tuts. Matteo climbs onto a chair and peers at the Sonos box on the wall, knocking his fist against it and muttering.

'Oh, here we go,' says Jenna. 'Matteo's about as useful in the electricity department as a Tudor king.'

'Hurry up, Daddy!' shouts Freddie.

The Papa Smurf entertainer starts scrolling through his own mobile phone, and a series of Eminem expletives blare out of it.

'Let's use the old CD player,' blurts Tess.

'No, I'm sure I can get the Sonos working,' says Matteo.

Optimistic as usual, Tess thinks, pulling a battered beatbox from a large kitchen drawer and switching it on. Coldplay spirals into the air, drowning out Eminem. Matteo stares at the Sonos box, consternation reshaping his face. He's addicted to electrical gadgets. The motion sensor that sets off a camera at the front door, the robotic vacuum cleaner, the app that allows them to control the central heating when they're out. It's just a shame he doesn't know how to fix any of them when they go wrong.

Charles rejoins the circle of children. Freddie is hunched on a cushion, a *Happy 3rd Birthday* badge pinned to his chest. Matteo is tapping his foot, his ears so large and red that he looks like a toby jug. The music stops, and there are gasps as Charles unleashes the prize at the centre of the parcel – an art set of crayons and pencils and felt-tip pens.

Something stirs in Freddie's blue eyes then. He strides over to Charles, glares down at him then bends and suckers his mouth to the boy's fleshy arm.

'Ow!' Charles roars.

'No!' says Tess, marching over and pulling Freddie off, his mouth popping as it comes free. Charles starts to cry now in Lucinda's arms as she bellows, 'He's going to need a tetanus injection!' Her Elnetted bouffant quivers.

She rubs at the boy's red arm and presses her son's head to her chest. Tess closes her eyes briefly then lifts Freddie, twisting him sideways as if she's warming up for the Olympic shot put.

'Naughty boy!' she says.

She can feel everyone staring, and her face boils. They're probably thinking she's deficient, that she's not angry enough. Why can't she do what's required, taking control and getting Freddie into line? She was stupid to think that he'd changed.

'Freddie! This is totally unacceptable!' yells Matteo, clambering down from the chair.

Charles continues to wail. Tess moves closer to him, Freddie still in her arms and kicking. Sympathising with the injured child is just one way to stop your child from biting, according to an internet site she's consulted. 'I'm so sorry, Charles,' says Tess.

'You're sorry?' hisses Lucinda.

'Yes, I'm—'

'For God's sake!' Lucinda clamps Charles' football head harder to the romantic fabric of her dress.

'Go and get some arnica gel,' Matteo says to Luca, pointing towards the balloons netted on the ceiling.

Luca stomps away, rolling his eyes. The muscles in Tess' arms bulge as Freddie continues to kick the air.

'Put me down!' screams Freddie.

'He's an absolute menace!' says Lucinda. The fleck of chocolate cake falls off the side of her flaring nostril.

'It won't happen again,' says Tess. 'Poor Charles, poor little—'

'I knew I shouldn't have said yes,' says Lucinda.

Chris Martin carries on powering through his song.

'There's no need for that,' says Jenna, her arms held wide. Baby Frannie starts to cry, and she scoops her up. Ruby clings to Jenna's leg.

The only other mum in the room, Karen, mutters, 'We really should be going.'

Freddie kicks out more aggressively.

'Stop that!' says Tess.

Charles' sobs have glazed his mother's dress with snot. The Sonos kicks in again, grafting *The Wheels on the Bus* over Coldplay. A flustered Matteo presses a button on his phone and *The Wheels on the Bus* grows louder still. Charles lets rip another sob.

'Christ,' says Matteo, though Tess can only see him mouthing the word through the cacophony.

Phoenix comes into the room then, absorbing everyone's attention for a moment. 'What's going on?' he asks.

A strangled sound tips out of Lucinda's mouth. Tess puts Freddie down and he races away, taking hold of the string attached to the net on the ceiling and yanking. The overhead balloons float down; the children start to 'ooh' and 'aah.' Charles stops crying and gets up, forgetting the circle of broken skin on his arm. Freddie jumps, balloons bursting and banging beneath his feet, and the other children, including Charles, join in. *Pop-pop-pop.*

'Be careful, Charles!' shouts Lucinda.

Tess catches hold of Freddie's arm and tries to pick him up again, but he whips away from her hand and carries on jumping. 'No, Mummy, no!'

She tries again, and he pummels her arms, but she grabs him, kicking and punching, and strides out of the room towards her office. She puts him down and slams the door, twisting the key and pocketing it. Quick footsteps click across the hall tiles, the door shakes. 'Let me in!' shouts Matteo. Charles' arm, Ruby's face, the drawn-out moments after the car crash when she couldn't see Ruby, nor hear her. These things writhe inside her as she watches Freddie try to open the door.

'Daddy!'

She feels cruel, sharpened. Freddie thumps through the room, disturbing one of three abstract paintings on the wall and tilting it. Tess yanks him backwards by his arm and he falls, his other arm upending the Anglepoise lamp on her desk, which clatters to the floor, bulb smashing, the base coming apart and spewing wires. He crawls away on the parquet.

'Who are you?' she hisses.

'I'm Freddie,' he replies, defiance in his voice.

'Tess, for God's sake, let me in!' shouts Matteo.

She walks towards Freddie, her heart drumming her ribs. She crouches, bringing her face five centimetres from his. Sympathising with the bitten child. Time outs. Banishing him to his room. None of it has worked. She picks up his arm and starts to lower her face towards it. His skin is hot. She sinks her teeth in and bites.

He screams and breaks away, his mouth a rhombus of pain. He pelts over to the door and bashes it with his fists.

'Daddy! Daddy!'

'Open the door!' shouts Matteo.

Tess wants to snatch the bite back, to stuff it back into her mouth. Her little boy, with his thin face, and bright blue eyes.

The door vibrates. 'Let me in!' yells Matteo.

Tess takes the key from her pocket, eases Freddie aside and opens the door. Matteo gathers Freddie up, Freddie crabbing his legs around him.

'Mummy bit me!'

Freddie points at the inflamed circle of skin and Matteo's eyes grow too big for their sockets.

'What were you thinking, Tess?'

'It was something I read about on the internet. Showing him how it feels.'

'He's just a child.'

He exits the room with Freddie, and thuds up the stairs. The blood is pumping in her neck. She opens a drawer of her desk and tears the envelope open, ripping through the letter inside.

The results arrived this morning, but she's put off opening them because how could she face everyone at the party once she knew what they were?

DNA Test Report.

There are columns of numbers, the words *Alleged MOTHER, Alleged FATHER* and too many zeros underneath them.

She stares at the bottom of the page.

Probability of paternity. 0%.

Probability of maternity 0%.

A boulder crashes into the pit of her stomach and air leaves her throat. Her hands are trembling. She looks down at her engagement ring; too big for her like a worn-in shoe that keeps slipping off.

Splashes of memory come vividly to her. Freddie falling so violently on the cobbled ground in Puglia, his knee bleeding, her putting her arms around him, him batting her away. Cupping his face in her hands that day in the garden after he'd trampled the pansies into a purple carnage. She'd told him off, said he needed to start listening to her, 'Because I am your mother,' she'd added at the end. 'No you're not,' Freddie had snapped back. All of it is becoming clearer like a blurred view through a camera lens swivelled into focus.

Her knees buckle beneath her. She grabs the desk for balance. Here's the proof that Freddie isn't their son; but then, she's known it all along.

❗

Tess looks at the time in the corner of her iMac; it's after ten, and Matteo still hasn't sought her out. The guests left soon after the biting incident, Jenna saying goodbye and haring towards the front door. 'Thank you for coming,' Tess had said to each guest, averting her eyes. Afterwards, she crept back into her office and started work although she hasn't been able to concentrate. Only Luca said goodnight.

She looks at the DNA results yet again as if they might reveal a different outcome to the one she read earlier. She gets up; she sits down, she twists her chair round to face the darkened windows.

The clinic had reassured them there were all sorts of safety measures, including some kind of video system, so how can she have given birth to the wrong child? And what about their two embryos? Were they turfed into a bin, pushed into some other woman? She gets the taste of bile and swallows.

Her real babies could be out there somewhere. A new void has opened in her stomach, adding to the one that's already there. The results flap in her hand as she walks through the hall to find Matteo.

Inside the high-ceilinged living room, Matteo is staring at a notebook, a pencil in one hand, the other one worrying at his forehead. He looks up, closes the book and pushes it down the side of the sofa. His face is full of sympathy as he looks at her, and she's not surprised – Matteo doesn't usually stay in a bad mood for long; tonight has been an exception.

'I shouldn't have done it,' she says.

'You've never even hit any of them. Ever.'

'It was something I read about.'

'You hurt him.'

'I thought it might work.'

'What about calling that child psychologist Karen told you about?'

She sits beside him, the embroidered green leaves on the sofa pushing into the backs of her knees. A sizeable glass of whisky shimmers on the coffee table.

'Might as well make the call,' he says. 'If she's as good as Karen says, there's bound to be a waiting list.'

'There's something else.' She flattens the letter on her knee. 'The results are back.'

He takes a long, slow breath through his mouth and stares at her.

'It's not good, Matt.'

'Let me see.'

She lets him take the results. 'God.' His face shudders. 'How can this be?'

'I don't know.'

He finishes the whisky. 'Maybe they made a mistake.'

'It's pretty clear they've made a mistake,' she says.

'I mean, whoever carried out this test. Maybe we should do another one.'

He gets up and paces, the paper fluttering in his hand as he moves around the room, over to the glass cabinet packed with family photographs. The boys pressed around their nonna in Ostuni; Matteo and his precious boys.

'We've got to think very carefully about this, Tess. The parents, the real parents, they could try to take him away from us if we do anything about this.'

She dismantles a stack of photographic books on the table, then restacks them, putting the largest one at the bottom. He picks up his empty glass, goes over to the open bureau containing bottles of spirits and a crystal decanter. He pours himself a generous whisky and paces, the urine-coloured liquid sloshing about in the glass.

'But what about our embryos?' she asks. 'We need to know what happened to them – we might have a child somewhere.'

He sits down, leaning forward, elbows on knees. 'But there were checks. It's a reputable clinic. Maybe the fault was with the hospital where Freddie was born. They took him into another room. Is it possible they brought the wrong baby back to us?'

'They didn't.'

'But how can you be sure?'

'He had forceps marks on his forehead, under his chin.'

'If we approach the clinic, oh God, it'll be a nightmare. We could end up in court.'

'We need to know what happened to our embryos.'

'But if our embryos were born to someone else, we wouldn't have any rights to them, would we? All it would do is drive us apart, so what's the point?'

He gets up again, sits down, drains the rest of the whisky, the cupid's bow in his lips glistening.

'We need advice from someone,' she says, thinking of the handful of lawyers they know. 'What about Jack? He works in family law, he might have some ideas.'

Matteo puts his empty glass onto the table then slouches forward, caging his hands around his skull. 'The thought that our children could be out there somewhere, oh Christ.'

She takes a deep breath, but it does nothing to still the chaos whipping up inside her, the chaos that she's been trying to annex away for years.

'I can't lose another child, Matt.'

'We won't let them take him away from us. Over my dead body.'

She didn't mean Freddie, but she doesn't correct him. She pulls the results from his hand and folds them into a square, smoothing and pressing it, then pushing it into the pocket over her chest.

Chapter 6

An empty can of cider clatters along the pavement towards Tess. There's the distant sound of people cheering from a sports field. The takeaway tea is hot in her hand, a paper bag of pastries under her arm. Carrying her laptop bag, she walks in the direction of a man sitting on cardboard in the doorway of a shop, an upturned cap on the ground beside him.

'Spare any change, love?' he says through a yellow smile.

She chews at her bottom lip. 'This is for you.'

'Stick a couple of sugars in it, did you?' He takes the cup from her with dirt-grouted fingers.

'I didn't think.'

The tea trembles.

'And something to eat.' She passes him the paper bag.

He puts it into his lap, doesn't look at her. How old is he beneath that burgundy face?

'Why did you, I mean . . .' Her deep breath sucks the smell of stale alcohol into her nostrils. 'Why are you out here? Don't you have anyone you could stay with, family, friends?'

He shakes his head. She crouches and the silence hangs. Should she ask some more questions; should she walk away? Jenna would probably lean across and lay a comforting hand on the man's shoulder, but Tess is a trunk of tension.

'Are you okay?' she asks then presses her teeth together, realising how trite that sounds.

'Yeah.' He concentrates on the tea still with its lid on. 'Families aren't the answer to everything. My family, fuck . . .' His gaze jumps around, refusing to settle on anything.

'I'm sorry,' she says.

'What have you got to be sorry about?' He looks at her then, and she swallows hard.

He raises the tea up, and the beige liquid sloshes out of the small drink hole at the top. 'Cheers for this anyway.'

She's been dismissed. She stands, tries to paste on a smile. 'You're welcome,' she says softly and walks away.

She looks back over her shoulder at him, crosses the road and walks along the pathway running parallel to the river.

The sun comes out then, dappling the charcoal water with light. She wonders how Phoenix's maths test is going. Tests every week and he's only twelve. She has to knock before she enters his bedroom now. She offered to help him prepare for the test, but he refused. He's pulling away from her; it'll only be a matter of time before he's gone for good.

She tramps across the wedge of grass and sits on a bench. She pulls some objects out of her bag and lines them up on the wood, trying to equalise the distance between each of them. The memory box. Her phone. She stares at the river for what seems like a long time. After a while, her phone starts to ring and she picks it up.

'Jack's found us a lawyer in the States,' says Matteo.

'Who?'

'A woman called Gill Cousins. She's acted for a couple who've been through something similar.'

'An embryo mix up?'

'Their baby was born to someone else.'

'What happened?' She brushes her hand over the lid of the box.

'The hospital discovered the mistake while the woman was pregnant. She had to give the baby back to the genetic parents.'

So there is a chance she might get her real child back, if

there is a child. Her mind ripples with ribbons and ballet shoes.

'It was a completely different case to ours,' says Matteo. 'But hopefully she can advise us. I've emailed her.'

Tess looks up river. Two moorhens are paddling towards her, the water corrugating around them. She can't see further than the wall of trees.

'I'll keep you posted, but I'd better go,' he says. He stays on the line though, and she does too, listening to his abraded breath.

'Do you really want to do this?' she asks.

'It's only a first step. We need to hear what Gill's got to say. Are you okay?'

'Yes.' Something is materialising in her, alongside the dread. This is what hope feels like, she thinks, hovering, irresistible.

Matteo hangs up first. She takes the lid off the memory box and scoops out a tiny amount of ash. She walks to the edge of the river, the mud sloshing and sliding beneath her boots. Low-flying geese squawk and breeze past.

She lets the ash go, a tiny puff of grey speckles that touch the water for an instant then are gone. *You've just stepped into another room.* That's what it said on the funeral service card, but Tess has been going through doors for years, and Ava always stays hidden.

She looks over at the houseboat moored on the other side of the river. A large grey structure with leaded light windows. There are rattan armchairs on a deck in front of it with olive cushions. The houseboat nextdoor has a shattered pane of glass in one of its windows, the front door in need of a paint, a drying rack outside it festooned with underwear – a large pair of knickers, and a beige bra with massive cups. She shouldn't have let the dwindling ash go here. She replaces the lid, and sits back down, pushing the box into her handbag.

She's scattered pinches of ash in places she's holidayed to, but she can't bring herself to let go of all of it yet. It's the only thing she has left of her daughter, a grainy, grey reminder.

Another child could be out there somewhere, another girl. The need to find her, to fight for her, tugs at Tess. She bends and wrenches a snowdrop from the earth. She crushes the bud, feeling the soft white petals disintegrate between her fingers.

Chapter 7

It's three minutes past the time that Gill said she would Skype. Tess forces herself to breathe slowly, deeply, clamps both hands around the bottom of the dining room chair. Matteo sits beside her with a glass of water, the laptop open in front of them.

They wait, the fridge humming, the wind scraping a branch along an outside wall. She listens for Freddie, but the baby monitor doesn't light up. Finally there's the jingle of someone calling, a spinning blue circle in the centre of the screen. In a corner, Tess can see herself beside Matteo, her foundation as thick as Polyfilla, then Gill is there in front of them, light pouring into her office and glancing off a lens of her gold-rimmed glasses.

They say their hellos.

'I'm sorry for what you're going through,' says Gill. 'This must be incredibly harrowing for you both. As I said in my email, I'm more than happy to act for you in all your dealings with the clinic, and we'll be pushing for them to settle out of court.'

'They won't try to take Freddie away from us, will they?' The words rush from Matteo's mouth.

'Cases like this are extremely rare, and there's no precedent. There have been many different outcomes. Each case is a unique set of circumstances, but I don't see a judge taking a little boy away from good parents who love him, brothers too, especially after this length of time.'

'But what about our children?' asks Tess.

'Your other children?'

'Our embryos,' says Matteo.

'There'll be a thorough investigation into what happened to your embryos,' says Gill.

'And they'll find them?' asks Tess, sitting so far forward on her seat that the back legs tip.

'We hope that will be the case, but there is a possibility we may never find out what happened to them.' Gill smoothes her hand across her desk. 'There's also the possibility that they were transferred to you, along with another embryo, and that your embryos didn't take.'

Tess is so fired with adrenaline that her head is bouncing around like it's on a wire spring; the camera in the corner of the screen captures only her stillness though. 'How could an error like this happen? There were checks; they said they had some kind of video system.'

'It says that on their website, yes,' says Gill. 'It's certainly something I'll be exploring. Unfortunately, where people are involved, there's always the possibility of human error.'

Tess can remember only patches of detail about the day of her transfer – the hair tassels frothing from the doctor's nostrils, the way he was talking to his colleague – as if he wasn't really staring into her vagina – saying something about a conference he'd been to. The only thing she can remember about the colleague's face was his hazel eyes, his young skin.

'It could be that a pipette wasn't washed out correctly, that somebody else's embryo was inside it,' says Gill. 'Perhaps petri dishes were mixed up or names. If the video camera was operational, it might show what occurred. There should be computer records of all the transfers too. There may be information we can use to find out why this has happened.'

'If our embryos, our children, were born to someone else, I want to meet them,' says Tess. 'I want them back.'

'We don't know whether there are children,' says Matteo.

'There'll be plenty of time to consider what you would like to do,' says Gill. 'You can make sure that you're both in agreement about the way we move forward. I think it's likely that the clinic will want you to undergo another DNA test, one that they've sanctioned.'

'So what happens next?' asks Matteo.

'I'm going to draft a letter to the clinic, sending them a copy of the DNA results and informing them that I will be acting for you. I'll be asking them to commence an investigation. They're likely to contact all of the couples who had treatment in the clinic around the time you did. That was May 2015, is that correct?'

'Yes,' says Tess.

'And there's something else I'd like you to bear in mind,' says Gill. 'If and when they find out who Freddie's genetic family are, we can't predict how they'll react.'

Faceless figures stray into Tess' head. She hasn't considered who Freddie's real family might be.

'What do you mean, how they'll react?' asks Matteo.

'One of the people involved might try to sell their story to the media,' says Gill.

Tess sinks into her seat. Nobody knows that they went for IVF, let alone gender selection IVF. It wasn't something anyone else could understand. They'd have thought her selfish, immoral even, and so she'd pretended. 'We fell pregnant naturally,' she'd told her friends, her family, as if IVF was unnatural and somehow deficient. Now her careful, smiling lie could be exposed, her life cracked open.

'I don't want my name in the paper,' she says.

'As I say, it's just another factor to consider.'

This situation might be a wildfire; it could catch and scorch, burning everyone in its path as it spreads.

'Can we see this letter before you send it?' asks Matteo.

'Of course, you'll have a draft later this evening. I'll work on it now.'

'Thank you,' says Matteo.

'It's good to meet you,' says Gill. 'And if you have any questions at all, don't hesitate to get in touch.'

Tess clicks off the call; the screen returns to a picture of their three smiling sons in a swimming pool.

'How much is this going to cost?' asks Tess.

'A lot, but Gill believes we'll be entitled to substantial compensation.'

'It's not about the money though.'

'There's going to be a lot of expense involved, trips over there probably,' says Matteo. 'The psychological effect this is going to have on Freddie, on us, on the boys, the distress. They might need support. Besides we're going to need some of that money to pay Gill.'

'I wish we hadn't done it.'

'We can still change our minds, not take it forward.'

'I don't mean this. I mean the IVF.'

She looks up at him, feels her face moulding into an accusation.

'It's too late for what ifs, Tess; this is the card we've been dealt.' He scratches his chin.

'Daddy!' The monitor shrieks to life.

'I'll go,' she says.

'No, I will. Why don't you choose something on Netflix, take your mind off everything, wind down.'

She goes into the living room, picks up the remote and puts it down again. All those photographs in the glass cabinet, Freddie doesn't belong there, but where are the children that do?

Part Two

Chapter 8

Florida, USA

The coffee maker rattles and shakes, and Annie whips the jug out, the brown boil of it sloshing over the sides. She turns on the faucet and lets the cold gush over her seared fingers. A drip of coffee has stained the belly of her blue dress with the New York skyline along the hem. She pours herself a cup, heavy on the milk, then sits on a high stool at the counter cramped with sauce bottles. She turns on her little black laptop.

As she waits for it to boot up, Alan, their tabby cat, jumps onto the counter and upends a bottle of olive oil. She sets the bottle upright again and puts Alan onto the floor, which he decorates with greasy paw prints. He wanders into the furthest reach of the small room and jumps onto the worn couch, while she soaks up the puddle with a foul-smelling cloth.

The computer screen is filled with the flatlining stats of her website. No one around here is interested in her running a craft party for their kids, it seems, and the page where she uploaded some photographs of her artwork has only had two views in the past three months.

Someone knocks on the front door. She pushes her hands through the slats of the blind to see who it is. Christy from downstairs is standing there in beige patent heels, her long blonde hair framing a pixie-porcelain face. When Annie opens the door, the wooden heart dangling on the outside scrapes back and forth like a Skandi pendulum.

'Morning,' says Annie. 'Coffee? I just put a pot on.'

'I've given up the caffeine,' says Christy. 'Besides, we've got the realtor arriving any minute, you know, to price up.' She smiles and thrusts some letters towards Annie. 'I came to give you these.'

'Okay, thanks.'

'I lifted them from the mailbox by mistake, meant to give them to you yesterday, but it went clean out of my head.'

Annie looks at the envelopes. There's a bill from the electricity company – she knows it's a final demand – and something else, a familiar gold bird motif on the front. The Pavilion St Michael Clinic. Annie doesn't pretend Willow was anything other than IVF, and if Christy's seen the return address it might stop her asking when she's having number two. Annie fans herself down with the envelopes. It's not as if they can afford to try for a second child. Carl's mother paid for their one and only round of IVF, and they're still paying her back almost four years on.

'Just a few bills, no surprises there then,' says Annie.

'I'm so forgetful at the moment,' says Christy. 'Guess I have my mind on other things. I'm pregnant, you see.'

Annie peers at the pink T-shirt dress clinging to Christy's lack of flesh.

'You can't be!' she squeaks. 'I mean, well . . .' She throws herself full force into hugging Christy. 'Congratulations!'

Christy lets go first and they pull apart.

'Well,' says Christy, circling her hand on her size zero bump. 'I wouldn't want to make Tiger an only one.'

The smile blooms bigger and more determined on Annie's face.

'I was an only,' says Christy. 'And it was so boring, so lonely. No, I wouldn't do that to Tiger.'

'Well, thanks again for dropping these off,' says Annie, her smile so painful it's like a couple of tacks are keeping it in place.

Christy waves and Annie keeps her eyes on those heels, willing them to topple down the rickety teak stairs, not to hurt the unborn baby, but just to rid Christy of one of her Tippex-white teeth. She shuts the door and the heels continue to stab their way down. Annie digs into her handbag, unwraps a strip of Juicy Fruit and stuffs it into her mouth.

'Mama!'

'Coming, butterbean!'

Annie opens the electricity bill – only a week left to settle. She'll have to borrow the money from the savings account she opened for Willow; she'll pay it back eventually. She pins the bill to a board, a busy collage of receipts, photographs, and recipes torn from magazines. She opens the letter from the clinic.

Dear Mr and Mrs Amstel,

We are carrying out an investigation into an incident that happened around the time that you were treated at the clinic, involving one of our medical staff.

As part of this, we are writing to everyone who underwent fertility treatment, and would be grateful if you could contact the clinic at your earliest convenience to answer some questions.

What kind of incident? Sexual harassment? Abuse of trust? Some kind of infection? Could there be something wrong with Willow? She thinks of the girl's webbed toes, the two toes nearest the big one joined up right to the base of the nails. 'Nothing to worry about,' said the doctor at the hospital where Annie gave birth, but perhaps that doctor was wrong.

Willow bounces towards Annie now, the skinny arm of her ragged one-eared teddy bear in her hand. Annie scoops Willow up and kisses her button nose, pinches her cheek where the dimple is.

Willow looks outraged. 'Stop!'

Annie kisses her again and again. 'Stop, Mama!'

'Do you want a pop tart?'

'I could fix you some pancakes before I go,' says Carl, who

has come into the room now, yawning. Knee-length yellow cargo pants so low on his waist that Annie can see his faded underwear, his blond hair so thin it's failing to disguise his impending baldness. And that beard – like he's about to audition for a *Grizzly Adams* remake.

'There's a letter from the clinic,' says Annie.

'What?'

'The IVF place – they want to ask us some questions.'

'What? Why?' Carl's face is animated with shock, his mouth hanging.

'I don't know; it's a bit vague.'

'Oh, but why would they . . .?' His mouth still hasn't closed.

'I want pop tart,' says Willow.

Annie sticks one under the grill on the counter, and turns the knob up to high. Carl shakes his head in Annie's direction.

'She likes them,' says Annie.

'It's got about as much nutrition in it as a piece of paper.'

'Well, the world's gone crazy with gluten free this and low sugar that. There's a name for that kind of obsession . . .' She twirls a finger in the air. It's coming to her. 'Orthorexia.'

'Well, at least that's one condition you sure as hell don't have.' She flicks his chest, smiling.

He laughs, loops his arm around her and kisses her cheek. 'I've got to go,' he says.

He collects his tool kit from the floor in a jangle of metal. She stares up at him and puckers her expectant lips. He kisses her nose. Her nose! Then he lifts and twirls Willow around and around.

'I'm fying!' she shrieks.

He throws her over his shoulder in a firefighter's lift.

'Jesus, Carl, be careful of her neck.'

He slots Willow into her raised wooden chair, and Annie clips the harness around her, testing that it's secure. The front door slams behind him; his footsteps are slow on the stairs. Annie pulls the overdone pop tart out of the grill and knifes away the black bits. She sets it in front of Willow who pats Annie's belly.

'Baby?'

Annie looks down at her slight bulge.

'Er, no.'

'Yes.'

Willow's face doesn't possess the kind of beauty most parents see in their own children; Willow is silly pretty, child-model material, nothing like Annie or Carl. The thought clogs up Annie's head. Willow is vibrant and vital, surely the clinic can't have done anything that'll affect her health adversely. The line of *House* and *ER* boxsets packed onto a shelf from the days before downloads catches Annie's eye then. She's watched enough hospital dramas to know that sometimes things can go terribly wrong.

Chapter 9

Surrey, England

i

Freddie is a comma on top of his quilt, Tess kneeling beside him. He turns away from her, closing his eyes, his lashes feathery pale. She looks at the knobble of his elbows. Those are not Rossi bones nor Rossi eyelashes. Even his tiny ears are the opposite of her boys', which protrude like their father's.

Freddie being here is wrong, the past years have been wrong, as if she's been method acting, and now the filming has ended. The green, white and red stripes of the Italian flag are pinned to the wall above Freddie's head. 'Kick it!' Matteo had yelled once as he flung the football towards a motionless Freddie. Freddie was Matteo's last hope.

Who does Freddie belong to? Are his parents tall or short? Would his real parents love him the way that Tess isn't able to? Are they kind people, kinder than she is? A lit-up globe of the earth sits in a stand on top of the walnut chest of drawers at the foot of Freddie's bed. Where are his parents? Where are her children?

She thinks back to the riptide of pain in her pelvis as the oxytocin dripped into her arm. She lay on the hospital bed, twisted one way then the other, her hand on her tightening stomach. She'd been going for 24 hours when the nurse flannelled her forehead and said, 'Three centimetres dilated'.

As time wore on and the contractions started getting closer it was as if someone was ramming the broken neck of a bottle into her vagina. She lowed like a cow; her other babies hadn't hurt like this. She would have been more up for having her leg severed off with a rusty saw yet still she didn't ask for serious pain relief.

When it was time to push she felt the centre of her stretching with fiery agony, but still the baby didn't emerge, then that doctor came in with the metal forceps. It was an excruciating, hot liquid entry into the world then the floppy newborn was rushed into another room.

When a midwife put him into Tess' arms a good while later, there was a spherical bloodied bruise on his forehead, a cut beneath his chin. Tess opened the white towel. The baby was limp and cadaverous, something of the extraterrestrial about him.

She looks up at the lopsided pencil grey drawing hanging on the wall at the side of Freddie's bed, a picture of a girl with pigtails, circles for her hands with lines sticking out of them. Tess touches Freddie's face. Why can't she love him properly? The way a mother is meant to love a child, instantly, unconditionally.

'Go away,' he says.

She can do better than this surely. Motherhood was meant to come naturally to her. Since her mid-twenties, she'd been longing for a child, and then she'd had Ava and Ava had been wrenched away. Tess had held her daughter's lifeless body and cried a delta of tears, her every cell contracting, pleading. *Let her live.* It's still there inside her, everything that happened, rubble in the foundations of a house.

She looks at Freddie. *It's not your fault,* she thinks. 'Goodnight,' she says. A dish shatters distantly.

Downstairs, she pads across the cold, chequerboard hall tiles. Matteo is in the kitchen, lifting shards of glass from the butler sink. The light is faint from the cooker hood.

The blood from his hand has marbled the white enamel, and in a corner is a shard of crystal, a leaf carved into it. He's broken the last one of the crystal tumblers they got as a wedding present.

His skin is puce, the stench of alcohol radiating from him. He lays the broken glass on top of a piece of damp newspaper.

'It's late. Where have you been?' she asks.

'I had to get the plumbers in to sort out a leak,' he says. 'It's been so busy. I should have called.'

'You've got a manager to deal with that kind of thing.'

'It's my business, Tess!' he snaps.

He winces, touches a hand to the base of his back and arches his spine, vertebrae cracking. He pulls some painkillers from the cupboard, swallowing one dry, the blood from his hand leaking into his sleeve.

She folds the newspaper around the broken glass and pushes it into the bin.

'The sooner you get the bathroom refurbishment underway the better,' she says.

He tears off some kitchen roll and presses it to the cut. It turns red, saturated. He throws the painkillers back into the cupboard and fills a new tumbler with Johnnie Walker.

She's biding her time before she asks about the lawyer again, keeping up the pretence that the clinic's negligence is not a constant, background thought in her head. 'Your back's bad again then.'

His eyes are somewhere faraway. 'It's not great. How was work?'

'One of my clients has recommended me to somebody else, a life coach.'

He laughs bitterly. 'Wonder what she'd advise about our situation.'

'Has something happened with Gill?'

He draws in air, puffs it out. 'She heard from the clinic. They can't find our embryos; they say they weren't frozen. They're trying to contact other patients.'

She leans her backside against the polished steel counter. 'Do they have any idea who Freddie's real parents are?'

'We're Freddie's parents. It doesn't matter about any stupid test. Besides, they can't make anyone have a DNA test; they don't have to comply legally.'

'But wouldn't everyone want to know that they have the right child?'

He scratches his face. She scans him from stubbled chin to dirty shirt, down to his socked feet, his little toe poking through a hole.

'Imagine if the truth only came out three years from now, ten,' she says. 'At least we have time.'

'Time for what?'

'To get to know our children if they're out there.'

He lets out an exasperated breath. 'Even if we do have children, a child, who in their right mind would let us meet them?'

'So why are we doing this then?' she asks.

'To make sure the clinic can't put anyone else through what we're going through. I want them to pay.'

He dumps the bloodied mound of kitchen roll into the sink, then pulls another two sheets from the roll and presses them to his hand. She puts on rubber gloves and mops up the rest of the shards from the sink with a clump of kitchen roll.

'If our embryos made it, I want to meet the children,' she says. 'I'd need some sort of contact. And because I know how desperate I'd be if our children were out there, it's only right that we let Freddie's parents meet him.'

'Christ, no way.'

'They're his flesh and blood.'

'And we are his family.'

'We can't cut them out of his life; think about how he'll feel when he's older, he'll hate us if we do that.'

'The clinic might not even track them down, Tess.'

'But they'll try.'

'They say they'll try. Even if they do, it's likely to take years, and I wouldn't bank on them ever discovering what happened to our embryos.'

'We went there to have a daughter, Matt. They screwed that up for us.'

'Don't make this about Ava. This is not about her.'

'I know that!' Bright geometric shapes oscillate inside her head, Doctor Michael's loud ties.

'The only thing they can give us is compensation,' says Matteo. 'It might help to pay for all the bloody therapy Freddie's going to need to come to terms with this.'

'And that's why you're doing it, for the money?'

'It's not just about the money. We put our lives into their hands, and we ended up with a baby that was meant for someone else. We deserve a payout.'

We deserve to have our own children, she thinks, eyeballing a photograph stuck to the fridge with a magnet – Freddie jumping on a fountain spraying from the ground in central London, his hair wet through, his eyes shut and streaming, a wide smile on his face. Matteo finishes his drink then walks out of the kitchen, rubbing his back.

She opens a cupboard, pulls out his painkillers and stuffs one of the amber-coloured jellies into her mouth.

Chapter 10

Florida, USA

Annie drops the garbage sack into the dumpster and turns to look at the realtor post plunged into the ground like a victory flag. She walks back towards the apartment and looks up at the rickety balcony where there's a hole in the boards big enough for a small foot to slip through. She hasn't contacted the landlord about repairing it, not when he's been so under-standing about them being late with the rent for the past four months.

She climbs the stairs, heaves a plant pot, containing a now dead shrub, over the hole and pants. She's better at paper flowers than real ones. She goes inside.

Willow has pulled a gill off the fish Annie made from thin strips of coloured paper. She drops the gill to the floor, and stares at it.

When Annie went downstairs Willow was busy playing schools, her dolls lined up on the couch, her toy bear on a small wooden chair. At least Annie came back in before Willow ruined the whole picture.

'I thought you were playing schools,' says Annie, picking the squashed paper shape off the floor.

'Can I do dis?' Willow points to Annie's quilling paraphernalia.

'Well, I don't know, honey; the pieces of paper are very small.'

The little girl's face squashes up, her nose wrinkled. 'I try.'

'Okay.' Annie lifts Willow into her raised wooden chair and

straps her in. The girl leans her elbows into the turquoise Formica table, which barely fits into the room.

Annie had planned on completing three artwork pieces this week and adding photographs of them to her website. She'll have to work on them after Willow goes to bed. She lifts her fish with its decapitated gill and puts it beside the coffee maker to dry.

She pushes a thin metal spindle into a square of polystyrene. Taking a ribbon of yellow paper, she coils it round the spindle then lets Willow turn the spindle, but it's too hard for her little fingers.

'You help me,' says Willow.

Annie puts her hand around Willow's and together they coil the paper more, then Annie pulls it off the spindle. She pinches the spiralled paper, turning it into a petal shape.

'Fower!' says Willow.

'Flower power,' says Annie and winks.

Willow scrunches both of her eyes shut and laughs. Annie squeezes some glue into a saucer, so that Willow can stick the papery shapes to a piece of card for Granny Lina's birthday. Willow's tongue pokes out from between her lips as she works. Annie's phone starts to ring.

Caller Unknown. Six rings, seven. Annie picks up.

'It's Doctor Michael here.'

'Oh, hello doctor.' She's hyper-aware of her breathy, grateful voice.

Her expectations were low when she'd produced only two eggs during the IVF procedure. Doctor Michael had managed to work a miracle anyway, and Willow had filled their lives with all the light that was missing. Without Doctor Michael, their bedroom would still be littered with thermometers and ovulation kits. Back then, before they'd known it was all pointless: no amount of temperature-taking or timing could counteract Carl's decrepit sperm.

Doctor Michael clears his throat. 'Did you get our letter?'

She eyes the junk drawer, so full it opens only partially. She's mentioned the letter a couple of times to Carl since they got it, and all he could muster was, 'I'm not sure what to do.' But if Doctor Michael is calling, perhaps there's something seriously wrong with Willow.

'What's going on?' she belts out.

'I'm so sorry to call you like this, it's just, as we said in our letter, we're running checks on some of our patients and, well, I'd like to ask you some questions about your treatment.'

She's been around panic as a child, and knows how to read it. The urgency in the doctor's voice, the breathing not quite right. He's building up to something; something large and dark beneath his carefully chosen words.

'Well, fire away,' she says.

'Did you agree to egg donation?'

'I wasn't exactly the golden goose, I only had two.' She slings her now cold coffee into the sink. 'What is this about?'

'An accusation has been made against one of our staff.'

'What kind of accusation?'

'We're trying to clear his name and as part of this we're asking a number of patients to visit the clinic for a DNA test.'

There's the sensation of falling, a screech in her ears. She can't seem to take in enough air.

'What's he being accused of?'

'I'm afraid I can't really say.'

'Lord, Jesus.'

She picks up her empty mug then puts it down again, a memory in her head. That time at Crystal's Cake Shop, a woman from her baby group had laughed at how ridiculously alike her husband and baby son were. 'It's a primal thing,' Christy had said. 'The baby always looks like the father in the first few months, so the father recognises himself and bonds.'

As Annie walked home, she tugged away the muslin covering the stroller and looked at Willow. Her brown hair lusciously thick for a newborn, that swarthy skin. Annie could find no sign of Carl in Willow's face, but what did it matter anyway? Carl wasn't having any problems bonding, that was for sure. Talking to Willow in that soft voice, churning out ice cube trays full of healthy purees when she went on solids; thrusting Willow into Annie's arms whenever she cried with a pained look on his face.

She walks into the furthest reach of the cramped room and shout-whispers into the phone. 'Is there a chance that Carl might not be Willow's father?'

His voice drops, gentle. 'We want you both to come in for the test.'

She walks around the room, bumping into things, skidding on one of Willow's books. *Willow is ours.* The phrase pulses through her like an antibody, but tears are pushing their way out of her eyes.

'I don't know, I mean, I'll have to talk to Carl.'

'Yes, yes, of course.'

She cuts the call, looks at her daughter, her illuminated, beautiful child. The person who Annie loves most in the world, her reason. If there's been a mix-up, so what? She doesn't need to know. She remembers that big word Dr Michael had said, his verdict that their infertility was down to Carl; there was nothing wrong with her at all. 'Oligozoospermia,' he'd said. 'But I've never smoked,' Carl said. 'I hardly drink.'

Dr Michael had recommended specialist IVF – Intracytoplasmic Sperm Injection. He'd take a single sperm from Carl's poor repertoire and inject it into Annie's egg. But first things first, Annie would have to produce eggs by pumping her body full of drugs and there was no way she wanted to do that. Besides there were plenty of children in the world who she could be a parent to. In the car afterwards, Carl sat there with his head hung low, staring at his own bitten fingernails.

'Adopt, that's what we'll do,' Annie had blabbered, taking up his hand, but Carl said he couldn't dedicate years of his life to a child that wasn't his. It seemed like she wouldn't get to be a mother after all. Then Lina had offered to pay for a round of

IVF. Annie had injected herself with those drugs, telling herself that the sacrifice would be worth it. She'd nullify the negative effects by becoming a walking advert for five-a-day. Hell, she even stopped buying cookies. And then their minuscule chance had arrived. When her period didn't come and the pregnancy test was positive, she did a cartwheel on the beach (she'd always been good at cartwheels) while Carl uncorked a bottle of sparkling wine that she didn't touch a drop of. For a month afterwards, she worried that her cartwheel might have dislodged the precarious life growing inside her.

They have a child, their child. Annie is the one who gave birth to her, who plaits her hair, who soothes her when she falls. She's Willow's mother, no matter what. But what if she isn't really? What if neither of them are Willow's parents, or just one of them?

'You sad, Mama.'

'I'm not sad, butterbean.'

'It's bad to lie,' says Willow.

Chapter 11

Surrey, England

Sorry we could not log you in. Please try entering your account details again. Tess types Matteo's email password into her computer, but the same message flashes up. She wants to update the hotel website with some quotes that satisfied customers have sent to him, so she tries phoning him. He doesn't pick up.

There's not much time left before she has to collect Freddie from nursery and she doesn't want to be late. She's trying to be a model parent to make up for his frequent bad behaviour. They've always been so patient with him, calmly explaining why he mustn't throw things or shout at other children when he's angry, and they're unfailingly kind to Tess. Still, at least Freddie hasn't bitten anyone since his birthday party. Upstairs, she goes into his room, shakes and spreads his quilt. She picks up the pillow, presses it to her nose and gets the pungent smell of sleep. It's like when someone has borrowed her children's T-shirts and the clothes are returned washed in a different detergent. There's something jarring about that smell.

If only she'd made a different decision before the embryo transfer; if she'd had just one embryo put back inside her, she might have ended up with the right child, a little girl. The phone rings, and she runs to their bedroom to pick up the extension.

'Mrs Rossi?'

'Yes?'

Children are chattering in the background, and the woman at the other end of the phone doesn't seem to register Tess' reply.

'Who is this, please?' asks Tess.

'It's Kim – I'm afraid you're going to have to come and get Freddie. He's pretty upset.'

'Why?'

'One of the children has been taken to hospital.'

Tess picks up the photograph of Freddie on Matteo's bedside cabinet. 'What's he done?'

'It was an accident,' says Kim. 'I'm sure it was nothing malicious, but Freddie pushed a button up a little girl's nose, and we couldn't get it out.'

Tess lays the photograph facedown and balls her fist.

'He won't stop crying,' says Kim.

'I'll come and get him.' Tess doesn't recognise the tired tone of her own voice.

She cuts the call, tilts her head to the ceiling. How foolish she was to think that he could change. She swallows the compulsion to swear.

It's half past ten at night when Tess comes down from her shower, the towel turbaned on her head.

'Okay, thanks.' Matteo puts the phone back into the cradle.

She hovers in the kitchen doorway. 'Who was that?'

It takes several seconds for him to turn around, and when he does he has a twisted expression on his face.

'Gill again?' she asks.

'The clinic want us to take another test. They want to be sure about Freddie.'

She ties her dressing gown tighter.

'They want us to go over there,' he says. 'But we can't just drop everything.'

She feels the weight of the water in the kettle then flicks it on.

'The lawyer for the clinic is insistent,' says Matteo. 'Gill says we don't have to, they can't force us.'

'Then we won't.'

He sips at a glass of water, ruffling his salt and pepper hair. 'They're disputing the test we've taken though.'

Steam spouts from the kettle and she holds a hand over it, feeling the warm moisture collect on her skin.

'I could do without this,' he says. 'On top of everything, but if we don't go, it'll drag the whole thing out. I want to settle as soon as we can.'

She pulls a cup from the cupboard and slings in a herbal teabag. 'Money, money, money.'

'What's that supposed to mean?' The kettle boils.

'I want to find out about our children. I want to know them.'

'Look, say we do have children, a child – they're not going to be ours, Tess. We won't have any rights.'

'You don't know that.'

She pours the kettle, missing the cup, the water puddling the counter.

'If you're feeling like this, what on earth are Freddie's genetic parents going to want from us?' asks Matteo. 'Maybe they'll make all sorts of demands. They might want to be part of his life, strangers, people we don't even know. Christ, of all the clinics we could have gone to . . .'

'You can't blame the whole thing on me,' she says.

'I'm not, it's just . . . Oh, I don't know.'

'We should go. We need to resolve this,' she says. *Even though we both want different outcomes.* She takes a sip of tea; it burns her tongue.

'But what'll we tell the boys?' he asks.

'We'll make something up. Why should their worlds be turned upside down by what that clinic has done?'

'Phoenix is bound to work out something is wrong though,' he says.

'Then maybe we should leave them here with Jenna.'

'Fine, but we'll have to be honest with her.'

'No!' She turns away from him, blows on her tea, cupping the mug in her hands. 'We'll invent something, say we've got to go to an important business meeting or something.'

'You're going to have to confide in someone about this eventually, Tess. Let the facade crack.'

She hears the barb in his voice, and straightens.

Chapter 12

Florida, USA

The office of Sure Water Publishing Services is a fog of throat-scuffing smoke. A desk is littered with polystyrene takeaway boxes, and a black ashtray overflowing with lipstick-smudged cigarette butts. Annie stoops to avoid the slants in the gabled ceiling; Willow coughs beside her.

'What time do you call this, Frida Kahlo?' asks Roz, spinning backwards on the wheels of her office chair, a cigarette sagging between her cherry-red lips.

Annie touches her finger to the hairy island between her eyebrows, and blows out air, thinking of the text message Lina sent her this morning. *Cannot babysit today. Have flu.*

'Lina's sick, so I have to look after Willow. I can't stay.'

'So what the fuck are you here for then?' asks Roz, smoke belching from her nostrils. She coughs and looks at Willow. 'No offence, Willa.'

There are columns of piled-high books dotted about the place. Annie picks up a paperback and fans Willow's face. 'I thought I'd take Tom's cover over, get him to sign the approval document.'

Roz stabs her cigarette butt into the ashtray with such violence she could be killing a cockroach. She shoves another Marlboro Light between her lips, flicks her silver lighter and puffs. Annie's got to get Willow out of here before she contracts secondary lung cancer.

'Yeah, about that cover . . .' Roz skids her wheeled chair back to her clogged desk and starts sifting through the detritus, then it's there in front of her, Annie's design. Annie made it by coiling thin ribbons of different coloured paper around a spindle then building up the tiny spirals into petals and corollas. The piece of card is covered in flowers.

Roz looks at it with a curled lip. 'It's like something out of a church craft class for seniors,' she says, screwing up her nose and turning the picture this way and that.

'It's called quilling.'

'It's called expensive.' Roz drops the picture onto the desk and spins closer to look up at Annie.

'But Tom's paid $4,000 for a 500 copy print run,' says Annie. It's not all that often she gets to look down on people.

Willow sneezes.

'I'm not running this publishing company for the good of my health you know; I'm doing it to make money!' Roz breaks into a hacking cough. 'Show him this instead. It's less complicated, much more eye-catching.'

Roz lifts a simple print of a red flower that a seven year old could have produced on a computer.

'Oh, come on,' says Annie, taking it from her.

'Show it to him!'

An unfinished graphic design degree. Five years at the photography shop and then, oh, please, has it really been that long – six at Sure Water Publishing Services? Annie's got to quit and go somewhere else, but where to? The island isn't exactly a seething metropolis of opportunity, and she needs a job.

'Okay . . . I'll see what Tom says,' she mutters.

'Make sure it's a yes,' says Roz.

Annie pushes the picture into her art folder along with the quilled one. A stuck-on flower shears off and topples onto the floor. Willow picks it up and they leave, Annie stomping her frustration all the way down the steps.

The windscreen is dotted with rain. A sperm-shaped droplet rolls down and joins a circular one – as easy as that. Oh, but just stop! Annie looks at Willow in the rearview mirror, hugging that bedraggled teddy of hers and kissing it, stroking its fur.

She swings a sudden left at the junction without indicating. A white car passes, the driver leaning hard on the horn. The honk blares and fades away. She switches on the wipers and presses, a pathetic froth of soap spraying over the windscreen. The wipers push and pull, leaving the mottled glass only a fraction cleaner than before.

There's the grassy roundabout with the water fountain in its centre, and beyond that, a pink building with turrets like a castle, windows the height of a grown man. She rolls the Versa into a car park space and pulls up the handbrake so hard it threatens to snap off. The door on the driver's side is still jammed shut from that collision with a tree a few months back, so she struggles over the handbrake and climbs out of the passenger door. She gathers Willow up, the art folder like a shield against the girl's back. The American flag, speared into the manicured grass, sags, rings chinking.

'*Giddy-up, Mama!*' Willow pats her mother's arm.

Annie walks on, past the spread of grey-blue water in the bay, the base of an old tree with exposed roots like a gnarled brown hand.

She climbs the stone steps to the vast reception with its pillars and corniced ceiling. Behind the curved counter, there's a concierge with scissor sharp hairs sticking out of her chin.

'I'm here for Tom.'

'I'll ring you up,' says the concierge.

Herb appears, brown-slippered and shuffling, a clear tube snaking into one of his nostrils, his belly bulging inside his short-sleeved plaid shirt.

'Hey there, Herb,' says Annie.

'That your girl?'

'That she is,' says Annie, pride swelling her chest.

Herb looks at Willow then regards Annie suspiciously.

'Must look like her daddy, I guess,' he says.

Willow points at Herb's belly.

'Baby!' she says.

'Ssssh!' says Annie.

'Der's a baby in der!'

'What's that?' Herb's mouth hangs as he looks at Annie. 'You're having a baby?'

'No, you are!' Willow jabs her finger towards Herb.

'Oh, there you are, Herb.' A male nurse is beside Herb now, and starts to lead him away.

'Well, nice seeing y'all!' calls Herb.

Annie's flagging inside, but she lifts her hand and waves.

'Baby!' says Willow.

'Honey, men can't have babies.'

'Daddy can,' says Willow.

Oh, Jeez. Annie grabs Willow's hand and heads towards the spiral staircase.

Tom's place is on the fifth floor, but there's no way they'll be taking that elevator, metal box teetering on tightropes. Besides Annie could do with the exercise. Her platforms clump against the antique tiles as she climbs. Willow's dress swishes, neck to knee in pink even though Annie can't stand the colour. The kid won't wear anything but. Willow lets go of her hand, but Annie keeps bounding on and up, her bosoms bouncing, a tiara of sweat beads forming on her forehead. Willow manages to keep pace.

'Hold onto the handrail now,' says Annie. Willow clutches at it with her slim fingers.

Each floor has its own smell. Tobacco on two, over-boiled broccoli on three. On four, there's that graffiti tag, the name Cheryl in marker pen, a smiling face inside the curve of the C.

On five, Annie lifts Willow who presses the bell, even though Tom's oak-panelled front door is already open a chink. *Ding-dong.*

'Hello there!' Tom's faint voice.

They go inside. There's rubbish overflowing from the swing bin in the galley kitchen. Wooden cupboards top and bottom, a grey counter speckled with crumbs. In the lounge beyond, Tom's beige chinos are sticking out from the easy chair, which is the colour of MasterFoods mustard, his upper half hidden by its velvet wings.

'Hi, Mr Tom,' Annie calls and barrels into the yellow and brown room, too dark and stale-smelling.

She picks up the glass vase on the sill containing tea-coloured water and drooping, dried roses that used to be red; she knows this as she was the one that bought them. A marble fireplace that resembles an enormous shell is topped with photograph frames and childish artwork. There are four mismatched easy chairs in all, and a pink brocade pouffe. The yellow shade on the standard lamp is fraying and a long piece of silky twine is hanging down.

Tom gives a half smile, the skin crinkled around his left blue eye. His poorly shaven face is twice the length of Annie's. He has a full head of soft grey hair and either side of his considerable red nose, lines curve to his mouth like brackets. His left hand is trembling with the effort of trying to push himself out of the chair.

'Oh, no, Mr Tom, don't get up,' says Annie.

'Wish you'd quit it with the honorifics.'

'Oh, sorry, Mr . . .'

'I mean it was okay when you were a kid, but . . . hey, what's wrong?'

Her mouth hefts an unconvincing smile while Tom continues to wrestle with the chair.

'Hey, precious one,' Tom says to Willow who climbs onto his knee and covers his face – half-frozen from a stroke – in kisses. Tom laughs.

Annie moves on through to the thin kitchen where she dumps

the old flowers into the swing bin and pours the stinky vase water away. She fires some dishwashing liquid into the sink and sponges it down then wipes the crumbs off the counter. Clean and fresh smelling now, unlike her own place. She peeps her head around the door.

'You want me to fix you something proper to eat?'

'Oh, hell, you people, all you want to do is feed me!'

She wipes her wet hands down her dress and goes back into the living room.

'The place is a bit of a tip,' says Tom.

Annie looks down at the boxed photographs on the coffee table. 'Doing some more research for your book then?'

'Just picking out some pictures. There's going to be four pages of them.'

She tried to persuade him that publishing a book with Sure Water was a waste of money, and when she failed, she tried to get him the 20 per cent discount that employees and their families are entitled to. 'But he's not family,' said Roz.

Willow starts poking through Annie's handbag, pulls out a big box of toffees and shakes them.

Tom breaks into a smile. 'My favourite!' he says like he always does; Annie brings him the same box every week.

He winks at Willow and she tries to wink back, but doesn't quite manage it. She finds a game in Annie's bag too – matching baby animals with their mothers.

'Play, Mr Tom,' she says, handing it to him.

'Well, okay, as long as it involves sitting down,' says Tom. He puts a goat beside a lamb on the coffee table.

'Dat wrong!' says Willow.

'Is it?'

'Der!' says Willow, moving the sheep beside the lamb, the goat beside the kid.

Tom lets her win.

'You want to get the cookie jar?' he asks.

Willow nods and runs in the direction of the kitchen.

'So . . . I have your cover,' says Annie quietly, thinking back to the plugs in the kitchen. They were all off, so no danger of Willow being electrocuted. And the toxic cleaning products in the cupboard under the sink, she's sure the lock was on. She takes a deep breath, zips open the art folder and pulls out the design. A large piece of card slips out and lands on the carpet.

With one hand Tom opens his glasses case and perches the tortoiseshell frames on his nose, his rheumy eyes magnifying into bulging blue circles. Annie hands him Roz's cover.

'It's kind of simpler than I thought it would be,' he says.

'It's all about the colour; it'll really grab people's attention.' The usual high pitch of Annie's voice is flattened under rock.

Tom barks a laugh. 'I'm under no illusions, Annie. The only person who'll read this book is me, and maybe you'll give me a sympathy vote.'

'That's not true.'

'The book's garbage!'

His eyes travel to the window, strung with a sun that Willow made from transparent yellow paper. 'I wanted to do something for Marie. Apart from her plaque, there's no sign that she was ever here at all.'

Annie shouldn't have got his hopes up with the mood board, all those old photographs and the pictures of flowers he knows everything about. Whether they like sun or shade, what kind of soil, their Latin names.

Tom's good arm creaks and reaches to the floor; he picks up the fallen piece of card. It's covered in Annie's paper flowers. The redring milkweed with its mop head, the spiky queen of the night bloom.

'What do you call this?' asks Tom, rubbing a finger over the rough shapes. 'It's really something; it's different. It's good.'

'Good?'

'Better than good. You did this?'

She nods.

'But not this one, right?' The simple design ripples in his shaking hand.

'Right.'

'Well, I'd like the best one to be the cover, and this is the best one.' He lifts the quilled picture.

Annie closes her eyes briefly.

'What?' asks Tom.

'The thing is, Roz doesn't like it. Oh, hell, I'm sorry Tom. You've paid all that money, and—'

'What else am I going to spend it on?' He holds her gaze. She looks away.

'Too damned independent . . .' He shakes his head. 'That self portrait you did when you were a kid, your hair a mess, a butterfly in it, lightning strikes behind. So the paint dripped a bit, so what. It's beautiful.' His eyes wander towards the top of the fireplace where it's propped. 'I never get tired of looking at it.'

He traces his fingers across the ribbons of colourful flowers on his lap, their stalks, the reeds rising from the bottom of the card. 'I've never seen anything like this before though.'

Willow comes into the room, chomping, the clear plastic cookie jar in her hand, her chubby cheeks encrusted with Oreo crumbs.

'Are you going to share them around?' asks Annie.

Willow continues to crunch and doesn't answer. Annie gets up and looks at the photographs on the mantel. Willow standing beside Tom in the gardens down there, his good hand clawed on her shoulder. The frame next to it shows a three-year-old Annie in a flowery bikini on the beach, a pair of men's brown socks pulled up to her knees.

'Come here,' Tom says, and Willow climbs back onto his knee. He rests his huge chin on top of her head and takes a cookie.

'She's a good kid,' he says. 'Takes after her mother in that regard. Just like you took after yours.' He often sings Nancy's praises. Annie takes the cookie jar from Willow and lays it on the coffee table.

Willow's missed out on hundreds of kindnesses because Nancy is gone. She was tightly strung, given to occasional fits of rage out of proportion to Annie's misdemeanours – leaving her bag on the school bus earned a slap around the face; dropping an egg that oozed goo onto the floor resulted in Annie's ear being pulled. But Annie's convinced being a grandmother would have smoothed out Nancy's jagged edges.

Tom starts to munch on his cookie then looks at Annie. 'Hey, Willow, you go on into the bedroom and bring me my wallet, will you?' he says.

'Come on,' says Annie smiling. 'You don't have to—'

'You can't stop me giving her pocket money. Now, tell me, what's up?'

Tom comes from a time when they put sanitary napkins on the top shelf; she hasn't ever told him she had IVF, but she's wearing it on her face now. She might not be Willow's mom; Carl might not be Willow's father.

'Turns out Willow might have relatives I didn't know about.'

His eyes skirt the room as if they're in search of something. 'What? But . . .?'

'There's things I haven't told you.' She sits down on the pouffe.

His loose cheeks jiggle. 'What things?' he asks, cookie crumbs specking the air.

'About our family.'

He looks at Annie with alarm. 'Oh, Annie, I—'

'I went to a fertility clinic to have Willow.'

He takes a breath, scratches his head. 'We used to hope for a miracle, Marie and me. Back then, we didn't have that option.'

'The thing is, the clinic, they're running these tests on some of the people who had treatment there. They say they're checking because someone's made an accusation against one of the staff, but it's obvious they think there's been some kind of baby mix-up.

What if Willow's part of it? Maybe they mixed up my eggs with the wrong sperm.' *Did she really just say sperm in front of an 83-year-old man?*

Tom finishes his cookie and shifts, the chair creaking beneath him. 'But Willow's your daughter.'

'They've asked us to do a DNA test.'

'It's all a bit much for my simple brain, Annie. *Brave New World* in the twenty-tens.'

'Maybe they put one of my embryos into someone else by mistake. Maybe Willow has a sibling somewhere.'

'It doesn't matter what any stupid test says. That girl was given to you to look after. You're her mother, no matter what.' He starts drawing some invisible shape on the arm of his chair with his frantic finger.

'But if something went wrong,' says Annie. 'If she's someone else's child genetically, it'd be wrong to keep that a secret from her. She deserves to know.'

He bites his bottom lip so hard his false teeth leave a dent in the flesh. Willow returns to the room, Tom's battered brown leather wallet in her hand. He takes it from her, riffles out a fifty dollar note.

'That's way too much,' says Annie.

'Mama will buy you a new dress with that, or something else, a new toy maybe,' he says to Willow.

Tom picks up the quilled picture again.

'Can I keep this?' he asks.

'Sure you can,' says Annie.

'And if it has to be that other dreadful cover, that's just the way it is.' He shrugs a shoulder.

Willow hands him another Oreo and he begins to munch again. Willow helps herself to a second one, or is that a third or fourth?

Annie wanders over to the mantel and looks at that photograph of her red-headed young self with the brown socks on. She must have been about Willow's age when it was taken, the slightly squinty eye, the gappy milk teeth. She looks at the photograph of Willow, her pink butterfly T-shirt riding up so that her pot belly is on display. Her long, silken hair, that olive skin, the moles under her eye.

The girls in these photographs look nothing alike. But maybe Tom's right; maybe none of that matters.

Chapter 13

Tess feels stodgy with aeroplane food, her armpits in need of a wash. The building in front of her is orange, a collection of air bricks forming a white rectangle in one of its walls. An awning is fixed above the glass doors, *Johnson Rowell Estate*. The clinic has footed the bill for everything including the flights. She combs her hand over the grainy interior of the hired Ford Fusion.

'This is the place?' she asks.

'It doesn't look like it did on the internet,' says Matteo.

'It's a dump.'

She turns to see Freddie in the back, his head wedged against the glass, his closed eyes, the rasp of his breathing.

'Let's hope it's better inside,' says Matteo.

He opens the boot. The wheels of the two cases scrape the tarmac as he pulls them along and goes inside.

From the car rental place next door, a skeletal man inside a battered pick-up truck leers at Tess, his elbow perched on the sill of his open window, his entire arm covered in a lacy black tattoo. She gets out of the car and leans into the back to unclip Freddie who starts to wake, yawning and stretching his arms.

'We're here,' she says.

She thinks of Jenna's face last week when she told her they had a business meeting in America and would be taking only Freddie with them. 'Of course, I'll have the boys,' Jenna had said, suspicion swirling in her eyes. 'Is everything okay?' 'Everything's good.' Tess had painted on a smile.

Deep in the pocket of her dress, she touches the marble she took from Phoenix's drawer, a splash of blue through it. She massages the little giraffe-shaped eraser that belongs to Luca. Though her boys are far away, she feels them right here beside her like an amputee sensing phantom limbs.

Freddie is heavy in her arms as she pulls open the glass door and goes into the tobacco-brown foyer. Some of the linoleum floor tiles are stuck down with peeling red tape.

'There's been a mix-up,' says Matteo. Their eyes catch. 'They haven't booked the villa for us. It won't be available for another couple of days.' Four of his fingers are pressed into the counter, bloodless at the tips. Freddie wakes and climbs down.

The woman behind the counter chews on a piece of food, the dough of it churning around her mouth. 'Sorry about that, Ma'am. We've got a room in the main hotel, but y'all are gonna have to bunk in together.'

Matteo sighs.

'It'll be fine,' says Tess.

Freddie is running around in circles; he trips and falls on a torn tile. Forced wails tumble from his mouth and Matteo lifts him. 'It's okay, my boy.'

Freddie stops crying at once.

'It's number 14, up here on the left.' The woman starts going down the corridor in front of them, the heels of her flip-flopped feet caked in hard skin.

They step into a lilac room stale with cigarette smoke, a pink valance frilled around the base of the double bed. A single bed is pushed against a wall. Tess catches the woman staring at her hand and stuffs it into her pocket.

'Just holler if you need me!' The woman leaves.

Freddie climbs onto the double bed and starts to trampoline. Tess runs her fingers over the dresser, collecting a dustball the size of a baby mouse. Matteo goes outside to collect the rest of their luggage. She watches him through the window, his collapsing posture, his head bowed. The bed continues to creak, Freddie laughing.

In the bathroom, a pubic hair is stranded on the avocado green sink. She runs the tap, and the cascading, circling water collects the wiry hair, spinning it down the plughole. She splashes water onto her face, then dots on some cleanser and rubs it off with cotton wool.

Stripped of foundation and mascara-free, her eyes in the mirror put her in mind of raisins. She doesn't look like she should, and she turns away from the disappointment. Freddie starts bashing on the bathroom door; it's then that she realises it's locked.

'Mummy. Let me in!'

She counts to fifty before she pulls back the bolt.

Chapter 14

Annie wrestles her way over the handbrake of her car and gets out of the passenger door. She smoothes out her dress, patterned with penguins, and opens the back door, an eggy smell wafting over her.

Willow, in her car seat, is waggling her finger in front of her toy bear like she's telling him off.

'What's he done this time?'

'He farted.'

'I think it might have been you who did that.'

Annie climbs the stairs with Willow in her arms, her rubber-soled sandals soundless on the wood.

Opening the front door, she sees Lina and Carl in the kitchen, Carl with his back to her, Lina in an old brown dress, her feet slumped over in her black block heels, more Colour-Me-Dowdy than Colour-Me-Beautiful.

'You could at least try to make me feel better,' says Carl. The heat of anger is in his cheeks though he's aggravatingly quiet even when he's cross.

'Well, you wanted me to be honest,' says Lina, her German accent becoming more pronounced. A horse-grunt shoots from her nose, her mouth puckering into an entry wound.

'Ganny!'

Carl jumps, shock stamped across the forest of his face.

'I didn't even hear your car,' says Lina, smiling, the skin around her eyes crinkling as Willow runs towards her. She crushes the child into a hug that looks painful. 'Hello, *schnuckel*.'

Annie catapults her leopard-print bag onto the couch; it tumbles to the floor instead, a pick 'n' mix of used tissues and empty candy wrappers spilling out. Carl tents an oil-smudged hand over his mouth.

'All that money that you paid, that *I* paid!' Lina gores a house-worked finger into her chest as she looks at her son.

'Leave it!' snaps Carl.

Lina sneezes.

'Bless you,' says Annie.

'Granny better go now,' Lina says to Willow. 'I don't want to pass anything onto you, my dear love.'

'Ganny, stay!'

Lina kisses her hand and pats Willow's head almost violently with it. She unlocks herself from the girl's grasp and heads towards the door.

'And you should do this test,' Lina says to Annie as she passes her. 'They might even give you a refund. *Idioten!*'

Carl's eyes roll towards the ceiling as she shuts the front door behind her and clacks down the stairs. His cheeks are going up in flames.

'You told her!' hisses Annie.

He chews his lip, eyes as big as plums.

'What did you go and do that for?'

'I dunno,' he shrugs, mouth like a plughole. 'It just sort of came out.'

'You know what she's like, she'll be up there tomorrow demanding her money back.'

She moves in front of him, leans a hand on the table; an earring made from a red feather skewers her skin. Ten years of making small adjustments to each other – her untidiness, a battle he didn't win; her encouraging him not to tell his mother everything. It looks like they've failed on all counts.

'Mama angry,' says Willow

'I'm not angry.'

'With Dada.'

'I'm not angry with Dada, honey,' says Annie. 'Hey, why don't you go and find a lollipop in Mama's bag?'

Willow dips into the leopard-print bag, grabs a lolly and runs into her bedroom. Carl loads the tools into his bag, his pants on their way down, revealing his butt line like the seam of a speckled peach.

'I can't stop thinking about it,' he says. 'And that doctor phoning you like that.'

Look at him standing there in his royal blue knee-length trousers, the red T-shirt and Birkenstocks, a spanner in his hand. He's like Wonder Woman minus her crown.

'I can't stop thinking about it either.'

He collects some crumbs on the kitchen counter with the tip of his other finger then rubs them off. 'The thing is . . .' His voice trails off and he turns the spanner in his hands as if he's rolling a cigarette. 'It's just, well, I'd been thinking, even before the clinic contacted us, that Willow doesn't really look like either of us.'

She meets his hangdog gaze. He gives a drawn-out sigh and closes his eyes. Why does he do everything in slow motion? If Annie believed in reincarnation, she'd put money on it that Carl had been a sloth in a previous life.

'When I told my mom about the test just then, I thought she'd say there was some old family resemblance. 'Cept she didn't, she said only a rogue gene could have produced a gem like Willow.'

Annie's wobbling about like a blancmange on the back of a quad bike. She leans her backside against the table to try to steady herself. 'It's this that's been bothering you all this time, isn't it?'

The spanner slips out of Carl's hands and clanks onto the floor. 'Yeah, but I'm not so sure I want to know whether she's really ours or not.'

He picks up the spanner, lays it on the table then looks at his own empty hands. 'She's our world,' he says.

'But maybe we're jumping to conclusions,' she says. 'Maybe they want us to do this test because of something else, because they're worried about Willow's health or something.'

'Maybe.' He stretches out the word so it takes up seconds.

'I think we should do the test, Carl. If there's something wrong with her, we should know about it.'

'I don't think this is about her health.'

'But we should know what it is, so we can deal with it. You've been stressed out for months, and since that letter I've hardly been sleeping.'

'I don't know, Annie.'

'Let's do it, put this whole thing to rest.'

He picks up his bag, stares at the floor. 'Well, maybe you're right, maybe we should do this stupid test.'

He folds her into a hug, cups the back of her head in his enormous hand.

'See you later, kiddo,' he shouts into her ear, and she flinches. Willow rushes out and clings to his legs.

'Bye, Dada.'

'I'd better go.' He strokes Willow's hair, releases himself from them both, and the door clatters closed behind him.

Annie pushes it open and something scuffs the balcony boards as she does.

He guns the engine of the *Pools for U* van, gears clunking, his teeth gritted as he stretches up his neck to look in the rearview mirror. The van reverses, and drives off at speed.

Willow is beside Annie then. 'Dada gone!'

The sun is high in the sky, but doesn't penetrate the damp balcony. The little girl bends and picks something up from the decking – the wooden heart, a fractured line running right through its centre.

Chapter 15

Matteo squeezes Tess' hand as they sit in the reception area at the clinic, awaiting the results of their DNA test. They've left Freddie in the playroom along the corridor, supervised by two staff.

The alcoves in the wall are filled with objects – a vase of orange flowers in one, in another the polished curves of a marble figure with a bowed head and swollen stomach. A seated woman in trainers whispers in her husband's ear. In another chair, a woman sits dabbing a balled-up tissue to her red-rimmed eyes. It might be full of peach soft furnishings, but this is the green room for desperate people.

Gill unravels a mint and pops it into her expectant mouth. 'Would you like one?' She crinkles the packet.

Tess shakes her head and stares down at the body that doesn't seem to belong to her today, the string bows on the front of her black pumps wilting; her black dress. She drinks one cup after another from the water dispenser, then stuffed-full, flicks through her mobile phone and checks that the blog she wrote for the landscape gardener has uploaded. She stars the two comments that have been left and tweets a link.

She walks through to the ladies' loos. There are mirrors along the wall, a long trough-like sink. Inside a cubicle, she pushes her phone on top of the high toilet cistern.

Nerves always go to her stomach, liquefying her insides. Afterwards, she douses her face with water and looks at herself in the mirror. She's like a stranger, this woman standing here all dressed in black, the stubble beneath her eyebrows. But that's what comes of deleting photographs of yourself that aren't good enough – too thin-lipped there, the chin double in that one. You can't recognise yourself when you see your own face in the flesh. She'd never get rid of any photographs of her children though. Not the one where Phoenix had tonsillitis even though they didn't know it yet, his face a sickly yellow, nor the one of Luca when he played Peter Pan in his school play and someone had smeared his cheeks with too much fake tan. *Pictures of you, Ava, if only we had some.*

Back at reception, Gill is still chomping on her mint. Tess sits beside her, searching her burgundy fingernails for a place to pick off the polish.

'Mr and Mrs Rossi,' says the clinic lawyer, Lynn, who they met when they did the DNA test the other day. Lemony sunshine pours in through the windows and lights up the downy hairs on her cheeks.

They follow her into an office where Doctor Michael comes out from behind his desk. There's another woman here too, a white line slashed through her hair like skunk fur.

'I so appreciate you coming all this way,' says Doctor Michael holding out his hand. Matteo shakes it; Tess doesn't. She sits on one of the chairs arranged in a circle, beside the woman with the unusual hair.

'I've invited our counsellor in,' says Doctor Michael. 'This is Broo Fisher.'

When everyone is seated, Matteo settles a hand over Tess's clasped fingers. Her palms grow clammy.

'The DNA results are through,' says Lynn. She fixes her gaze on Tess. Tess looks away and takes Doctor Michael in. He folds his arms, his entire body tensing.

'Well?' asks Matteo, his voice as soft as a child's.

'It's as you had discovered for yourselves,' says Lynn. 'Freddie is not your genetic child.'

The confirmation goose bumps Tess' arms – the sum of her part relief, part disappointment.

Doctor Michael hangs his head. 'I'm so sorry, I truly am. I can't believe this has happened – we adhere to strict guidelines at all times.'

He's not the God-like figure she remembers from years ago, a man unafraid to take up his space in the world. His limbs are jumpy, a twitch to his face, his eyes darting.

'Well, on this occasion, it appears that you didn't adhere to guidelines,' says Gill.

'There were a number of staff involved in Mrs Rossi's treatment,' says Lynn.

'And all of them employed by Doctor Michael,' says Gill.

'We have an embryologist and a doctor working together, double checking every stage of the IVF procedure,' says Doctor Michael. 'We even have video cams recording what goes on.'

'But I understand from my notes that the video cam in the treatment room where Mrs Rossi had her transfer was not operational, is that correct?' asks Gill.

Doctor Michael glances at Lynn. 'That's correct,' she says.

Tess can't bear to look at Doctor Michael anymore. The counsellor's legs are crossed, her Scholl mule dangling from her long-nailed toes. She regards Tess, a line down her forehead like a paper cut.

'Are we any closer to finding out at what point the mix-up occurred?' asks Gill.

'We're interviewing all our staff, but we haven't been able to ascertain that yet,' says Lynn, 'we're continuing to work on it.'

Tess is slipping into her seat, jabbing her fingers into the underside of her thighs, the sensation of falling headfirst over the edge of a cliff, gravity accelerating, pulling and plunging her down.

'We've spoken to a number of people who were treated at the clinic around the time Mr and Mrs Rossi were,' says Lynn.

'We've run tests, but so far we haven't found Freddie's genetic parents.'

'And what about our embryos?' asks Tess.

'We're doing our utmost to find out what happened to them,' says Lynn.

Gill scribbles in her notebook. Doctor Michael lays a quivering hand on his colourful tie.

'You planned to put two embryos back inside me; did another woman get them instead?' asks Tess.

'We don't know what happened to your embryos yet,' says Lynn. 'The investigation is ongoing.'

Suspicion wrings Tess' neck. Matteo's face is rigid. A faraway phone begins ringing beyond the door.

'We could have children out there. We could have a daughter,' says Tess. 'That's why we came all this way, to have a daughter.'

'And I can assure you, the investigation will be comprehensive,' says Lynn.

'But how did it happen? In the lab? In the transfer, what?' snaps Matteo.

'We're making every effort to determine that,' says Lynn.

Matteo shakes his head. 'The incompetence.'

Freddie is an imposter. The last three years have been a lie. And Tess is going down and down, falling. Freddie is a lie; Freddie is wrong. She looks out of the window at the paths and grassy knolls, the faraway cubed buildings hazed in heat.

'You'll find them though, won't you? Freddie's parents, my embryos?'

'We're doing our very best,' says Lynn.

Tess' real child could be out there, a daughter, her daughter. The thing she's craved for so long might be about to come true. Hope pulls her upright again.

Chapter 16

Annie is on her knees delving into the box of books in the waiting area of the IVF clinic with its peach leather chairs, and the pictures of magnified cells lining the walls like an ice cream parlour.

'Look at this, butterbean.'

A book with piano keys is in her hand. She braces herself for the piercing electronic music as Willow pulls her fingers from her mouth and gets up from lying down across two chairs. She takes the book from Annie and presses, but mercifully, the batteries are dead. The clinic promised to turn around the results of the DNA tests after an hour. Annie and Carl opted to wait, but it's been almost two and a half hours, and still they're waiting.

Willow pitches the book sideways, hitting Carl's leg. He's like a straitjacket made from limbs, his legs knotted, his arms wrapped around himself.

'We could play musical chairs; I spy; rock-paper-scissors,' says Annie.

Willow stuffs her fingers back into her mouth and sits down again, sucking.

'Or how about doing some drawing?' continues Annie. 'I think I've got some pens in my bag. We could sing a song, or play snap. How about musical bumps, Dada could hum a—'

'Annie,' says Carl.

'I mean, we shouldn't be here too much longer. And then, well, we have the whole day. A picnic at the beach, ice cream at Gerry's. Maybe we'll—'

'Annie, please,' says Carl.

She's babbling like she always does when she's nervous, and this is the most nerve-inducing thing she's ever done. Carl tried to talk her out of it all the way here. She drove, rocketing over speed bumps, watching his leg flexing in her peripheral vision as he reached for the brake that wasn't there.

His loose jeans are sliding down his hips, his flip-flopped feet turning outwards. When was it that he got so baggy? He used to look like a man who could impregnate a woman just by touching her.

Annie pulls a puzzle book out of her bag along with a bunch of felt-tip pens. Willow climbs onto the floor and kneels, the puzzle book on a chair open at a paper maze, her bare skin touching the floor. *Listeria? MRSA?* Annie gulps – Lord knows what could be lurking invisible on these floors.

'Honey, maybe you should . . .' She clamps her mouth shut and watches Willow figuring her way out of the paper maze, drawing a pink line straight from entrance to exit. Annie stands and does a wiggling circuit of the waiting area.

'Are you okay, baby girl?' she asks.

'Candy!' says Willow.

Carl looks at Annie, but she digs her hand into her bag anyway. This is no ordinary day after all. Annie ate two bacon hoagies for lunch, the bread spread with enough butter to fix a tile. Carl bites at the skin around his thumbnail, gnawing, digging his teeth in woodpecker style. He seems more nervous than she is, which is saying something.

She peels the plastic off a lolly spiralled with colour and hands it to Willow who gets up and wanders off, licking. Willow is as she's meant to be, and surely she's meant to be with them. They look like any regular family: Carl, his eyes somewhere far away, lacing his fingers then pulling them apart again; Annie with her ironed-flat hair, though God knows why she's made an effort for this occasion, and Willow – beautiful Willow – looking like an advert for BabyGap with her sun-kissed skin and the bright pink sundress she insisted on wearing even though Annie tried pulling that green striped number over her head. A regular family. This is as near as Annie's ever going to get to being part of one. Just her and Nancy when she was growing up. Then her and Carl. When he'd asked her to marry him nine years ago, it had crossed her mind that he didn't have any brothers and sisters, and she'd so wanted a big family, cousins for her kids; she imagined she'd have three kids. Who gets the perfect package, though, right?

Annie pulls a stick of Juicy Fruit from her bag and starts to chew. *Chomp-suck-chomp.*

Over the past few days, Carl's calmness has shattered into a million tiny pieces. He went out with Chalky one night and came back drunk – Carl, who prefers eating a gastronomic meal to drinking.

'Maybe we shouldn't have done this,' says Carl.

His mobile phone starts to vibrate in his pocket. He pulls it out, looks at it, then turns it off.

'There's no way we're involved in any mix-up,' says Annie. 'They're just going to rule us out.' She swallows a bubble of air.

'What?' asks Willow, sitting up.

'Nothing,' says Carl, his teeth lodged in his thumbnail.

Doctor Michael appears in front of them, looking like he's aged ten years since she saw him earlier.

'If you'd like to follow me, Janine will stay with your daughter.' His saliva arcs through the air and splats onto the marble floor.

A woman in her twenties is beside them then, her hair dipped grey – why in the world would anyone want to look old before their time? Annie's heart is threatening to burst out of her chest.

'And what's your name?' asks Janine, bending over Willow, leaning her hands on her own knees.

Willow folds her arms.

'You go with this nice lady here, and Dada and me, we won't

be long.' Annie tries to make her voice all upbeat television presenter, but it comes out flat.

'No!' says Willow.

Carl's face crinkles up as Willow's chin wobbles.

'My name's Janine,' says the young woman whose waist is so thin it'd fit into the centre of Annie's cupped hands.

Willow starts to cry as Janine takes her hand and leads her away. Annie and Carl follow Doctor Michael, his shoes clipping. Willow's fading sobs burrow into Annie's chest, but this is no conversation she wants her child to hear.

Inside Doctor Michael's office, there's a woman wearing a pendant with a small metal boat fixed to it, a slash of white through her dark hair. Doctor Michael introduces her, but as soon as Annie hears her name, it floats away. The woman is some kind of counsellor. Annie feels nauseous and too-full as if someone has stuffed her with sand. Carl sits on a chair, his Adam's apple bouncing as he swallows repeatedly. He crosses one leg over the other, his foot working so fast it's like there's a motor inside it. The woman with the medallion is seated at Annie's side, Doctor Michael tucked behind the desk. There's a chinless woman beside him who introduces herself as the clinic lawyer, Lynn.

'There is no easy way to say this,' says Lynn. 'I'm sorry, Mr and Mrs Amstel, but Willow is not genetically related to you.'

A twister gathers momentum inside Annie's stomach. 'I can't . . . What does this even . . .?' The word 'No,' blares inside her head like a klaxon.

Carl's chest starts to rise and fall like there's limited oxygen in the room. He turns to her, his eyes wide and blinking. 'Oh, Annie . . .' He reaches over and snatches up her hand. 'How could this have happened?'

'We don't yet know,' says Lynn. 'We're interviewing every embryologist who worked on your embryos, and the embryologist involved in your transfer. We are being very thorough. We have a number of staff working on the investigation.'

Dr Michael clears his throat, eyes flitting to Lynn then back towards Carl.

Why won't he look at her? She's the one that carried someone else's child around in her belly for nine months for God's sake – the stomach that hasn't snapped back into shape, the episiotomy scar. Oh, but who cares about any of that, it brought Willow to her, didn't it? Willow who's not actually her child, Willow who could be taken away from her at any moment. Right now, Annie wants to grab the old fool's tie and pull it into a garrotte.

'It's an error of the gravest nature,' says Doctor Michael.

'So what happens now?' asks Carl. He's squeezing her fingers too tight. She pulls her hand away.

'There will be some form of compensation, of course,' says Doctor Michael.

Annie roots inside her handbag for another stick of gum. She turned herself into knots to have Willow. Forcing Carl to have sex every night for two weeks each month. Once when he had a cold, two bits of tissue paper shoved up each of his nostrils. Then taking all those fertility drugs. Annie unwraps the gum and pushes it into her mouth.

'Who are the real parents?' asks Carl.

Real? What are we then? The chewing gum snaps in half inside her dry mouth. She kneads it and combines it with the tasteless lump lodged against one of her teeth.

'We're looking into that,' says Lynn. She catches Doctor Michael's eye and something definite, something they're holding back, hangs heavy in the air.

'You know who they are, don't you?' says Annie.

Medallion woman touches Annie's arm. 'This is a harrowing situation, and I'm here for you whenever you need to talk, however long you need to talk for.' The kindness punctures a hole in Annie and she starts to cry. Carl lays his hand on her back and leans towards her.

'What about our embryos?' he asks. 'If Willow didn't come from them, where are they?'

Doctor Michael and Lynn exchange that loaded look again.

'Just tell us!' snaps Annie.

'We've run some tests on another family,' says Lynn. 'You have given birth to their genetic daughter, and their child is in fact yours genetically.'

The marble floor tiles roil in front of Annie's baffled eyes. This isn't happening. Except she's sitting here about to detonate. She chomps harder, faster. She leans forward and snatches at the tissues on the desk until her palm is full. That got Dr Michael's attention. He meets her gaze, his eyes with lightning strikes of fear in them. He looks away, he who delved into her nether regions so many times, and now he can't even look properly at her face. She glares at him and scrunches the tissues into a ball.

'Will they try to push for custody of Willow?' asks Carl.

'No one can predict what the other parents will want!' screeches Annie.

'Do they know about Willow?' asks Carl. He's sinking lower, like he's melting right there in front of her eyes.

'Not yet, no,' says Doctor Michael.

'They can't know,' says Annie. 'You can't give away any of our private details.'

'We won't be sharing anything about you unless you want us to,' says Doctor Michael.

'We don't want any contact with them; they can't know anything about us at all,' says Carl. He has never sounded so definite.

Doctor Michael nods. Her real child is out there, her other child. The thought skewers her heart.

'Is it a boy or a girl?' she asks.

'Sorry?' says Doctor Michael.

'Our child, their child?'

'A boy,' says Dr Michael.

She laughs, or maybe it's a sob that leaves her mouth. She

isn't sure of anything anymore, but Lynn and Doctor Michael look at her with slightly open mouths. She has a son, a daughter that isn't really hers. Talk about blended family.

'You're going to need an attorney,' says medallion woman.

'Why?' asks Annie.

'For so many reasons. You might want to have contact with this other child eventually.'

'What good will having contact do?' asks Carl. His throat makes an involuntary yelp, his chin corrugates. 'What's happened has happened, we can't change that. We just have to live with the consequences.' He shovels his hands into his pockets.

'Getting an attorney is something for you to go away and consider,' says medallion woman. 'You don't need to make a decision today.'

Carl sits forward in his chair. 'We haven't got that kind of money.'

'Please rest assured that the clinic will pay all your legal bills,' says Doctor Michael.

That man sitting there gave them a child, but because of his clinic's errors could they lose her?

'A son, my God,' says Carl. He sits there crying quietly, Carl who's never cried in front of her before.

All the nerve endings in her chest are tingling, her pulse walloping inside her neck. She'd been anticipating relief, and now she's pinned down and trapped by this new knowledge. Why couldn't she have ignored that damn phone call? *Her little boy. The cute face that she's never even set eyes on . . . Molecules, cells, breath, the bulk of him, God knows where.*

She stands, her handbag clattering onto the floor. A tampon spins across the nylon carpet along with a dollar coin.

'Those people are not coming anywhere near my daughter!' she says. But then if she doesn't let them, they won't allow her to see her son. *Her son.* Already it's there, an invisible thread stitched into her heart and pulling insistently, painfully.

She clambers onto her knees and grabs the tampon then she's stomping towards the door in the noisiest way possible, sobbing, sniffing, her red Mary Janes clicking. *Take me back to Kansas, Toto, right freaking now.*

She sucks in oxygen through her nostrils. There's no way anybody is splitting them up, not another set of parents, not some court.

'Please take a seat Mrs Amstel,' says Lynn. 'We have a lot to discuss.'

Her son, her daughter, her whole damn life. She goes back to the chair and sits on it, slightly broken, pressing and twisting the tampon in her fingers like a worry bead.

Chapter 17

Tess picks up Matteo's phone and dials her own mobile again. She listens, but there's no sign of her phone ringing in the motel room.

She goes out into the corridor and follows the scribbled arrow on the A4 piece of paper that says Pool. Outside, it smells of bins. There are broken slabs of concrete near the pool, an inside out ice lolly wrapper smudged with pink juice. A sopping towel has been flung over a plastic chair.

A woman in a stringy bikini is kneeling with her dimpled backside in the air, changing her baby's nappy, her long finger-nails curved like talons. Matteo is in the water, holding Freddie's hands, making a circle with him. Tess climbs in, the water creeping up her flat bare stomach, closing over the black triangles of her bikini bra.

She breaststrokes lengths, her head above the water, her chin raised to avoid the chlorinated blue. Pulling herself out, she stretches on a sun-bed. Freddie climbs out too, Matteo following. Matteo sits, propping his feet on a chair, Freddie playing with toy cars beside him.

'I still haven't found my phone,' says Tess. 'I've been using yours to call it, but no luck.'

'You had it at the clinic this morning.' He pushes his Ray-Bans on top of his head and pinches the red marks they've left at either side of his nose. 'That bloody place.'

'I phoned them a while ago, but they can't find it.'

'They couldn't organise a piss up in a brewery.'

'I'll go over there, take a look myself.'

The woman in the thong waddles away, her tremendous thighs undulating. Now Tess and her family are the only ones left. The swell of the old nappy remains folded at the side of the pool.

Matteo scratches stripes into his unshaven face. The pressed shirts, the floppy hair have been stripped down to this stale-smelling version of her husband, and she always thought he was the strong one. Freddie is on the other side of the pool now, and out of earshot.

'If there's a child,' she says, 'maybe he or she'll look like Phoenix and Luca; they're a matching pair.'

'Don't get ahead of yourself, Tess. Our embryos were so unlikely to have made it.' He lowers his voice to almost a whisper. 'If Freddie's genetic parents don't have a child, that could be a massive problem. It might make them more determined to push for custody.'

His knee starts to jerk. Freddie should have sunscreen on; he burns so easily, but the sun is dipping lower now, making way for the evening. A mosquito starts to buzz around her face.

'I don't want to lose him, you know,' she says because however diluted her love is, she does love Freddie. 'But if there is another child . . .'

She leans an elbow on the arm of the sun-lounger and puts her chin into her hand. She wants there to be another child despite the complications and heartache it'll bring.

Matteo smoothes his hand along the wooden arm of his seat. 'All we can do is try to get compensation, and if there is another child, meet the family perhaps, try to move forward somehow.'

Moving forward. Yes, she thinks. Hope lies ahead and she's hurtling towards it.

'There's so much that we need to know.' She can hear the forced restraint in her own voice, slowed down and over-enunciated. 'For one thing, maybe this family can shed some light on Freddie's behaviour. Maybe they have a history of mental health problems or something.'

'Freddie doesn't have mental health problems. He's just a child who doesn't know the boundaries yet.'

'It's more than that.'

'You say you don't want to lose Freddie, but it doesn't sound like you love him all that much,' he says quietly.

'I do.'

'Moping around after he was born like you did, as if he was a disappointment. The way you left him to cry . . .'

'But I read that book on controlled crying.'

'Then as he got older, sighing all the time whenever he did anything wrong. Like you do now, in fact.'

'I don't sigh.' Her emotions are an impenetrable package; what is he talking about?

'You crashed the car. It was a write-off, a brand new car and now it's in the scrapyard. If you hadn't crashed, we wouldn't have known about any of this. How I wish I didn't know. But now we do know, we need to put it right.'

'You think money can put it right,' she says. 'You think money can put everything right.'

The way he'd thrown himself into borrowing it and buying the hotel. The late nights. All those travel journalists she'd invited to stay in the executive suites free of charge in return for nothing but a news in brief.

'It's not about the money,' he hisses. 'It's about the clinic taking responsibility. This will be a terrible burden for Freddie to carry around, but he's my son, and I want to do what's right for him.'

'But he's not your son. And he's not mine either.'

The light to the side of Tess alters; she turns her head and standing beside her is Freddie, his nose crisped, a globule of snot peeking out of a nostril.

'Whose son am I then?' he asks.

Tess folds her arms, and lowers her head. Freddie slaps her

hard across her upper arm and runs away. He batters onto his knees and starts to cry.

'Well done, Tess,' snaps Matteo. Arms pumping, he marches over to Freddie and lifts him to his feet.

‖

A warning alarm beeps as Tess reverses and parks outside the clinic. She walks towards the entrance, stepping over a flower bed packed with mop-headed purple blooms. Is it hope that's heating the centre of her chest, or fear that there is no other child?

She walks into a wedge of the revolving door, pushes through and climbs into the lift. The woman who gave birth to her daughter might have touched this metal wall, these silver buttons. Tess lays her fingers on the buttons as if she might absorb some stray molecule, some microscopic connection with the child.

When the lift arrives on the fifth floor, she pushes through the door of the clinic and pads past the receptionist on the phone.

In the ladies' room, there's a line of shiny beige cubical doors. One of them is locked. Tess hears the trickle of urine. She goes into the third one along and looks up at the tall boxed-in cistern. There on top of it is her phone pushed up against the wall almost out of sight.

She looks at it, fourteen missed calls, all from Matteo's mobile. There's a rip of tissue paper from next door, the shift of fabric. Tess goes out and waits for the lift. People arrive beside her and wait too, but Tess doesn't look up. She climbs into the lift, and the people follow.

'Are we going home now, Mama?' A child's voice.

'Yes.'

Tess drops her phone into her bag and takes the people in. The little girl's eyes are coal-dark, her skin the colour of manuka honey.

Yellow discs dangle from the woman's ears, and hairs tuft

between her thick eyebrows. Her hair is sharply cut, layered and loudly red, but mostly she's the fluorescent yellow of the dress that's clinging to her spare tyre.

'I'm too hot,' says the little girl, yanking at her mother's arm.

The woman jams her hand against the wall as the lift descends, staring up at the ceiling, and breathing deeply like she's trying to remain calm. There's a little man in the lift too in a Spiderman T-shirt, a large tattoo covering the inside of one of his lower arms, an indecipherable name in loopy black script.

'You'll be fine,' he says to the woman. 'It's only a few floors down.' He's scratching his beard, his baggy trousers about to slip off his hips.

Words push their way up Tess' throat. *Don't waste your money here: save yourself some heartache; go somewhere else.* She bites down on silence instead.

The woman starts to cry, her head turned to the wall, the little girl sucking her own fingers, and the tattooed man lost in thought.

The lift pings and grinds to a halt. A woman with short, black hair steps into it and the doors rub shut once again. This new woman is in her sixties, with angular cheekbones and a handbag resting in the crook of her arm. She stares at the red-headed woman, concern blooming across her face.

She stretches out her hand and lays it on the younger woman's arm, and the eyes of the two women meet as if joined by some invisible cord. And Tess goes on staring at the red-headed woman, feeling the motion of the descending lift, unable to tear her gaze away.

There is grief etched into the younger woman's face, her downturned mouth, her wet cheeks, something devastated about her green eyes. And the comfort of the older woman's hand is still placed softly on her arm.

Tess goes back, right back to all those years ago when they lost Ava. *Passed away, taken, gone*; people dressed it up in all sorts of euphemisms, instead of saying the word 'dead.' They fidgeted in her presence and weren't able to meet her eye. Her friends with children stayed away. But whatever it is that's wrong with the younger woman, the older woman isn't squirming. She's making an offering and the younger woman is accepting it, the way Tess hadn't been able to. She hadn't been impatient or ungracious; no, that had been Matteo's forte. 'I don't really want to talk about it,' Tess had said if anyone brought it up. Because what could they give her, they who knew nothing of what it was like to lose a child? But perhaps if she'd allowed herself to be touched like that woman standing there crying, perhaps if she'd really let go, she might not be crumbling inside. So she stands there, absorbed in this moment, not at all sure of what's unfolding before her eyes.

The crying woman swallows hard, wipes the bottom of her nose with the back of her hand and sniffs her tears back in, and still they stare at each other, the older lady gripping a little firmer now. If Tess had reached out to touch someone like that, she'd be deliberating when the right time would be to take her hand away. There'd be something robotic about the way she removed it.

The lift halts and the doors open, and the older woman gives one final, squeeze to the younger woman's arm and steps out.

Something falls onto Tess' bare toes and she crouches. The younger woman has dropped a teddy. Straggly, dirty fur of no discernible colour, a nose made of fraying black thread, a missing ear. She looks at the girl's sandals then, a thick silver bar velcroed across the toes. The toes?

Tess stops breathing, the sound of fire crackling in her ears, her head spinning as if she's about to keel over. She stays down, wedging her free hand on the floor to keep herself upright. The flesh between two of the girl's toes is fused right up to the base of the nails, as if the toes were one. Tess looks at the girl's face properly. There are dimples in her cheeks, her chubby face topped by a too-short wonky fringe, two moles under an eye. This can't be . . .

'This is it,' says the man in a long, slow drawl and the lift doors open. He rubs a circle on the woman's back.

And still Tess holds onto that teddy. The girl is moving away, her hand locked inside her mother's fingers.

The doors close behind the family, and Tess stands there in the compressed box, her heart throbbing inside her ribcage, panic rising around her like ocean swell. She can't let them go. She presses the button to open the doors, but they stay closed. She punches her finger again and again then she's free, stepping through the shine of the ground floor foyer with its profusion of plants.

She rushes towards the revolving doors, and goes outside, her skin blasted by the sudden warm air. Where are they? There are so many rows of cars. A woman is edging her pregnant stomach between two of them. Holding the teddy to her heart, Tess jogs, going over on her ankle and wincing. She can see her own hire car gleaming in the distance. Then she spots the family, the flash of the woman's red hair, the dot of the girl beside her, and that sack of a man.

He's opening the boot of a battle-worn silver car. Tess might have enough time to reach them before they drive off. She looks at the scrawny teddy in her hand. The engine of the car is starting now; she's going to miss them. Her mouth is lizard-dry. She starts to sprint, her bag on her shoulder banging her side. Not much further; her knee joints are practically ossified. She jumps into her car and reverses and there it is, the silver car gliding along, the wheels barely visible beneath its sagging suspension. The rust bucket doesn't look roadworthy.

They are on the highway then, the wide lanes of traffic and the signs overhead. Large car parks roll by, their entrances flanked by palm trees, and boxy shops and cafes.

The silver car is in front of Tess, but all its back windows are blacked out. She tries to see the driver's face in the wing mirror, but she can't.

A car in the left lane indicates to move in front of Tess' car, but she presses her foot harder on the accelerator and doesn't let the car cut in. Tess who's never run a red light, who usually smiles back at the smiley face speedometers that tell her she's driving a tad below the 30mph limit. She passes Wendy's Drive Thru and a stack of numbers announcing petrol prices.

They are cresting a bridge now, and the traffic is thinning out. She looks at her hands locked on the wheel, her pulse thumping, her dress moist with perspiration, the teddy on her lap. *I mustn't lose them. My darling girl.* Thoughts batter through her head and none of them are rational. She feels unhinged and dizzy. Some chasm has opened up beneath her and she's fallen in, her insides pulling upwards. *It's her. It's her.*

She presses on, the bonnet of her car practically kissing the rear of the one in front. What sort of people are they? Where do they live? Will the girl already be missing the teddy? Luca pretends not to be attached to his toy monkey, yet still he hugs it to his chest when he goes to sleep.

Tess picks up the teddy and smells it – mouldy cheese meets feet in need of some odour eaters. The stench collides with her heart. *They were going to call her Sophia or Erin.* The girl in the lift looked like an Erin . . .

They're putting distance between themselves and Tess. They skid slightly and Tess notices the bashed door on the driver's side. She presses harder on the accelerator. Oh, but it's hot. She twiddles knobs, and the windscreen wipers come on. She tries another, and Tammy Wynette blasts the interior with a crackly version of *Stand by Your Man*.

Tess passes ranch houses with clapperboard fences around them. There are pebbled front yards, an anchor festooned in rope poked into one of them. She glimpses the sea at the end of the lanes running perpendicular to the road, sand like golden caster sugar. She rolls down her window and the smell of the ocean spills in. The people she's following slow down, and she does too.

Their silver car turns off the main road into a driveway without indicating. So much for mirror, signal, manoeuvre. Tess rolls past, taking the place in – a wart on the nose of this pastel-coloured street, a dilapidated shed of a building, a two-storey wooden block with a rickety staircase rising in a diagonal up its side.

At the top of the street, Tess makes a U-turn and parks on a balding patch of grass.

She gets out, the teddy pressed to her stomach. The sea is at the end of the road, the crashing blue of it framed by two houses, brambles in between. The wind lifts a lid off a bin and frisbees it along the road, until it skids and scrapes to a stop. A seagull lands on the pitched roof of a house and squawks.

She heads back to the building where the family have parked their car. Standing on the other side of the road, she can see a large white van parked in the driveway too, *Pools for U* painted on its side. There's a crumpled plastic bottle on the ground, a crisp packet blowing in circles, and the man is leaning into the boot of the car, the strip of flesh above his trousers jiggling, the cleft of his buttocks on show. He takes a bag from the boot and slams the lid, dawdling up the stairs. The front door shuts behind him.

Her daughter's feet have been on those steps, her hands have touched that wooden handrail. It's as if Tess' insides have disappeared and the breeze coming off the sea is blowing right through her. There are no windows on the part of the block that faces the road. The front door must be around the side. Tall hedges are fencing the place in, casting it in darkness.

The teddy. She has to give it back. Her sandals on the grey pebbles make too much noise. A car whizzes by. The teddy is in her arms like she's holding a fragile newborn. She goes past the steps and looks up at the apartment on the first floor. Is this really where the little girl lives or maybe they're visiting friends? There's a wooden balcony over her, and through the slats, she sees a purple ball. She goes upstairs. The place reminds her of one of those diagrams of a kitchen that invite you to circle all the dangers lurking in it. A plant pot containing something dead not quite covering a large hole in the wooden decking, a plastic princess castle and two miniature chairs. There's a wooden heart with a split down its middle hanging from a ribbon on the mint-green front door. The air is darkening and the wind pulls through the hedges fringing the property.

A large wooden W is perched behind the glass on the sill of one of the windows. *Wendy, Wanda. Winifred.* Names sift through Tess' head. She feels an almost irresistible urge to press her nose against the glass, to sense the coolness against her skin, to put her lips onto the dusty surface and leave their imprint there. She holds the teddy tighter to herself instead. She looks at it, a faint smile in its sewn mouth. This could be a way to keep the girl close.

She patters down the stairs and heads out of the yard, with the teddy squashed against her stomach. She looks over her shoulder to make sure no one has seen, then jogs all the way back to her car.

Chapter 18

Gill makes a long play of settling herself behind her desk, smoothing her skirt and jumping her chair forward. Tess takes in the enlarged pores speckled over her nose, the knot in the gold chain of her specs as she pushes them on. If you really look at them, even the faces of still people are constantly ruffling, eyes twitching, the muscles in the cheeks flexing and rippling beneath the surface of the skin. Gill wouldn't say over the phone what it is that she wants to talk to them about, and anticipation is making Tess hold her breath and listen hard, her gut squeezing.

'The clinic have discovered who Freddie's genetic parents are.'

Matteo bangs his mouth with a fist.

'And there's something else,' says Gill. 'They have a daughter. A daughter who is, in fact, your genetic daughter. There's been a direct swap.'

It takes all of Tess' strength not to crumple onto the floor. Burping silently, she feels as if she might vomit, and covers her mouth with a hand. Anaesthetised by shock, she watches Gill speak for a while without really hearing what she's saying.

'I want her back,' says Tess.

'You might want that, but you're not the birth parent,' says Matteo. 'And anyway, if you do that, they'll take Freddie. Think about what you're—'

'She's my child. We know nothing about these people. Who they are, what kind of people they are.'

'I don't know anything about them either at this stage, apart from the fact that this girl is their only child,' says Gill.

'When can we see a photograph?' asks Tess.

'Unfortunately the family are refusing all contact.'

'Of all the things to happen,' says Matteo. 'Christ almighty.'

'We can push for a contact order,' says Gill. 'But I think it would be better if we waited. This is a shock for everyone, and the other parents have only just found out. Once things settle, they may change their minds, start to come to terms with what's happened. They might be more amenable to having contact with you.'

'I presume the child is three,' says Matteo.

'She's three, yes,' says Gill.

'I can't take this in,' says Tess. 'Our daughter, and we don't even get to see her. Don't they want to know about Freddie?'

'I haven't had any communication that they do, but as I say, it's early days.'

'We should let them know what Freddie's like,' says Tess. 'I could write them a letter, send it to them.'

'No,' says Matteo, nails digging into both of his cheeks.

'If you do decide to write a letter, I can pass it to their attorney,' says Gill.

Their attorney? Surely the people she saw in the hospital couldn't afford a lawyer, but then perhaps they're not the ones. Freddie's parents, the people who have her daughter, could be anyone, anywhere.

'We can't do anything rash,' says Matteo.

Tess focuses on the jumbled office – the framed certificates on the wall, the volumes of books and files in a bookcase, the stacked chairs in the corner of the room. She can smell dust.

'We leave the day after next,' says Tess. 'We need to do something now. We haven't got time to wait.'

How she'd wished she could blow life back into Ava as she held her, and now that grief-stricken centre is breaking the banks of Tess' body all over again. She has a daughter who she might never see, never touch, a daughter who will never sleep in the next room to her, a daughter whose voice she might never get to hear.

She gets up, sits down again, clutching her handbag to her stomach.

'This must feel overwhelming,' says Gill. 'But since both you and the other parents are in the same situation, I'm hopeful that they will eventually want some kind of contact, and if they don't, we can pursue it through the court.'

Tess scuffs her shoe across the floor, sending a wave through the blue carpet.

'The clinic will pay for counselling for you all,' says Gill. 'If that's something you want to pursue back at home, let me know the details and I'll sort everything out.'

Matteo stands, thrusts his hand out towards Gill who stands too, her grey pencil skirt wrinkled around her thighs. She comes out from behind the desk, her suede stilettos so high it's like she's standing on tiptoes. Even then she's only half Matteo's height.

'Well, we're thankful you're acting for us,' says Tess.

Gill and Tess look at one another; Gill lays a hand on Tess' arm and Tess stiffens.

'This is going to bring up a lot of emotions for you both,' says Gill, pushing her glasses up the ridge of her nose, the chains glinting. 'But I'm here to help you, to find some sort of resolution that you can both live with.'

There are sweat patches in each of the armpits of Matteo's pinstripe short-sleeved shirt. He opens the door and lets Tess walk out.

Freddie is sitting on a sofa playing a game on Matteo's phone. He looks up and past her. 'Daddy!' He flings the phone to the side and runs towards Matteo who scoops him up.

'Thank you for watching him,' Tess says to the receptionist.

'Oh, he's such a good kid,' says the woman against the back-drop of sound from the water trilling over the pebbles in the water feature.

'You were a long time,' says Freddie.

'I know, my boy, but we're here now. Who wants ice cream?'

'Meeeee!' says Freddie.

A red-headed woman in a flowery dress walks past the window, and Tess' heart leaps. It's the woman from the hospital – the same sharpness to the ends of her hair, the same padded upper arms. Tess opens the door and goes outside, the smell of burning rubber up her nose, the heat sticky on her skin. The woman is getting further away, her flowery dress billowing out.

Tess walks quickly after her, her arms working, her right pump slipping off her foot like a slingback. She is closing the distance between her and the woman.

'Wait!' calls Tess.

And the woman turns around and Tess sees that she's not a woman at all, but a teenage girl, her tanned face crooked with confusion.

'Can I help you?' the girl asks.

Tess shakes her head and starts walking away, throwing a muttered 'sorry' over her shoulder.

She's slightly breathless when she gets back to the parked red car. Matteo finishes clipping Freddie into the back.

'Who was that?' asks Matteo.

'I thought I recognised her,' says Tess.

But Matteo isn't listening. He climbs into the driver's seat and she looks back up the road. The girl is a smudge in the distance now, then she's gone as if she was never there at all.

Chapter 19

'Bug Bear has gone on an adventure, honey,' says Annie in a faltering voice.

She is crouching on the pre-school pathway, holding both of Willow's hands. People pass, bags on shoulders, small sandalled feet.

'Bug's in hopital,' says Willow. Her face is pillowy and pink, but at least she's finally stopped crying.

She keeps insisting that she left her teddy back at the clinic, but Annie has rung them and they can't find the teddy, so Willow couldn't have dropped it there. Annie stands, lets go of one of Willow's hands and leads her along the crazy-paved path, past the play cars on springs poking from the sandy ground, the two swings on ropes.

Fast footsteps scurry up the path behind them and Annie turns to see Christy's daughter Tiger catching them up, deely-boppers on her pig-tailed hair.

'Hello Willow,' says Tiger.

'We've had five viewings already,' shrills Christy, fast approaching. A pink shirt dress, her hair backcombed and topped with an Alice band. 'All developers, of course.'

'Go on in now.' Annie bends and kisses Willow's plump cheek.

'Find Bug, Mama,' says Willow.

'I'll try.'

Tiger waves to Christy then takes Willow's hand and leads her through the door.

'She looks as if she's been crying,' says Christy.

'It's that little toy of hers, the teddy . . .'

'Her lovey?'

'Yeah, we can't find him anywhere. I don't know, she must have dropped him or something. I can't think where.'

'Oh, that poor sweet child. It's like a little friend, a baby, a brother . . .'

Here we go . . . Annie breathes in, and stands a little straighter. Christy gives her own non-existent bump a gentle pat.

'Let's hope it turns up,' says Christy. 'After all, every child needs someone.'

Annie mutters 'goodbye' and hurries away. There's a line of neat cars parked bumper to bumper along the grass verge outside the pre-school, then there's Annie's skew-whiff Versa. She passes a couple of moms on their way to drop their kids off at class.

'Hi Annie.'

'How you doing Annie?'

'Oh, yeah, great.' Annie keeps the smile tacked to her face and looks at her sandalled feet, the sole coming apart underneath her toes. Willow in second-hand clothes. If she could sell one of her pictures it would help their ailing finances, but who in their right mind would pay for her work? She's not an artist, she's a mom, that's all, Willow's mom. But then that's just something else she's been pretending at.

She's a fake.

Later, on her way back from work, Annie opens the mailbox outside their flat. She pulls out a padded envelope, and a couple of letters. Climbing the stairs, staples fly as she opens the envelope. There's a pristine teddy bear inside, well, maybe pristine's overdoing it, straggly threads that resemble fur. This brand of toy looks old even when it's new. But even so, it could do with a bit of weathering before she gives it to Willow. A dunking in a vat of mud and gutting it of some stuffing might help to make it look the part. Hell, maybe Annie should rip off its ear.

Not that any of that would fool Willow. Annie shoves her nose into its clean plumpness then stuffs the teddy back into the envelope. She could improvise a note from the fairies. *We've mended Bug Bear and brought him back to you as good as new.* She's a terrible liar, but all she'll have to do is feign a bit of joy, and that should come easy to her.

She climbs the stairs and opens the front door. Willow runs towards her in her damp Dora the Explorer swimsuit, the crotch sagging too low, the wet tendrils of her hair about her face.

'Hey, kiddo! You need to have a shower!' Carl calls.

He stands in the lip of the kitchen door, his *Will Cook for Beer* apron tied around his waist. Willow's feet are encrusted with sand as she clings to Annie. The apartment is full of the smell of cooked meat.

There's a cling-filmed meal on a piece of slate. Why Carl can't serve food on a normal plate is anybody's guess, but then eating off a roof tile certainly beats a microwaveable tub.

'It's a composition of seared duck breast and triangles of rösti potato,' says Carl in a voice so slow she looks at the wall-mounted clock. She would have been happy with mac and cheese, but who's complaining.

'You've been swimming again,' Annie says to Willow.

'In the sea!' says Willow.

'A regular mermaid, this one,' says Carl. 'Takes after her mother.' His gaze falls away and smacks to the floor.

Mother. The word doesn't fit anymore. A woollen sweater that's shrunk in a hot wash, the yarn too close together, tight and scratchy.

'You found him!' says Willow, prodding her finger into the envelope under Annie's arm.

'Oh, this, it's erm—'

'Bug Bear!' says Willow.

'No, I mean, well kind of. The fairies put him back together and . . .' Could her hesitant voice be any less convincing, but what the hell? She pulls out the teddy, labels and all.

Annoyance flickers over Willow's face. She pouts her lips. 'Dat's not Bug.'

'No, honey, it, er, the fairies, like I say, they made him all new again.'

'No, dey did not.'

Dear God, that's how bad a liar Annie is; even a three year old doesn't believe her. Willow takes the bear from her and flings it across the room like a crash dummy. It collides with the edge of the two quilled pictures behind the couch, unleashing puffs of dust, then falls spread-eagled onto the floor. Willow stomps into her room and closes the door.

'Hey, hold on, butterbean!' Annie tries the bedroom door, but it won't give; Willow must be sitting behind it. 'Let me in.'

'Leave her; she'll come round.' Carl bends and picks the teddy up. 'You've been found out,' he says to it. 'You're an imposter and she knows it.'

He catches Annie's eye, a twitch to his whiskery face. Annie fills a glass with water and downs it in one. Their child, that boy, whoever he is, is an imposter in another family's home, and Willow is an imposter in theirs. How different their lives would be if they'd given birth to the right child, how much more straightforward. She thinks of the mothers she knows with teenage children – *'Oh, it's her hormones.' 'Hey, don't worry about it, she's a teenager, she's meant to be as moody as hell.'* What kind of teenager will Willow turn out to be once she knows the truth? She might run away; she might shout, 'You're not my mother!' She might want to know them, her real parents. And if she does, will Annie support her?

'Those people. I can't stop thinking about them, and that little boy.' She wipes her sweaty face with the back of her hand. 'Maybe we should try to connect with them somehow.'

Suds fly as Carl starts to wash the crockery, heat dyeing his cheeks red. 'I dunno. Shit, Annie, Willow is our everything, but this other kid . . .' Froth has attached itself to his eyebrow.

'Maybe we should meet them,' she says.

'But they could be complete crazies. Fruitarians, Republicans even – no.'

She rolls her eyes.

'Once we go down that route, we might be powerless to stop them gaining access to her,' he says.

He rubs at a saucepan, creating waves in the basin, the soapy water lapping over the draining board at the side.

'But I need to know that they're alright, that they're good people,' says Annie. 'They've got our son.'

'He's not our son though.' The clank of a dish.

'He came from our bodies,' says Annie. 'Oh, Jesus, it makes me feel violated, Carl – that they took him away from us.'

'And we got Willow instead. I wouldn't want any other child.'

And yet he'd been so against looking after a child that wasn't really his. Maybe there's still a chance to persuade him to adopt after all, then again Willow already has a sibling of sorts.

'We can't risk having contact with them, Annie. They'd make judgements about us, like we'd do about them, and what if we don't like them? We wouldn't have any power to help the boy.'

She pulls back the cling film from the tile and shoves a fried potato into her mouth then picks up the rest of the mail.

A letter from the landlord, putting up the rent by a hundred dollars per month.

'Lord, no,' she mutters, but Carl doesn't seem to hear her through his vigorous scrubbing.

There's something from their attorney, Susan Purcell. Annie opens it and reads the enclosed letter handwritten in neat, tiny words.

His name is Freddie. He's three years old. He likes pizza and cucumber and Paw Patrol, *and dogs – whenever he visits his auntie's house, her black labrador sits at the bottom of the stairs and waits for him.*

A noise bursts from Annie's throat, her legs start to give way beneath her. Why didn't their attorney warn them a letter was coming their way? Something prickles inside her lower abdomen as if the place where her son should have spent nine months is reacting to this description of him.

His name is Freddie. It makes her think of eighties horror films and short, hairy-chested rock stars.

'His name's Freddie,' she says.

Carl twirls round and sees the letter in her hand. 'They wrote to you?'

She nods.

'They know where we live?'

'Susan sent it on.' God, she can't get used to calling their attorney by her first name, even though she insisted on it. 'Ms Purcell,' Annie adds.

'But we said no contact.' Carl's shoulders slump further forward, his neck too. He pulls the letter from her; it dampens in his hands, water plinking to the floor.

He shallow-breathes through his mouth. 'I think we should . . .'

'What?'

'Let him go.'

Why us? she thinks then sighs. Annie may do hypochondria on a daily basis, but she doesn't do feeling sorry for herself. She elongates her spine and feels it, that pure empty space inside her chest, waiting to be filled with this boy.

She tries to take the letter from Carl, but he keeps hold of it, and it stays there trembling between them like something alive.

Out of breath from the stairs, Annie knocks on Tom's partially
open front door, but he doesn't call out to her. She pushes her
way into the darkened apartment. He's not in his chair.

'Mister Tom?'

Nothing.

'Tom?'

She goes into his bedroom, a musty sweetness to the air like
somebody died. The memory of Febreze in her mother's ward
room . . . dear God, no.

'Tom?'

He snuffles and wheezes and relief descends. She heads into
the lounge. The seat cushion on his chair is flattened and worn,
his desk stacked with A4 paper, and an uncapped red Biro.

On the top page, there's a box around the printed words. *It's
a Funny Old Life by Tom Pearson*, an old-fashioned spidery font.
She takes a stick of chewing gum from her handbag and chomps,
the sugar dissolving in a rush on her tongue. Sitting down, she
flicks through and spots a page with red pen marks on it. She
starts to read:

> *I would have given up after they put a bullet between
> Eddie Stewart's eyes, but the Captain kept saying:
> 'We're a family now; only sacrifices we make are for
> each other.'*

Tom's book is an autobiography. He sent it to a couple of big
publishers, but when neither replied he decided to pay for it to
be published as a tribute to his late wife Marie. This part must
be about his time in the Vietnam War. 'Shame does strange things
to a man,' he'd said when she'd asked once what it had been like.

She fans through the proofs, looking at the changes he's made.
Roz won't allow most of them as they'll cost too much at this
late stage. A comma here, a question mark there, a red line
through a sentence. Something on page 84 catches her eye then,

a scrawled red arrow, and two torn holes like a staple's been removed.

She shuffles backwards in her seat and looks into the trash can, a jumble of ripped paper inside. This is Tom's private stuff, she tells herself, but nosiness wins and she's already lifting the strips and piecing them back together. She sees her own name written there in Tom's shaky hand.

When our next door neighbour, Nancy, took off, we looked after her baby daughter for two whole years. Finally, we had the child Marie and I had always wanted. Instead of sleeping in our spare room only when her mother was on shifts, Annie slept in our house every night. She filled the cottage with childish chatter. I worked construction during the day and when I came home, the kitchen had been turned into a bakery, icing daubed on top of cupcakes and through strands of that little girl's red hair.

That sounds like her alright, a trail of crumbs following her everywhere. But what does Tom mean '*two whole years*'? She combs her thumb over the words scored deep into the paper, anxiety escalating.

'Now and again,' that's what Tom had said when Annie asked how often he and Marie had looked after her, but two years. After Nancy died, Annie wanted to know every small detail about her mother, details she should have known when she was alive. With no more new memories to be made, she needed old ones to cling onto.

Tom coughs. There's the rustle of blankets. She gets up and goes to the bedroom door. The lamp on the bedside cabinet comes on, pale light shining through the fringed shade.

'Are you okay?' she asks.

'My sheesh . . .'

He reaches for the denture pot, upending it, liquid spilling. His tut comes out as a slurp.

'Here, let me.'

She hoists him up and plumps the pillow behind him, the loose skin beneath his long chin wobbling, his mouth curved over his bare upper gums. She puts the pot on his lap then turns away.

'I'll fix you a drink,' she says.

He tries to say something else. The kitchen is a picture of loneliness. Four chipped stained mugs inside a cupboard, beside them a shrivelled orange with a badge of mould. The brown cooker hood is glazed with oil, and a tea towel is folded over the handle of the oven door, the squiggled faces of Willow's pre-school friends printed across it. Annie was the one who put it together, placing the pencil into the children's hands. There were lines for smiles, circles for hands; Willow had topped the drawing of her face with scribbles. Annie takes a glass, clouded with dirt and fills it with water then tromps back into the bedroom.

'What are you doing in bed at this hour anyway?' she singsongs, pulling back the curtains and flooding the room with light. 'Have you been partying?'

'Yeah, as it happens.' His voice is whole again. 'With my friend out there.' He's bleary-eyed and stubbly, cowlicks sticking out of his hair.

'Your book.'

'I was having second thoughts about one of the chapters.' His arthritis-curved fingers play with a button on his burgundy pyjamas. 'How long have you been here for?' he asks.

'Not long.' She sits on the bed and hesitates. 'I pulled something out of the trash can,' she ventures, smoothing out a crease in the comforter.

His eyes are shock bright. A shiver plays at the back of her neck. He's going to say he made a mistake; she wants him to say he made a mistake, that he should have written two weeks, not two years. She wants him to say, 'Forget my own head if it wasn't screwed on,' the way he often does, except he's blinking fast.

'Did my mom run off and leave me?'

'She was a good woman, your mother. Decent . . .'

'Why did she go, Tom?' Annie straightens herself up to take the blow.

He shakes his head, mutters to himself. 'She didn't, she—'

'I saw what you wrote.'

She covers his hand with her own. He is shaking, or maybe it's her that's shaking.

'I don't know why I wrote that.'

'Please, Tom, I need to know.'

He swallows hard. 'When your daddy died, well, you can't even begin to imagine how hard that was for your mama. It wiped her out. She stopped turning up for her shifts at the hospital. They ended up giving her a final warning and she resigned. Money was tight, but even so she kept on spending.'

His eyes skirt around the comforter as if the old faded lemon thing might provide him with some answers.

'You've got to understand, she loved him so much and she was young. When someone's taken from you like that, nothing can lift you.'

He takes his good hand from underneath hers and covers his mouth with it.

'What did she do?'

'She started drinking to perk herself up. Not much at first.'

'She never drank.'

He looks at her, then away, setting his hand back on the bed.

'She tried so hard to make the grief disappear. She didn't know how. It was just at night to start with, then I went next door one morning to fix a dripping tap for her, and smelt it fresh on her breath. I suggested she talk to someone, a doctor maybe, but she refused to admit there was anything wrong. I guess she was ashamed.'

Annie can feel her whole body sagging, her shoulders, her head, her heart.

'I didn't know what to do,' says Tom. 'I kept pressing her to talk about it, but she wouldn't. Marie tried too, but every time we went next door, the place smelt of liquor. We were so worried about her, about you, and we'd done gentle, so I decided to try something else. One day when she opened the door, I searched the place, pulling the cushions off the couch, opening cupboards.

'She was shouting at me, bashing me on the back, but I carried on anyhow. I found all this hooch. I poured a bottle of brandy down the sink, vodka. I told her if she carried on, I'd phone the authorities, and they'd come on in and take you away from her.' He hangs his head.

'The following morning I went next door again, but she didn't answer, so I got the spare key that Marie kept and let myself in.'

There's a V in his wrinkled forehead and he sighs.

'Tell me,' she says.

'She was gone. You were there in your cot crying.'

His face clenches as if he's taken a bullet and is waiting for the pain to arrive. He looks at her again. 'Like I say, she was grief-stricken. She left a note, said she'd be back in a couple of weeks and could we look after you.'

'She abandoned me? How old was I?'

'Two and a half.'

It's like hands are crushing her heart. 'A baby.'

'I never wanted you to know any of this.' His good hand is straight like it's praying on its own. He lays it against his other one, which stays clawed and curled on the cotton. 'We brought you in with us and for a while we had the family we'd always wanted.'

She turns away from him, the stench in the room overwhelming her. Two weeks, Nancy's note said. Two years, Tom wrote. He must have got it wrong.

'She came back after a couple of weeks?' asks Annie.

'No.'

She doesn't want to ask it because she already knows the answer, but the question is nailing holes in her chest like she's a lump of Swiss cheese.

'She stayed away two years?'

'Yes.'

'She must have contacted you though, to make sure I was alright?'

His eyes find some place over her shoulder.

'She must have!'

Tom licks his chapped lips. 'There were postcards.'

'Postcards?'

'She didn't stay in one place for too long, but at least we knew she was alright.'

'And what about me? Did she even ask about me?'

'No.' The word is dredged up from somewhere deep inside him.

A heavy weight presses her insides towards her feet.

'But she was my mom.'

She gets up, her hands hanging heavy by her sides. It's as if some vital part of her has been torn away. She waits, expecting to list to one side, to fall, but she just stands there, the room spinning around her, blurry and too fast.

'Her little girl, and she left her,' she says. Tears spring into her eyes, her nose starts to fill. She sniffs hard and loud, putting the heel of her hand into an eye and rubbing.

'You had us,' says Tom. It sounds like the most pathetic thing anyone has ever said to her.

'You lied to me.'

'I never lied.'

'You didn't tell me. You should have told me.'

'You didn't remember. It was best that way. For a few demented moments last night, I thought maybe I should include the details about what happened in my book. It was a bad idea. That's why I ripped it up.'

'You're not who I thought you were, and neither is she, my mom.' The word tastes like ruined milk.

He reaches out to her, and she steps backwards towards the door.

'No one is one thing only,' he says. 'Your mother made a mistake, she was ill, not right in the head, but she did the most wonderful things too. She cared about people. You knew her, Annie. If anyone fell over in the street, your mother would be the first one out there, making sure they were alright.'

'Jesus, Tom, she left me. I could have been taken into care, just like you said to her.'

'But you weren't! She knew that we'd look after you.' His loose jowls shudder. 'Me and Marie, we—'

'What happened after that?'

'She straightened herself out, came back dry. She begged us to forgive her; she begged us to give you back.'

Her mother's bracelet with the cross on it glints inside Annie's head. That Jesus picture in the bathroom with the bulb underneath that didn't switch on.

'And you did, just like that?'

'Not just like that, no. We kept our eye on you, but at the end of the day, we weren't your parents.'

'Fuck.' She moves a little further back towards the door. 'My mom was such a fucking hypocrite.'

'This is why I didn't tell you.'

'Well, you should have, then I wouldn't have spent years being deluded about what kind of a person she was.'

She looks over at the empty side of the double bed, the crisp white pillows on top of each other, a gallery of photographs on the cabinet beside it. Marie in a white dress smiling into the camera, one eyebrow arched like a question mark. In another picture, Tom is sitting on a stoop with a sandwich in his hand, looking down at Willow beside him.

Her own mother walked out on her. And this old man, the one that she confided in before she ran off to get married in Vegas, the one who she planted potatoes with in the soil, the one who always let her win at Battleships, he's been covering things up for all these years.

'I used to watch parents with their kids, and I'd think we weren't a real family, her and me,' she says. 'But we were even less of one than I thought.'

'That's not true.'

'She left me with strangers.' She looks at Tom then, a nerve plucking at his baggy left eyelid.

'We weren't strangers.'

She thinks of the way he usually tries to keep her talking, so she won't leave. She backs out of the room.

She hears him sniffling. She wants to walk back in there and shut her arms around him, but she just listens, his quiet crying slashing at her heart. He's someone different now – someone who knew something so fundamental about her yet didn't say a thing. Layering on the lies like papering over names and dates on bare plaster. *Annie woz here.*

She knows she should go back in there right now, and tell him it doesn't matter, but she pulls the front door shut behind her and heads down the steps.

She passes an arched window, sees her dirt-frosted car, something moving beside it, a person too faraway to make out. Someone dressed in black pulling open her back door.

'What the?'

Annie didn't even think to lock it, because who'd want to steal that heap of junk anyway? All those candy wrappers strewn on the floor, the crumbs wedged between seats.

Annie clacks down the stairs fast then faster still, toppling backwards and saving herself by grabbing onto the handrail. At the next landing, she looks again. The person is inside the car now.

The crumbs on the back seat of the car are skewering Tess' knees like gravel. She can smell cheap perfume, floral, synthetic. In the tray behind the gear stick, there's a mystifying array of screwed-up receipts. *Chocolatey chip waffles; hot pocket frozen sandwiches.*

Tess pushes her hand into the seam of the seat and pulls out a little hair grip shaped like a pair of glasses. She stuffs it into her pocket, wipes her hands down her thighs and shuffles her way out. Thank goodness there's no one around. She rushes away, the crumbs fluttering from her knees, and gets into her hire car.

As she pulls away, she sees a distant figure heading down the stairs at the front of the building. Her foot presses the accelerator hard.

Chapter 20

Two months later

i

Surrey, England

Tess moves the cursor along the street pictured on her iMac. There's a dirt track and a blurred image of a woman at her car. It's that street in America where she followed those people back home. She should be working – she's only got an hour before she has to collect Freddie from Montessori – but she can't stop clicking closer to their apartment, the weathered wood, the bin with the lid that's not quite shut in the driveway. She's the closest she can get to the apartment, given she's more than 4,000 miles away.

There's a flash of lightning outside and the rain types the skylight. *Give her back to me.* She lets the thought rise into her head, pushes it out through her skull. She wills it to fly across land, across ocean, down that street and into that tumble-down flat. She wants those people to hear this thought and act on it. *Please.*

The letterbox creaks, the pat of letters landing on the mat. She scoops them up and knives some of them open at her desk. Tickets to another of Jenna's private views; an invitation to try a new credit card; a cheque for £15,000. Matteo's cashed in a bond, the bond that they only opened a few months ago. She opens the last envelope. It's a letter from Gill Cousins. Her heart tries to break free from her chest as she reads. Gill has enclosed a note from Freddie's real mother. Loops and points and swirls. There's something decorative about the way it rambles across the page. Her eyes blink over the words too quickly to make any sense of them. She snatches out '*devastated*' and '*feel as you do*' then she locks onto a phrase, '*We would like to meet.*' She reads it again and again until she's sure she's not mistaken. There isn't a single detail about the girl, not even her name, and the letter is unsigned. Does this handwriting fit the woman that she saw in the lift?

She goes over to the cupboard with its sliding doors and kneels, pulling out files and loose papers. There, at the back, is the teddy. She feels guilty as she sniffs its musty tang. It belongs to a child, and that child has probably been crying for it. She wants to put that right. Perhaps that might go some way to settling her haunted head. It hasn't mattered what she's been doing over the past months, that girl she saw has still been making her presence felt, in the corner of Tess' eye as she drives to business meetings, a shadow in a room that disappears as soon as she walks in. She opens a drawer, feels the hair grip inside an envelope. There were no hairs attached to it, nothing that could be used for a DNA test, but despite this Tess is holding onto the thought that the girl is the one.

▌

A few hours later, Matteo comes into Tess' office, an inflamed circle of skin on the edge of his top lip, a whisky sloshing in his hand.

'The family have made contact,' she says.

His eyes are glazed.

'They've written to us, Freddie's family. They want to meet.'

He dumps himself into the leather chair, air deflating from its cushion, the whisky splashing over his fingers.

'So we should go back there,' she says.

'Going away is not an option for me right now.' He can't get the words out fast enough, and the muscle in his cheek starts to flex.

'This is important.'

'The hotel's important. I've got a million things to do.'

He takes the letter from her with an air of fatigue, and reads.

'You wouldn't have to be away for long,' she says. 'If they've made this offer, we should take them up on it, before they change their minds.'

'That was never the purpose of . . .' He looks at her and swallows. 'Anyway, we can't go. The children, we can't leave them with Jenna again.'

'So we'll take them with us.'

He glugs at his drink. 'We can't risk the boys finding out.'

'But I want to meet my little girl,' she says.

He scratches his cheek, dry skin snowstorming.

'If they want to meet, they mean just us,' he says. 'We're not even going to get the option of meeting this child.'

'But it could lead to that.'

'A long time down the road perhaps.'

'We should tell the boys.'

'They don't even know about Ava, you didn't want them to know, so why would we tell them about this?' asks Matteo.

'To get them used to the idea of their sister.'

'No, Tess.'

'You know what Phoenix is like, he's bound to pick up on what's happening, we can't lie to him.'

'I want to protect them from all of this.'

'And you still can,' she says. 'If they know now, it won't be such a shock to them in the future. Think about it, Matteo, this little girl might track us down eventually, might want to get to know them.' She can feel the hope shining out of her own eyes. 'You're the one that's always saying we should talk about things.'

'I don't know.' He lays his empty glass on the floor.

'The boys break up for the summer holidays in three weeks,'

she says. 'We could go after that. We could get a babysitter if we have to go to the meeting alone.'

He breathes in, holds it then lets it out as if he's forcing himself to stay calm.

'What's really bothering you?' she asks.

He straightens in the chair, 'I'm busy, that's all, and this mess . . .'

'You've cashed in that bond.'

He folds his arms. 'We're still not getting all that many book-ings, I needed to use it for wages – short term only. I'll open another bond when things pick up.'

'It's because of that wedding, isn't it?'

All those upset stomachs, that white dress. The Carrara marble restrooms looking more like public conveniences on a ferry in rough seas.

'That didn't exactly help.'

'But we gave them their money back,' she says. 'I answered all the awful comments on TripAdvisor. We were in Condé Nast Traveller before that for goodness sake.'

'Well, it's a good job Condé Nast Traveller didn't write a feature about 120 people puking in our loos.'

The stench. That's what she remembers from when Matteo had phoned her to come and help out. That and the mother of the bride shouting. Tess would have shouted too if her wedding reception had ended in a bulk buy of oral rehydration solutions.

'Look, Tess, if we go over there, they might change their minds about seeing us. It could all be a waste of time.'

'Let's just do it.'

'I can only stay for a few days. Just . . .' He swallows. 'Don't get your hopes up.'

These are her hopes: her daughter falling in love with her, Freddie hitting if off with this other family; everyone agreeing that the best course of action is to swap these children back. Pulling out the pieces of a jigsaw puzzle that don't fit, and righting them. She feels hot with anger then it subsides, and in its place, the guilt swells.

i

Matteo steeples his fingers underneath his chin and looks at Phoenix and Luca sitting on the couch opposite. 'We've got something to tell you.'

Tess can hear the television filtering in from the kitchen diner as she closes the door. She's left Freddie watching a cartoon.

'We're going to Disneyland Paris!' says Luca, eyes ballooning.

'No,' says Matteo.

Tess sits between the boys, hooking her arms over their shoulders. Phoenix pulls away.

'It's something to do with Freddie,' says Tess.

'Has he been bad again?' asks Luca, biting a nail.

Phoenix tuts.

'Do you remember that holiday we went on about a year before Freddie was born?' asks Matteo.

'No,' says Phoenix.

'When we went to America,' says Tess.

Phoenix shrugs.

'Well, while we were there your mother . . .' Matteo clears his throat.

'We made a baby,' says Tess.

'Oh, no,' moans Phoenix, covering his eyes with a hand. 'Yuck.'

'Sometimes, when two people find it difficult to have a child, they have a procedure called IVF,' says Tess. 'That's when doctors take the woman's egg and the man's sperm, mix them together and make a baby. Well, that's what the doctors in America did for me.'

'Doctors made us?' asks Luca.

'No,' says Matteo.

'How were we made then?' asks Luca.

Matteo draws in air.

'Doctors made Freddie,' says Tess.

'Can we go now?' asks Phoenix, scratching his fingers along the arm of the couch.

'Hold on,' says Matteo. 'What your mother is trying to say is that the doctors made us a baby, but instead of putting that baby back inside her, they put Freddie there by mistake.'

'So Freddie isn't related to us?' asks Phoenix.

'No,' says Matteo.

'But he lives with us,' says Luca. 'I don't get it.'

'Think of it like adoption,' says Matteo. 'He came from someone else's body, but like you, he's our son.'

'But he did come from Mummy's body,' says Luca.

'What is wrong with you?' Phoenix asks Luca.

Luca leans over Tess and bashes his brother's arm. Phoenix bashes him back, and they carry on fighting.

'Stop it!' yells Matteo.

Tess looks at the door.

'He belongs with us,' says Phoenix.

'Yes, he does,' says Matteo.

'Freddie doesn't know about any of this yet,' says Tess. 'We're going to tell him when he gets a little older, but we've got to go back to the clinic. They want to talk to us about what went wrong. And so we're taking you all with us, back to America.'

'A holiday, goody!' says Luca.

'But you said we weren't going on holiday this year,' Phoenix says to Matteo.

'Well, now we are,' says Tess. 'The clinic are paying for our flights, a villa.'

'I want to stay here,' says Phoenix.

'We leave in a week,' says Matteo.

Phoenix leans his elbow on the arm of the sofa and sinks his chin into his hand.

Luca stands and does some star jumps. 'We're going on holiday!' He puts his arms around Tess' neck and kisses her. She smiles at Matteo over the boy's shoulder.

'If you got the wrong baby, who got the right baby?' asks Phoenix.

'There's another family,' says Tess. 'They had a little girl, our girl. They want to meet us, well, just Daddy and me to start with.'

'We have a sister,' says Luca, breaking away, his eyes bulging brown orbs.

'She's not really your sister,' says Matteo.

'But she's . . .' starts Tess. 'Well, we don't know anything about her yet.'

'Is she going to come and live with us too?' asks Luca.

'No,' says Matteo.

'I'm going to watch telly,' says Phoenix, standing.

'You mustn't say anything to Freddie, or to anyone,' says Tess.

Phoenix rolls his eyes and walks out. Tess looks at the floor, feels her face folding.

'Oh, Mummy, it'll be okay,' says Luca, laying his hand on her cheek.

Will it? she thinks. 'Of course it will,' she says. She moves her face sideways and kisses his fingers.

Chapter 21

Florida, USA

The sun is glaring through the windscreen of the hire car, the air-conditioning doing little to quell the heat. Tess didn't sleep on the flight and fatigue is weighing heavy on her eyelids. The road stretches empty ahead of them, Matteo driving with both hands on the wheel.

Luca's iPad game pings as they pass a grizzled, leafless tree. Telegraph poles and wires loom stringily above them. Eventually, the tidy black of the tarmac turns to a thick dusty stripe sand-wiched by palm trees, and signs slashed with blue words. Tess eyes her scribbled notes: *310, Sunshine Drive.*

A bare-chested man, his doughy paunch bulging over his board shorts, holds a gushing hosepipe, the water puddling on the grass. The wheels of the hire car slap through it. The road is lined with street lamps and pink bougainvillea. Instead of pavements, there's just sand.

'You have reached your destination,' says the sat nav, and though Matteo presses a button, the robotic voice repeats. He stabs his finger again and it stops.

He pulls up outside a house with green timbered walls, a staircase on stilts rising up the side. The L-shaped front garden is swathed in shells. Tess gets out of the car and the sea announces its nearby presence with a steady hiss. She turns in its direction a hundred metres away, the sand almost white through the gaps between the villas closest to the beach; it is pitted with shells and driftwood. She can smell the briny aroma of the sea.

Matteo crunches over to the house, climbs the wooden staircase, his shoes dangling in his hand, Freddie following. Tess heaves one of the cases from the boot and heads upstairs too, Luca so close behind that he steps on one of her heels, unhinging her sandal strap.

'Sorry, Mum.'

'It doesn't matter,' she says, lassoes her arm around his shoulder and kisses his cheek.

Matteo tries the combination on the key drop and retrieves the single key. The front door gives. Freddie goes through first, thundering across the spongy blue carpet in his Crocs.

'You need to take your shoes off!' calls Tess, but he's already going through one of the doors off the living room.

Each step of the slatted inner staircase is carved with outlines of starfish and conch shells. There's a mezzanine level above with a bookcase and a potted palm on it.

Everywhere there are signs nailed to the wall. *Life's a Beach. Mermaids Welcome*, and a large piece of driftwood half-painted blue. A basket brims with shells on the coffee table.

There's the sound of creaking springs and Tess goes towards it. Freddie is jumping on a king-size bed in what must be the main bedroom, his shoes pounding the quilt, his head knocking the gold chandelier above him, setting the crystals in motion.

'Get down!' she says.

He bounces harder, gleefully, the crystals on the light shimmering like broken glass.

'I said get off the bed, Freddie.'

Still he jumps. She takes a deep breath and grabs his wrist. He yanks it away. The apartment where the girl lives is a ten-minute walk away. *Their girl.* Tess calculated the distance between the properties before she booked this place.

She lies on the bed, the puffy cotton quilt cushioning her

head. Her whole body vibrates as Freddie continues to jump. She closes her eyes and transports herself to that lift in the clinic. If Tess could get the girl back, she could erase these wasted years. It's not as if children can remember the details of their early lives anyway. She'll be left with brief flashes, but undocumented by photographs, the girl will forget. Tess focuses on a bird's-eye painting of the island on the facing wall and closes her fist, her polished nails digging crescents into her skin.

'Can we sleep up here?' shouts Phoenix from elsewhere in the villa.

Freddie jumps off the bed and bounds out as Luca wanders in and curls himself beside her. He puts his fingers into hers, chubby and pliable. She gets up then and starts to unpack the folded squares of Matteo's clothes – all things she has bought for him, designer shirts, and boxer shorts, crisp summer trousers. At least he came.

Luca stares up at the ceiling with a smile on his face, her boy who fits despite his difference, how she relishes his difference.

'Look at this place, isn't it lovely?' she says.

'It's cool.'

'Come on, let's take a look at the swimming pool.'

She goes into the open-plan living room where Matteo is on his mobile phone, one arm folded flat across his chest.

'I can't say when!' he snaps.

There's a crash of metal like furniture being moved about somewhere. Matteo turns to the noise and notices Tess. He smiles like someone has told him to say 'cheese.' A cold sore is crusting his upper lip.

'We'll speak later,' he says and clicks his phone off. Luca is rattling the key in the lock of the sliding glass doors to the back garden. Tess examined the floor plan carefully before she chose this place, so she knows those doors lead downstairs to the outdoor swimming pool.

'What was that about?' she asks Matteo.

'Never off duty.' He gives a small laugh, but his face stays serious.

Luca opens the back door and goes outside.

'I'll grab the last of the luggage,' says Matteo, the bottom of his chinos dragging on the carpet.

He steers himself around the open door of a cupboard underneath the stairs; two deckchairs have fallen from it. Tess can hear Freddie cooing from inside the cupboard. She goes towards it and crouches, her knees clicking. Freddie's strawberry blond hair shines in the gloom.

'Baby,' he says.

The low ceiling of the cupboard is strung with cobwebs. A dead beetle is cocooned inside a wispy globe.

'Come out of there.'

She pushes her hand in and takes hold of Freddie's wrist. He resists, something dragging behind him. She pulls him out with force.

'Ow!'

Now he's standing beside her, she can see what it is in his hand: an upside down baby doll, her brown hair salted with dust and sweeping across the carpet, blood gleaming on both of her cheeks, her lifeless chipped brown eyes. Tess tightens her grip on Freddie's wrist, pressing fingers into bone.

'You're hurting me!' He starts to cry.

She drops his wrist and he rubs it. The dried scab where he skinned his knee the other week has gone, in its place a crater dribbling blood.

'What *have* you done?' she asks.

He drops the doll to the floor and stares at it, blood caught beneath his fingernails. She reaches for her handbag, fumbles inside it for some wet wipes then picks the doll up and cleans it, cradling it in the crook of her arm.

'She's not real,' says Freddie.

Tess pushes the now clean doll back into the cupboard and closes the door as Matteo reemerges with another case in his hand.

Chapter 22

Two days later, Tess and Matteo are in a hotel conference room waiting to meet their son's genetic parents. Her cheeks are too hot, her black dress soaked in sweat. The tension in the room is amplifying and she feels the need to open a window, a door, to let out some of the pressure. She looks at her phone instead, scrolling through her Twitter account then setting it to silent. *Please let the babysitter keep Freddie under control.*

Digging inside her bag, she finds the painkillers she pilfered from Matteo's wash bag this morning. She pushes one from the pack and when she's sure he's not looking, she slips it into her mouth. Taking hold of a thin flap of skin at the side of her thumbnail, she pulls. It comes away thickly, sore, but she carries on pulling anyway and it doesn't bleed. Another cold sore has sprouted on Matteo's upper lip.

A first impression has never counted so much. This meeting could be a passport to seeing her daughter. It feels like the most important thing she'll ever do, the precision landing of a lunar space module. She checks that her lipstick hasn't coagulated in the corner of her lips then fishes for her phone again, looking at herself in the camera, checking her black hair is behaving, that there are no bogeys up her nose.

Gill comes in then. 'The other couple are in the conference room now. Are you ready?'

Tess feels paper-thin. She wants it to be over, to be out the other side, to have her daughter sitting right beside her, or rather she wants a reversal – to step back in time so that what's happened can be undone. Following Gill, Tess can smell the woody notes of Matteo's aftershave.

Then they're going through a door, and there she is, the woman from the lift. It really is her: the brassy red hair, crystal globes dangling from her earlobes. Something turns over inside Tess because the woman might recognise her, might have seen her as she stood on the deck outside her apartment with the toy in her hands. Annie Amstel, that's what Gill said her name was.

Annie stands up so quickly that her chair topples onto the floor behind her, its metal legs pointing in Tess' direction like spikes. Adrenalin surges through Tess, swerving her sideways, making her heart batter and her hands shake.

Annie can feel herself smiling manically at the woman in black.

'Hello there.' She laughs raucously then shuts it down.

The woman's face is so serious it could freeze warm water. Sharp nose, paper-straight black bobbed hair. Morticia Addams after a trip to Lavish Locks.

'Hello.' Her voice is so posh it has edges. Her foundation is spread thick and nothing about her moves, but there's an echo of Willow in that face.

The man puts her in mind of Benicio del Toro then he turns his head and she sees the cold sores sitting on his lip like sequins. He towers over her and Carl. She jabs her elbow into Carl's side, but still he doesn't stand straighter. Limply, he shakes the man's hand.

'Matteo,' says the man, an accented voice.

Carl mutters his own name and looks away. Annie and Carl's attorney, Susan Purcell, is standing beside Annie with that face that's always smiling, gummy and invisible-lipped.

'So this is Tess and Matteo,' says Susan then introduces Annie and Carl.

Everyone sits on chairs in a group-therapy circle including

that counsellor called Broo who keeps massaging her own naked earlobe. The Rossis' lawyer has hairspray-hard hair.

'What's my . . . your girl's name?' asks Tess, loud and definite.

Annie flits her eyes to Susan, then what the hell – 'Willow,' she says.

Tess' nostril gives the smallest of flickers; perhaps she's not all that keen on the name. Carl plunges his hands into his pockets then pulls them out and crosses them behind his back. Lord, if Carl is falling apart, what hope is there for the rest of them? Nobody is speaking. The silence rises as if someone's broken wind and everyone's pretending not to be able to smell it.

'So this is a first,' Annie blurts.

Matteo coughs.

'We could all start by stating what we'd like to get out of this meeting,' says Broo.

'I'd like to meet my daughter,' says Tess.

Every fibre of Annie's body urges her to get up, to run from the room right now.

'Your biological daughter, you mean,' says Broo.

Tess raises her chin. 'The clinic has mixed everything up. I want to try to make it right.'

Broo nods. 'And how about you, Annie, what is it that you want to happen?'

Annie tries to send her voice out on a low volume, yet she ends up screeching. 'Me? I don't really know what I want.' She swallows. 'I feel guilty even contemplating meeting Freddie.'

'Guilty about what?' asks Tess, her forehead furrowing.

'Guilty that I want to meet him at all,' says Annie. 'Guilty that meeting him diminishes what I feel for Willow. See, the thing is, I don't give a shit about . . .' The nostril quivers again. 'I mean I don't care about the biology; Willow's my little girl.'

There's a beat then Annie pushes more words out. 'Except that ever since I found out about Freddie, I can't stop thinking about him.'

'What do you think will happen if you meet him?' asks Broo.

'It could open up a wound,' says Annie. 'Something that won't ever heal.'

'You have to,' implores Tess.

'Do I? It's not as if we can swap them back,' says Annie.

Tess' eyes pop. 'Would you like to see a photograph?' she asks.

'Hold on,' says Susan, crossing her legs and making herself more upright. 'My clients may not be ready for that.' She trains her brown eyes on Annie.

Carl's face is failing to contain all the emotions colliding inside his skull. 'I guess we could take a look,' he says on a whisper and moves backwards in his seat.

'You'd like to see the photograph?' asks Susan.

Carl nods.

'I'd like to see it too,' says Annie.

Tess pulls a photograph from her bag and puts it into Annie's hand. The little boy has the same strawberry blond hair that Annie had as a child. She looks sideways at Carl who is staring at the photograph, gulping, and scratching his beard.

This is topsy-turvy, a birth and a death all rolled into one – her son may have made it, but he's lost to her. She's gazing at his face, but he's unmoored and floating away.

Annie wants to put this photograph down, to take the antiseptic liquid from her bag and wipe her fingers. But now she's seen the boy's face, she can't unsee it. It's like putting on a pair of tinted goggles that end up glued to your face.

Carl's eyes are tearing up. He sniffs, looks away from the photograph. 'Shit,' he says.

She places a hand over his and taps it. It feels like she needs to compliment the child somehow, fill her mouth with words that you say about other people's kids – *he's cute, handsome, he's just like you.* There's an itch in her throat like an urge to cough.

'I had it printed especially,' says Tess.

Carl slouches forward, puts an elbow onto his knees and leans his head there. 'We didn't bring any of Willow.'

'But I'd love to see her,' says Tess.

'Tess,' says Matteo, a warning glance.

'Is it okay with you if Tess and Matteo ask some questions about Willow?' Gill asks Annie, then looks at Carl.

'I guess so,' says Carl.

'Does she have a favourite toy?' asks Tess.

'She did have,' says Annie. 'A teddy bear, but we lost him.' A buzzer goes off in Annie's head like she's given the wrong answer on a television quiz show. What kind of impression are they making? She should have worn something more sober, something dark like Tess. She should have put on more make-up, gone on a diet. She should be better than she is.

'What does she like to eat?' asks Tess.

Ice cream, cakes, candy. 'Cucumber, zucchini. Eggs, she likes eggs.' Annie's voice squeaks the way it does when she's lying.

'What about friends? I bet she has lots,' says Tess.

'Oh, sure, there's Tiger, Claire, Jennifer and Jade,' says Annie. 'You know when she was first born I had her horoscope done – it said she'd be charismatic, people would be drawn to her, and that's pretty much how it panned out. Sometimes when she . . .' Annie is lifting out of herself, her cheeks heating, words cascading from her mouth and deluging the room. *Shut up* she tells herself as she sees Matteo squirming, Broo's forehead pleating with sympathy, Tess stiffening. Annie catches only some of her own tumbling, gushing words: 'The best thing that ever happened to me.' 'Love everything about her.' 'Love her so much I could marry her.' *Shut up.*

Then there's the weight of Carl's arm around her neck, his soothing voice in her ear. 'Annie, honey, Annie.'

And she clamps her dry mouth shut and stares at her stubby fingers in her lap. She's hot, shocked and shamed.

'And Carl, how about you, is there something that you're

particularly interested in finding out about Freddie?' asks Gill.

Carl's panic-stricken eyes switch from side to side. 'Well, does he like, er soccer?'

Matteo deflates. 'Freddie's not all that sporty.'

Like Carl. Annie manages to bite that observation down.

'Is he happy?' asks Annie.

'Of, course,' says Tess, her smile doing nothing to melt the icy expression on her face.

'And what about his health?'

'He's perfectly healthy,' says Tess, her lips puckering.

'What about your health?' asks Annie.

Tess touches her neck. 'I'm sorry?'

'Are there any illnesses in the family that we should know about?' asks Annie.

Tess looks at Matteo then back at Annie. 'There's nothing in our family, apart from a couple of cases of mild eczema.'

Annie's eyes land on Matteo's little finger, dry and cracked.

'What I don't understand is, how this could have possibly happened,' says Tess. 'They asked all sorts of questions, kept checking my date of birth. And it's unlikely we have the same surnames.'

'We don't need to discuss this yet,' says Susan.

'Mind you, I did use my maiden name at the clinic,' says Tess. 'I felt it might make me more anonymous.'

'I hardly ever use my married name,' says Annie. 'I usually go by Perry.'

Tess shudders in a breath. 'The same maiden name as me,' she says.

Gill looks at Susan. 'We were going to discuss this with you all as we had already established that,' says Gill. 'It does seem likely that the mix-up may have occurred because of this, but we'll have to look into it further.'

'Then they'll have to pay up,' says Matteo.

'But I don't understand,' says Annie. 'It's pretty clear we're not the same age, how could they have mixed up our dates of birth?'

'I don't know,' says Tess.

The blood sings in Annie's ears. *Why didn't I use my married name?* Her hands are shaking.

Tess looks at the wall-mounted clock. 'Please, let's get back to the children. I'd like to know more about Willow.'

Annie swallows bubbles of air instead of breathing. The pressure builds in her chest like a drowning. 'I can't . . . I don't . . .' She balls her hands in her lap, thinks of her little girl, and forces herself to speak. 'She's kind.' She heaves in air. 'Gets this look on her face when other kids are upset. She's good at directions too.' Annie bites her gum to stopper any more verbal diarrhoea.

'You have just the one?' asks Tess.

Just, when Willow is more than enough – she's everything. 'One's enough, one's good.'

'Freddie has two brothers,' says Matteo, his chest puffing. 'Luca who's ten, and Phoenix who's twelve.'

Tess may have porcelain skin, but Annie's sure she's an older mom, maybe that's why she had IVF, maybe she left it too late to have a third kid – although why bother when she had two to start with? If only Tess hadn't bothered, but then if she hadn't, Annie would never have known Willow.

'Do you think Willow suspects there's something different about her?' asks Tess.

'Different? In my baby group there was an artificially inseminated lesbian having a baby for some gay guys, and a woman who was pregnant through an egg donor. Everybody's different, every person everywhere, Willow fits right in.'

Matteo starts scratching his face.

'I don't think we'll be telling Willow anything about this, not for a long while anyway,' says Carl.

'I agree,' says Matteo. 'They're too young to understand.'

'How long are you here for anyway?' asks Carl.

'As long as it takes,' says Tess.

'As long as what takes?' asks Annie.

There's the crunch of Carl biting his fingernail.

'I'd like to get to know my daughter. I—'

'Your daughter?' yips Annie.

'I want to get to know Willow, that's all,' says Tess. 'Surely you must feel the same about Freddie.'

'I guess so,' says Annie. 'I don't know.' She shoves her hand into her bag and touches the packet of gum longingly.

'We've rented a villa on Sure Water Island,' says Tess.

'We live on Sure Water Island,' blurts Annie. Carl glares at her. 'Whereabouts are you staying?'

'I don't think you should be exchanging addresses at this stage,' says Susan.

Tess moves forward so she's perched on the end of her chair. 'But that's wonderful, we could arrange to meet.'

'We don't want to rush anything,' Broo interjects.

'But if we're so close, gosh, why not?' asks Tess.

'It would be helpful to pencil in another meeting shortly, especially as my clients are only here for a limited time,' says Gill.

'We can discuss this,' Susan says to Annie and Carl. 'I'll get back to you on that, Gill.'

'Perhaps you'll agree that you all want to meet the children,' says Broo. 'Or perhaps one of you won't want to meet the children. If you do meet, however, I'd stress that it needs to be on neutral ground, back here perhaps or somewhere else.'

'Certainly Tess and Matteo would very much like to meet Willow,' says Gill.

'Annie and Carl need time to think about this though,' says Susan.

'But Matteo is only staying for another week,' says Tess. 'And Freddie is here.'

'What? Where?' Annie turns and looks at the shut door.

'Back at our villa. We've got a babysitter for this afternoon,' says Tess.

Annie and Carl's son is on the island where they live. Thoughts of seeing him, hearing him, touching him moil inside Annie. An 'oh' comes out on a sigh. He's so close and if she doesn't meet him soon, she might not get the opportunity to see him for another six months, another year.

'As I say there's no pressure to decide now,' says Susan.

'It feels as if there's no right answer,' says Carl.

'Yes, there is. We want to meet him,' says Annie and looks at Carl who is slipping further into his seat.

Something flutters out of Tess' hand then. The photograph of Freddie lands on the floor, his pale little face staring up at them all like a ghost.

Chapter 23

Five days later, they are back in a hotel meeting room again, 'the holding room,' Matteo has called it. Freddie is kneeling on the floor, a toy car in one hand, a juggernaut in the other. He slams them together, and the noise jangles Tess' nerves. Matteo is breathing too fast.

She sets her phone to silent. There's an assortment of crayons, colouring books and plastic farm animals on the coffee table in the centre of the room. She hasn't told Matteo about seeing the girl in the lift. There's only a slim chance that she'll recognise Tess anyway. The teddy is back at the villa slotted onto a shelf, but she's not going to give it back; she's decided against that now. The toy is imprinted with her daughter after all. Luca cried when he lost his toy monkey all those years ago. When Matteo came home later, she retraced the steps she'd walked and eventually found the toy, its legs protruding from a hedge. She knows it's cruel to keep the toy, but it might be her only memento.

Gill flusters into the room in a navy pencil skirt, offering apologies for being late. 'Such terrible traffic,' she says.

Freddie digs into a box of crayons and flings a handful across the table. Tess is about to see her real child, that vital little girl with her cute voice. *Please don't let them change their minds.* The desperation has given her a tension headache.

'The other family are here,' says Gill.

There's a knock to the door, and Broo comes in, her mules silent on the nylon carpet. 'Hello, you must be Freddie,' she says, leaning down to him.

'Hello,' says Freddie.

'We've got some friends we'd like you to meet in the next room. Will you come with me?' asks Broo.

Some friends – that's what they've told Freddie. They can't tell him anything else yet, because these people might change their minds about getting to know him. And if they do want to be part of his life, Tess will have to introduce what's happened a little at a time.

'I'm staying here.' Freddie shuffles backwards on the floor, so his back presses against a plastic toy box.

'Come on,' says Matteo.

'There are more toys where we're going, Freddie,' says Broo.

'Is there?' he asks.

Broo nods.

Freddie gets up, takes his father's hand, and Broo leads the way.

'I'm hungry,' says Freddie.

'I've got some snacks,' says Tess.

They walk into a large, bright room with windows in the ceiling. Colourful balls are penned in by low plastic walls at the end of the room. There are children's chairs and beanbags, a netted climbing station with a padded slide.

And there she is, the girl, her luxurious hair, her brown eyes, the two little moles under her eye. It's obvious she's an Erin, not a Willow at all.

There is no one else in the room for Tess now except for her.

Freddie's knees poke inwards like Annie's, except his are knobbles on sticks. A wobbler, Nancy would have called him, head constantly on the move, ankles teetering, sprawling when he sits down, like now at the edge of the pen of balls, his indecisive, chubby hands in his lap then back at his side. Carl is staring at the boy, combing his fingers through his sparse hair.

The adults exchange hellos and Annie's stomach rises into her chest like a hiatus hernia. Freddie should have been hers. If he was hers she'd cut his hair for starters and it'd be Target specials instead of that Ralph Lauren T-shirt, a polo player riding across his thin blue chest. Annie goes over to the ball pen then, wading through and crouching beside Freddie.

'I'm hungry,' he says.

'You must be Freddie,' she says.

'I'm hungry.'

'And I'm Annie.'

He doesn't look at her, and before she can stop that tactile hand of hers, it's caught hold of his chin and is turning it gently towards her. His eyes rake her face. He smells of coconut. She misses him, oh God, she misses him even though she's never seen him before.

'And that's Willow,' says Annie, pointing to her little girl.

Willow looks over then carries on collecting balls in the basket of her arms; they keep falling through. Annie decides to leave them to it and walks barefooted back to Tess. It's not just the woman's height that makes Annie feel small. Annie's face is too plain, her hair too dry.

'I'm hungry!' shouts Freddie.

'I'll get something for you to eat in a minute,' says Tess, raising a smile.

They stand there, the four of them, the air-conditioning wafting, the balls tapping down, the awkwardness unfurling between them. Strangers in a hostage situation, and everyone too scared to speak.

Freddie stamps his foot. 'I want food!'

Annie marches over to her handbag still marooned on the floor. She pulls out a plastic-covered lolly encrusted with fat grains of white sugar.

'Here you go!' she says.

'He probably shouldn't have that,' says Tess. 'Sugar doesn't really agree with him.'

'Give him a break,' says Matteo. Freddie runs over, leaps towards the lolly, which Annie lifts out of reach. 'Well only if it's okay with your mom.'

'I want it!' shouts Freddie.

'Oh, alright,' says Tess.

Freddie snatches the lolly from Annie and runs back towards the coloured balls, surging and scattering as he jumps in.

Willow eyes the lolly in Freddie's hand. 'I want candy!' she calls to Annie, her hand pincering as she approaches.

'He's a bit excitable,' says Matteo.

'Family get togethers, eh?' says Annie.

'There's no need to apologise for him,' Broo says to Matteo.

A small noise escapes Matteo's mouth, his face breaking. He turns away, retreats to the other side of the room.

Carl gnaws at his fingernails and appears to reduce from pint to pocket sized. He comes closer to the pen of balls and watches Freddie.

Tess crouches, eye-level with Willow. 'My name's Tess.'

'Me see lines on your face,' Willow points at Tess' forehead.

The girl runs away. Freddie screams and throws several balls into the air. They batter down onto Willow's head. He clamps his arms around her and leans his mouth against her ear as if he's going to eat it. Tess gasps, her neck clenching. Freddie kisses Willow's ear and Tess' rigid body loosens a notch.

❚

Tess goes over to the play area with the balls again. She really should take her shoes off. That baggy man, Carl, is wearing socks and every time he moves, he presses sweaty footprints into the floor. Freddie starts to fill a bucket with balls, Willow bringing them to him.

'Gosh, Willow looks so much like my eldest son,' says Tess.

Annie folds her arms. Tess gazes at her own navy dress then looks at Annie's bright orange one. Oh, but Tess should be able to take hold of the girl's hand and drive away with her, and if it wasn't for this Oompa Loompa of a woman, she'd do just that.

Annie picks up a ball and goes towards Freddie. 'What colour is the ball I have behind my back?' she asks.

Willow reaches a slender hand towards her mother.

'No cheating,' says Annie.

'Blue!' shouts Freddie, spittle spraying the air.

'No.'

'Red!'

'No.'

'Green,' says the little girl.

'You got it!' says Annie, showing the ball to the children.

'You saw!' Freddie snaps at Willow.

Tess looks at Willow, the little girl whose future she'd planned for so long. Baking cakes, playing with her hair. She can't seem to drag her eyes away from the child. In her peripheral vision, she sees Annie pick up another ball.

'What colour is this one?'

'Red,' says the girl.

'Purple! Green! White! Yellow!' Freddie shouts.

'You got me there,' says Annie, throwing the yellow ball his way. He catches it and Annie tries to high five him, but he pulls his hand away. She mock chases him then, balls flying, and Freddie starts to laugh.

'Do you go to nursery?' Tess asks Willow. Her voice sounds out of place, alien, an English person in a Hollywood film.

The girl shrugs.

'You mean pre-school!' yells Annie. 'Sure you go to pre-school, honey.'

Tess notices the chewing gum stuck to the side of Annie's tooth. She tots up all the other things she can find not to like about the woman. That pillowy stomach, the stomach that housed Tess' daughter for nine months. Tess can smell excrement and starts to breathe through her mouth. Freddie dives into the balls and roars.

'That's boys for you,' says Tess.

'I always wanted a girl,' says Annie. 'I mean, don't get me wrong, I love boys too, but if you're going to have one child, a girl's pretty special.'

'Boys are too,' says Tess, feeling herself become ramrod straight.

'Oh, yeah, sure. I just mean I'm grateful for Willow, that's all.'

Matteo is leaning against a wall staring at Willow, while Carl slouches near Annie.

'It would be lovely for you to have a boy though,' Tess says to Carl.

'Girl, boy – just so long as they're happy and healthy,' says Carl, voice stretchy like caramel.

'Well, Freddie belongs to you really,' says Tess.

'Let's not go into this here,' says Broo. 'There are listening ears, and this is obviously very sensitive.'

'No, Willow belongs to us,' says Carl.

'Please . . .' says Broo.

Willow's laugh blares into the corners of the room, and showers down on Tess. She is steeped in the sound.

Sustenance, thinks Annie as the door opens and a woman in a too-tight beige uniform pushes in a trolley, trembling with cups and cakes. Freddie drops his lolly onto the floor, rushes over to the trolley and grabs a chocolate muffin. He stuffs it into his mouth, crumbs cascading. Tess closes her eyes briefly. Staring at the trolley, Willow hands her lolly to Annie.

'Would you like a cake, honey?' asks Annie.

'Yes, peas,' says Willow.

'Go on and help yourself, but remember to say thank you.'

Willow takes a cake and the uniformed woman smiles down

at her then leaves. The children move towards the pen of balls again, a pathway of crumbs spilling behind Freddie.

'Not in there, not while you're eating!' calls Tess, but Freddie ignores her and stumbles in anyway.

Willow stays put outside. Tess right-lefts over and heaves Freddie up, settling him onto his feet outside. Freddie glares at her, but when Willow sits on the floor, he does too. Annie pours herself a coffee, burns her lip as she sips. Tess arrives at her side.

'Would you like a drink?' asks Annie.

'Some water.' Tess takes a bottle, unscrews the lid and sips.

Annie helps herself to a buttercream cookie and crunches, watching Freddie cross-legged on the floor. His ear is peeping through his hair, and it's tiny, like Annie's ears.

'So, do you work?' asks Tess.

'Well, I work in art. Kind of,' Annie shrugs, and rushes out a question. 'How about you?'

'I run a social media marketing business.'

Annie isn't sure what Tess is talking about, and her lack of a response hangs.

'They're getting on well anyway,' says Tess.

'Completely oblivious to it all,' says Annie. 'Whereas us, Lord – it's a wonder we're not all on Prozac!'

Tess' eyes open a fraction wider, and the seconds tick by.

'I want Bug,' Willow says then, her chin wobbling.

'Remember what I told you, Bug went on an adventure.' Annie glances at Freddie climbing out of the ball pen now, and gasps as she notices brown sludge leaking from the hem of his shorts. It plops onto the floor like porridge.

Matteo rushes at Freddie and picks him up, stepping into the mess. He holds Freddie facing forward in his faraway arms and marches to the door, his moccasins pressing poo patches into the floor.

'Don't worry, we'll get someone in here to clean this mess up,' says Broo and goes out the door too.

'He must have an upset stomach or something,' garbles Tess. 'I'd better go and help.' She disappears through the door behind Matteo.

'Poo, poo!' says Willow.

The stench is invasive.

'Poo!' says Willow, pointing to the turdy slide on the floor.

Annie glances at the chocolate muffins on the trolley, which seem far less appealing now.

'I think we should make an excuse and leave,' says Carl. 'This is way too intense.'

'We can't just go,' says Annie.

'Maybe it was a mistake coming here.'

'It'll be a mistake if we just leave.'

He lowers his voice to a whisper. 'Did you see the way that woman kept on looking at Willow? I bet they push for custody.'

The woman in the beige uniform comes back in, unleashes an enormous roll of blue paper and starts wiping at the mess on the floor with her lace-up shoe. The air fills with the smell of lemon Ajax.

Carl climbs into the pen in his yellow socks and picks Willow up. 'That's enough for today, kiddo.'

'Dada, no!' says Willow.

Tess comes back into the room with Broo then. 'Matteo's cleaning Freddie up,' says Tess. 'They'll be back in a minute.'

'We're going to go,' says Annie.

'Okay, it was only meant to be a short introduction today anyway,' says Broo.

'But you've hardly spent any time with Freddie at all,' says Tess. 'Nor me with Willow.'

Willow buries her head into Carl's shoulder.

'I'm really sorry,' says Annie, hovering her hand towards Tess' arm then thinking better of it and snatching it back.

Carl is striding towards the door now, Carl whose speedometer is usually set to slow. Willow is in his arms, her hair blowing as they walk beneath the air-conditioning unit.

Tess takes three steps after them. 'Well, it was really lovely to meet you,' she calls as the door shuts behind them.

She rushes over to her handbag then and pulls an iPhone from it; that's when Annie sees the pink burn on her hand.

'I'll take your number,' says Tess.

'Oh, no, everything must go through your attorneys,' says Broo. 'That's what we've all agreed.'

Annie plunges towards the door, pushing on her sandals without doing them up and grabbing Carl's trainers with the green slashes along the sides. She hurries through the corridor, buckles chinking, and catches Carl up at the elevator.

'That was a shitty experience,' he says.

'Naughty, Dada!' says Willow.

Annie looks over her shoulder, and flinches. Tess is standing behind the glass door staring at Willow. The woman puts Annie in mind of the Virgin Mary ornament Nancy used to have on the mantel, a beatific look on its face along with a decapitated right hand.

Ping. The doors to the elevator slide open.

'I'll see you at the bottom of the stairs,' says Annie and rushes away.

Chapter 24

Tess plucks an orange scarf from a rack in the clothes shop. There are dresses and separates grouped into colours. Usually, she'd make a beeline for the black and navy rails, but here she is standing in citrus. She arranges the silk scarf around her neck, the yellow dress she's just tried on strewn over her arm.

'That looks good on you, ma'am,' says the shop assistant with the pierced nose.

'I'm going to take it, and these.' Tess lays the scarf, the dress, and a red bikini on the counter.

Outside again, she positions herself on a bench and looks at her phone – Annie and Willow have been in the soft play centre at the other end of the square for twenty minutes now. Tess pushes her Ray-Bans high up the bridge of her nose. Another ten and the child might have had her fill.

It's been two days since they met Willow, and still no word from Annie and Carl's attorney. That's why she drove back to Annie's apartment, and watched the place. She was desperate for the loo, and on the point of giving up when Annie's car reversed out of the driveway at speed, and Tess began to follow it.

She lifts the bodice of her black dress and lets air circulate in the space. A woman wheels her buggy past, the baby asleep inside, his head lolling. The sun is blazing yellow in the cloudless sky, and Annie fills Tess' head as an ache. Why has chance thrown them together like this?

She puts on her sunhat, counts to a hundred then starts again.

She stays there for a long time, then she sees them, Annie waddling, the little girl running to keep up. Tess stands and walks, keeping distance between them. They're heading for the super-market.

They disappear inside and Tess scissors towards the entrance, grabbing a basket from a precarious tower. There's the beep of tills as she makes her way to the bread aisle. Plastic boxes of pecan pies, cheesecakes, rows of freshly baked cookies. She puts a key lime pie into her basket. Walking across the aisle ends, she can't see them, so she walks back the other way. Still no luck.

She pauses in front of a shelf of mangoes and looks at her diamond ring – all these possessions that fail to fill her up. Her little girl, the smell of her breath, the sound of her laugh. All the yearning she feels for Ava has found somewhere to dock itself.

She walks and sees a red cotton thread caught in the spinning wheel of a supermarket trolley. Covering some more ground, she spots Willow, her little feet shut into *Dora the Explorer* sandals, but where is Annie?

'Mama! Mama!' calls Willow, her chin creasing.

Her eyes are frantic; she's sucking her fingers with force. Something electrical starts buzzing in Tess' chest – *Willow is alone, and she's right here beside me.* The sound of water fills her ears.

'Hello, Willow,' says Tess.

The little girl is about to cry. She pulls her fingers from her mouth like a bottle uncorked. 'Mama!'

Tess' whole body tingles. 'Are you lost?' she asks.

The air-conditioning has goose bumped Willow's arms. Tess pulls her new scarf off her neck and covers Willow's shoulders with it. The girl strides away, turning her head sideways as she passes the end of each aisle, and the scarf floats free to the floor.

'I'm sure we'll find her soon,' calls Tess, collecting the scarf and walking after Willow. She catches her up and grabs her hand, and when Willow tries to snatch it back, Tess is forced to let go. The girl paces away.

'Mama!' she shouts.

Tess tries to take her hand again.

'No!' shouts Willow.

A woman with a long swish of black hair extensions regards Tess then looks down at Willow.

'Do you know this lady?' she asks Willow in a gentle voice.

'No.' Willow stops and folds her arms.

'I'm going to call security,' says the woman, her shoulders slumped to one side under the weight of her full shopping basket, a box of dog biscuits about to slide off the top.

'I'm her mother,' blurts Tess.

'Hygiene to aisle four please. There's a spillage in aisle four,' goes a tannoy.

'You're not my mama!' says Willow.

'My God.' The woman hitches her lip. 'Is she trying to make you do something you don't want to do?'

Willow nods, stoppering her mouth with her fingers again.

The woman puts her hand on Willow's back. 'Don't you worry, I'm going to get someone.'

'There's really no need.' A lock of hair falls into Tess' face.

'Clearly there is,' says the woman. She reaches down to take Willow's hand. Willow takes it back again.

'Hey, we need some help over here!' the woman calls.

An elderly lady eyes the woman suspiciously through round glasses, the half-moon sunshades attached to them tilted upwards. She wheels her trolley away.

A security guard in brown overalls slouches towards them on pigeon toes. 'Is there a problem here?' His hair is a shiny black combover.

'This woman is saying she's this little girl's mama!' says the woman.

'Is she your mommy?' the security guard asks Willow.

Willow shakes her head then wanders away. 'Mama! Mama!'

Tess catches up with her in the alcohol aisle, the woman and the security guard in hot pursuit.

'Mama!' yells Willow.

There's a scatter of feet on the floor.

Annie appears beside them then, 'Oh, Willow, there you are, thank God!' She gathers Willow into her arms. 'I've been freaking out for the past five minutes.' She presses the girl harder to herself. 'I thought I'd lost you.' She kisses Willow's cheek.

'Is this your daughter?' the woman asks Annie.

Annie nods.

'Well, that woman said she was her mother.' The woman's finger is lifted and pointing straight at Tess.

Annie starts blinking fast, her mouth open, a blob of chewing gum stuck to a tooth. 'What did you say that for?'

The security guard walks in between Tess and Annie. 'We don't want any trouble here.'

'It's okay, we know each other,' Annie says.

The woman's eyes dart back and forth between Annie and Tess.

'Well, so long as you're alright, ma'am,' the security guard says to Annie.

'I'm fine, thank you.'

'Hmmmm . . .' A noise slips out of the woman's shut mouth.

'We're fine here, honestly,' says Annie, reaching out a hand and touching the woman's arm. 'And thank you so much.'

'Well, okay,' the woman concedes. She wanders away, turning back to look at them.

'You can't go around saying things like that,' says Annie.

'Like what?' asks Tess.

'That you're her . . .' Annie mouths the word 'mom'.

'But I am her mother, in a way.'

'You're not!' snaps Annie.

Willow looks at her mother and starts sucking her fingers. Tess wants to cover her own face, her neck. She's burning up and not just because of the ferocious hot flush that's drenching her body in sweat. She covers her chest with the scarf.

'All I want is for . . .' She feels a bead of sweat trickling down her face. 'Why don't we meet again, maybe later, maybe tomorrow?'

Annie puts Willow down. The child hides behind her mother's legs.

'I'm not sure I can do that,' says Annie.

'Why not?'

'This is such an impossible situation.'

'I feel exactly the same,' says Tess. 'But we should at least try to . . . I don't know, build some kind of friendship?'

Annie's chest fills with air.

'Please,' says Tess. 'Matteo goes home in a couple of days, and . . . can't we give it one last try before he leaves?'

'You're not going with him?'

'We're staying on for a few more weeks, the boys and I, but Matteo has to get back for work.'

'Well, I don't think Carl would be able to come.'

'You could come though, you and Willow, to our villa. Look, I'll write down my address.' She pulls a pen from her bag and scribbles on a Post-it Note.

Annie looks at it. Tess' phone number is there too. 'That's right around the corner from us,' says Annie. 'That is so weird.'

'Well then, it'll be easy.'

'Mama, I want to go home!' says Willow.

Tess keeps looking at the child, the neat fingernails, her shiny hair. Working hard to keep this serene look on her face is like holding a particularly challenging yoga pose.

'I'm sorry, I'm not reacting all that well to this,' says Annie.

'If anyone knows how you feel, it's me. Please. Today, tomorrow?'

'Broo said we should meet somewhere neutral, nobody's house.'

'But it's not my house, it's a rented villa. Please, just think about it, that's all I'm asking. We have a pool, the children could play in it, we could . . .'

'Alright, I'll think about it.' Annie takes Willow's hand and starts walking away.

Tess watches her go, an urgency in her steps. She takes a right and disappears from view.

And then it's as if someone is pulling the strings of Tess' puppet feet, lifting them up and placing them down and she is following Annie, the pots and boxes slipping around in her basket.

The doors to the outside slide open and Annie marches through them, Willow running along beside. Tess follows them out, and an alarm starts to shrill. Annie is opening the boot of her car.

'Ma'am! Er, ma'am!' A hand clasps Tess' bare arm. She turns to see the lopsided male security guard from earlier standing there.

'My daughter, she . . .'

'Ma'am, you are trying to leave the premises without paying your bill.'

Tess looks at her half-full basket and the alarm continues to sound.

'I'm not a thief!' says Tess.

The security guard clings wetly to her upper arm. He lifts his walkie talkie to his mouth. 'We got a dipper.'

He frogmarches her back through the store, heads turning to look at her as she passes. A woman with a hooked nose keeps her eyes on Tess as she pushes her groceries into a carrier bag. A man in a backwards baseball cap tiptoes to see.

'Do you want some help packing?' a cashier says to someone, but Tess is the main attraction.

There's a furnace in each of her cheeks. 'Please,' she says.

The security guard leads her through a door with a mirrored window in it.

'I'm not that sort of person,' she says in a withering voice. 'I would never dream of taking something that didn't belong to me.' Even to her, the words sound hollow.

Chapter 25

Annie hides the last piece of chocolate cake beneath the dollop of sprayed UHT cream on her leaf-flecked plate.

'Well, that was just lovely,' she says and takes another sip of her too-cold milky coffee to kill the lardy aftertaste. Carl certainly didn't inherit his cooking skills from his mother.

The only sound in Lina's dining room is Willow's jaw ploughing through the dense sponge, but then that kid will eat anything from anchovy foam to Slim Jims. Willow sneezes.

'*Gesundheit*,' says Lina, peering at Willow and holding a weathered hand over her forehead. 'I hope you are not going down with my flu. Oh, I thought it was never going to end.'

From here, Annie can see the cardboard boxes towering in the hall, an old pair of flippers sticking out of one of them, 'tools' marker-penned across another.

'I said I'd help you sort through that stuff,' says Annie. 'All that heavy lifting.'

'But I have the strength of an ox,' says Lina, flexing her twig arm, the loose flesh beneath it jiggling. 'Besides I want it all gone now. You take what you want, Carl, but after that – poof!' Her hand mimics a blade cutting her throat. 'There's a few bits in there you can sell, might make up a little for all those birthdays he missed.' She decapitates the remaining sponge on her plate and shovels it into her mouth. 'The swine,' she adds, her mouth scatter-gunning crumbs over the lace-covered table.

She rarely mentions Diedrich. He got together with another

woman when Carl was eight, and they had a whole gang of kids. Carl hasn't seen his dad since he left.

Annie catches Carl's eye and he smirks. Lina's given herself one of her DIY haircuts, layers sticking out at sharp angles around her face. The back came off worst though; it stares at Annie from the dresser mirror, short bits, and patches where it's still long. In front of the mirror, several cards are on display, a bear with a balloon declaring *Happy Bear Hug Birthday*. If Willow notices it, the questions about her lost teddy will probably start all over again. Willow's homemade birthday card is on the dresser, one of the quilled flowers already peeling off.

'You want another slice?' asks Lina.

'Yes, peas,' says Willow, her face messy with crumbs and cream.

Lina wields the knife at the sunken chocolate cake.

'Oh, no, that's okay, really. Willow's had enough.' Annie's laugh echoes around the minimalist room.

'But it's my birthday,' says Lina with the force of a sudden gust of wind.

And it's Willow's belly; Annie can't put her daughter through another slice.

'No, really, we have to think about her teeth,' says Annie.

'You don't think about her teeth when you give her *bonbon*!' declares Lina.

She plunges the knife into the sponge, cuts a wedge and manoeuvres it onto Willow's plate where it sits like a hard slab of mud.

'Carl told me about meeting those people,' she ventures, circles of orange blusher on her cheeks.

'Not now, Mom.'

'You must be very careful, Annie,' says Lina, waggling the knife in the air. 'You cannot trust them.'

'Why?' asks Willow.

'Nothing, butterbean,' says Annie.

There's a crash as Willow's cake and plate explode onto the cleaned-three-times-a-week engineered wood floor.

'Oh, no.' Willow slams her hand across her mouth.

'It doesn't matter, *schnuckel*, it's nothing that can't be fixed, not like . . .'

Lina rises from the table, a frilly apron tied around her slender waist. She returns with a dustpan and brush.

'I'll get that,' says Annie, rushing to grab the brush.

'I can do it,' says Lina, snatching it back again.

She bends, sweeps up the crumbs and broken crockery while Annie bins the ruined cake in the kitchen. Lina comes in and starts the washing up, water steaming.

'This is what comes of interfering with the natural processes,' says Lina, shaking her head. 'Wishes always come at a price.'

Like a fairytale. The smell of lemon dishwashing liquid curls into the air.

'Lina, I don't want Willow to know about this, could you—'

'The stress of it. I haven't been able to sleep since we found out for certain. And as for my blood pressure.'

Annie dumps the dish towel down. 'Maybe I'll take a look through those boxes.'

'The important thing though is not to catastrophise,' says Lina, clanking a dish into the drainer.

Annie opens a box – a screwdriver, a pot of nails, stained old rags. In another one there are piles of photographs. Lina, a cigarette pegged between her fingers, Carl, when he was a boy, standing knock-kneed beside her, and smiling. In another photograph, Lina has a ball of a perm, her round glasses outsized. And then there are older photographs, sepia-toned pictures of people in pantaloons, and black and white ones taken by a professional photographer – a woman holding a baby, a blond boy, aged around four, leaning on the side of her chair.

'Oh,' says Annie and her head starts to spin. The boy is so like Freddie. Except, instead of Freddie's long hair this boy has a short back and sides.

'Is this Diedrich?' calls Annie.

Lina comes out into the hall and takes the photograph with still-wet hands. She holds it close to her face and tuts.

'Even as a child, he was odd looking,' she says. She returns the photograph to Annie and walks back into the kitchen.

The longing to see her little boy again is an ache in Annie's chest. *Mother.* She's been hugging that word to herself like a pillow, but what does that even mean in relation to Freddie? Lina's dumpling stew sits too heavy in Annie's stomach, her back and neck are too hot. She lays her hand against the wall to steady herself.

Lina walks into the living room and tears the cellophane off her box of birthday chocolates.

'Now, who would like one?' she asks.

'Meeeee!' calls Willow.

'Mom, she's had enough sugar.'

'But it is my birthday – take two, *liebling.*'

Annie lays the photograph in front of Carl who catches sight of it, and looks up at Annie, stunned. They stare at each other, Annie's eyes filling with tears, and Carl squeezing her hand.

'What are we going to do?' she asks him.

'Dat's Fed,' says Willow, melted chocolate pasted over her chin.

'That is your grandfather, child.'

'No, dat's Fed!'

Lina rises, muttering, 'No, that is a good for nothing piece of . . .' Her words trail away as she goes out into the hall and fumbles with a box. 'There!' she says, returning with an old-fashioned camera and laying it in front of Willow. 'It belonged to him, you should have it.'

Carl smears his palm over his face. 'She can't play with that.'

'It was one of the few things of any value that Diedrich left behind when he walked out,' says Lina. 'A Yashica Mat camera, made in West Germany.'

Willow stares at it, unimpressed. Lina gathers Willow onto her knee and crushes her between her arms.

'I'm wrapping you up in my love,' she says.

'It hurts,' says Willow, and Lina smiles and kisses the top of her head.

Annie looks at Carl, leaning his elbows on the table, his hands laced together and his eyes shut like he's saying a prayer.

Chapter 26

Annie stuffs the pot of Jolen into the back of the overcrowded bathroom cabinet, bottles teetering on the edge of the glass shelf. *If a woman as old as Tess can look that good . . .* She slams the mirrored door shut.

A U2 song blares in from the kitchen and she taps her foot while tweezing the middle of her monobrow. The bleach is a frothy white moustache over her top lip. She might as well work on a picture while it's taking effect, and Willow's out at her swimming lesson with Carl.

Annie wanders into the kitchen diner, plonks herself at the table and starts fashioning blue ribbons of paper into feathers for the wings of her kingfisher. Humming to the music, she lays all the shapes onto an A3 piece of card.

Freddie plays ball inside her head like a Gif. There are four quilled pictures stacked behind the couch now, all of which she's photographed and added to her website under a tab on the menu called *My Artwork*.

She'd advertise on social media if she knew how. Last night, she clicked on and off her website hoping that might make it rise up the Google search, but it didn't.

A key scratches the lock. They're back already and she's only been working for about half an hour. Willow springs forward into her mother's arms, her hair still damp.

'Have you been on the cappuccino again?' asks Carl.

Oh my Lord! The bleach. Annie puts Willow down and rushes

towards the bathroom, tripping over the box of art supplies on the floor.

'I'll fix us some lunch,' calls Carl. 'Then I'm going to head off.'

Annie wipes the bleach off with a mound of toilet roll, then looks at the strip of inflamed skin over her upper lip. She was trying to get rid of a moustache not make herself a new one.

In the kitchen, Carl is pummelling a piece of chicken with a mallet. Willow is singing in her bedroom.

'I think I'm going to go,' say Annie.

'Where?'

'To see him.'

'Oh, Annie, we've talked about this. You need to run this by Susan first. I'm not sure it's a good idea.'

'Susan! Jesus, Carl, the clinic are paying her, so who is she really working for – us or them?'

He puts more force into the chicken beating. 'It feels too soon, and what about Willow? I'm working later, so I can't look after her.'

'I'm going to take her with me.'

The mallet pauses in mid-air. He shakes his head. 'I've got a bad feeling about this, I mean, really bad.' He sighs then bludgeons the chicken meat again.

'It'll give me a chance to work the family out,' she says. 'I just want to know a bit more about them, make sure they're alright.'

'I don't think you should go.'

'Well, I'm going.'

He attempts a particularly violent whack of the chicken and ends up thundering the mallet onto his thumb. 'Shit!'

Alan comes through the cat flap and climbs into the litter tray, the crunch and scrape of little stones.

'Freddie's never going to be our son,' says Carl. 'Even if you see him for a few hours, that's never going to make up for a lifetime, so, in a way, what's the point of seeing him at all?'

She fails to come up with an answer. Even so, she feels it, that steely determination sitting in her chest like a ball bearing.

Annie's calves ache as she climbs the stairs of Tess' green villa, Willow's hand in hers. The bleached skin above her upper lip stings beneath a smear of concealer. She would have been better off leaving the hairs russet-coloured.

'Twenty five steps,' she says, panting, when she and Willow reach the landing, Annie weighted down on one side by her basket bag, and a carrier bag with handles that are about to shear off.

'Tenty five!' says Willow, dangling from her mother's arm now and lifting her own feet off the ground.

A wooden rocking chair is loaded with towels, a bucket, a spade, a blue rubber ring. The doorbell doesn't make a sound as Willow presses it. There are windows at either side of the door, both with closed slatted blinds. Annie tries the bell too. A tile is stuck to the wooden wall with a bright blue starfish on it. Vague voices filter through the shut door, but there's no sign of anyone coming. Annie tries the bell again, flicking her eyes sideways to her beaten-up car down there, parked too close to the gleaming red one that Tess and her husband must have hired. Willow gives the door three hard knocks.

Annie's heart pummels in time with the approaching footsteps. When the door opens, Matteo is standing there, fragrant, tousled, tall.

'So good to see you again,' he says, that scabby lip of his descending on her. He kisses first one cheek then the other. Annie hopes those cold sores aren't catching.

'Hello, Willow.' He lays his smooth hand on top of her head.

Tess is behind him now, a hand plunged into the pocket of her yellow dress. 'Hello, little one,' she says robotically.

Willow clings harder to Annie's hand. 'Go way!'

Annie sends a hacking laugh into the air. 'She must be tired.'

'Have you been waiting here long?' asks Tess.

'We tried the bell.'

'It's not working. I should have said.'

Matteo drapes his arm around his wife, moving her backwards, swishing his arm through the air to usher them in. Annie stays put on the stoop. There's something stopping her from stepping inside and it's not just Willow pulling her backwards.

Freddie appears then, bare chested, inverted nipples. Annie straightens her bra strap and swallows. She scans his body for more signs that he's actually hers. His slightly bulging belly button, his feet turning outwards. *Oh, but just stop!*

Annie tries to pull Willow inside. 'Come on, honeybun.' Willow clamps her fingers more firmly to Annie's hand. Annie starts to walk inside anyway, heaving Willow while Tess stares at the girl. Annie reaches towards Tess and shuts her into a one-armed hug. Tess' body doesn't give, and Annie stays pressed to her chest as if she's in search of a heartbeat.

'Hello, Willie,' says Freddie.

'Wil-low,' says Tess, stretching out the two syllables and untangling herself from Annie's arms.

'Great to see you, Freddie,' says Annie.

The house is an indoor homage to the sea. An enormous flat screen television is mounted on the wall, and a sign has been nailed beside it, *Mermaids Live Here*. Everything's blue – spongy blue carpet, two blue sofas arranged in an L-shape, framed seascapes all over the walls. The sun, spilling in through the large windows, spreads everything with buttery light.

Willow lets go of Annie's hand and follows Freddie into another room.

'I bought some refreshments,' says Annie, handing over the torn carrier bag.

'There was really no need.' At the kitchen island unit, Tess pulls four bottles from the bag, lining them up like skittles: Dr Pepper, Crush Orange Soda, Sprite, Fruity King Fruit Punch.

'I've just got to make some phone calls, darling,' says Matteo, pointing towards the ceiling.

Some emotion flares in Tess' face then it's gone. Matteo climbs the stairs.

'I take it you need to change,' Tess coos.

'Oh, yeah, great.'

'The bathroom's over there.'

Annie goes in. There's a free-standing bath and behind it one of those taps that rises on a pole from the dark wood floor. She yanks off her dress and steps into her bright green bathing suit, all 155 pounds, 5 foot nothing of her. Just what is she doing here?

Annie wants Willow to know the truth about where she came from, but how will Annie even broach the subject with her? Forget fumbling over the birds and the bees; try telling a child that she was put inside the wrong mother's womb. Perhaps it would have been better if Annie had never set eyes on Freddie – because when she saw him for the first time, a kind of love started growing in her, and keeps on growing, so that she's feeling stuffed full.

She arranges her off-centre bosoms into the cups and tucks her cartoon towel around her. Grabbing her other things, she walks out and spots Tess struggling to open the French doors at the end of the kitchen.

A boy with thick hair in his eyes almost bumps into Annie.

'Oh, sorry,' he says, two crooked teeth jutting from his smile.

'This is my middle one, Luca,' says Tess. Luca gives Annie a little wave and disappears outside.

'Children, come along!' calls Tess.

Willow emerges from Freddie's room with a frown on her face. 'Bug Bear.'

'Honey, I told you before, Bug Bear has gone on an adventure,' says Annie.

'Der, Mama, der!' Willow points a finger towards the room that she and Freddie have just come from.

'Come along, there's more toys downstairs!' Tess declares, shovelling Freddie towards the French doors with her elegant hand, her diamond ring sparkling. 'Phoenix!'

There's footsteps overhead, then a boy who's taller than Annie appears – startled eyes, smooth skin, a fountain of quiffed hair. She can feel her mouth hanging.

'Phoenix often has that effect on people,' Tess says. 'Meet my eldest son.'

'Hello,' says the pre-teen. And still Annie stares at him, because there in his face is her daughter, the olive skin, the eyes so brown that the pupil and iris are barely distinguishable. He goes through the French doors.

How different Willow's life would have been if she'd been born into this family, the bustle and noise of older brothers, expensive holidays, a fancy education. Annie feels reduced and not good enough. What child would choose a damp, cramped apartment over this? Freddie is the one who got lucky. *My son.* The words are acid pouring through her. *Oh, but just quit it with the amateur dramatics!* Freddie looks at her as if he can hear her thinking.

'Pretty lady,' he says.

'My mama,' says Willow, smiling.

Willow and Freddie cling to the handles of a huge canvas bag full of plastic pool toys, and Tess follows them downstairs. Annie stays there at the top watching.

One of the older boys jumps into the infinity pool with a splash. It looks like a scene from a vacation brochure. The pool is huge and spherical, mosaic-ed in shades of blue. The two older boys are submerged and thrashing about, churning waves that swell over the sides. Stripped down to her pink spotted bathing suit, Willow sits at the edge of a circular jacuzzi beside the pool and bicycles her legs through the water. The buzz of a mosquito grows loud in Annie's ears as she steps down onto the concrete. Tess pulls off her dress to reveal a bright red bikini, a flat stomach. She lies on a lounger, chinks of light on her sunglasses. There's something about the angle of her face that makes Annie think she's staring at Willow.

Freddie is standing against the grey wall of the house. There are no windows down here; it must be a garage or storage unit of some sort. Freddie huffs and pulls at a pair of red armbands, not managing to get them past his skeletal elbows. Annie pushes on her scratched sunglasses and notices a thin, crimson scar creeping out from beneath the hem of his swim shorts.

Tess hasn't noticed that the boy is having difficulties. His face is pinkening with frustration, and Willow is sitting there in the full midday sun without any sunscreen on. Which child should Annie help first?

'Go away!' shouts one of the boys in the pool.

'No, you go away!' calls the particularly good-looking one, Phoenix.

'Can you both be more gentlemanly please?!' says Tess.

Annie whips up the sunscreen and heads over to Willow.

'Oh, no, Mama.' Willow shies away. Annie props a hat on Willow's head and slathers her in thick white cream.

She feels a whisper of something at the side of her neck and turns. Tess' head is still angled towards Willow, a line dissecting her forehead. Freddie hasn't had any success with those armbands yet, so why isn't Tess helping him?

Annie marches over to him. 'Here, honey. Let me.'

Crouching, she smoothes his armbands on. Someone jumps into the pool and Annie looks sideways to make sure it's not Willow. Phoenix's head bobs up and out; he flicks his hair. There's the sound of thrashing water. Annie turns back to Freddie. The long thin face, the blue eyes, his tiny ears, the bloom of a bruise around his wrist like a purple bracelet.

'How did you do that?' asks Annie, caressing a finger over the outer edges of the bruise.

'Mummy did it.' Freddie's quiet voice is almost eaten by the splashing water. 'She bit me too.'

'She bit you?' whispers Annie. The bitter taste of worry coats her tongue.

Freddie's nostrils widen like he's about to cry. He puts a finger to his lips and makes a shushing sound.

Annie gazes at the scar on his thigh. 'Why do I have to be quiet?'

He shrugs. Annie swallows a bubble of air, stands and looks at Tess smiling in the direction of Phoenix's mobile telephone as he snaps a photograph of her.

'Let's go swimming,' says Freddie, taking hold of Annie's hand.

They reach the edge of the pool.

'Want to jump?' asks Annie. Her mouth is dry, her heart insistent.

'No,' says Freddie.

'I'll go first,' Annie says.

She jumps in, the water cold against her hot skin. She opens her eyes to bubbles, the water gurgling in her ears. She somersaults backwards then pushes her flat hands out in front, kicking her legs and gliding under the surface, the water giving her a grace that's absent when she's on land. She can count on two fingers the things she's good at, and swimming's one of them. She won medals for it at school; she never came first, but somewhere in the junk drawer at home are bronze and silver circles attached to a tangle of blue ribbons. She rises up and sees Freddie still standing at the side of the pool, his body so pale it's almost blue.

Willow is smiling. 'Jump, Fed!'

'Do it in your own time,' says Annie.

'But he can't swim,' says Tess.

'The armbands will make you float, and when you jump, I'll be here to catch you,' calls Annie, lifting her hands out of the water. So help her, she's going to make sure Freddie enjoys himself.

The bigger boys are chasing each other around the concrete now. Freddie's eyes are wide with fear as he contemplates the water. A small noise scrapes from his throat and he jumps, his legs bending and shooting sideways, his body breaking the water with a painful slap.

Annie goes under and watches Freddie, the bubbles fizzing around him, his face knotted, his eyes squeezed shut. His hands are splayed and struggling, stretching towards her. Her fingertips touch his. She gathers up his hands and pops her head out of the water. His head pops out too, smiling and streaming.

'Good job, Freddie!' she says.

'More!' claps Willow.

Freddie tries to doggy paddle through the water, but stays in the same spot. Annie pushes him in the direction of the metal ladder and he climbs up and out. Freddie and Willow hold hands at the edge.

'Now!' Willow shouts and the pair of them jump, the water exploding around them.

Annie watches them both underwater, Willow's smile bubbling as she doggy paddles. *My little water baby.* She waves at Annie and Annie waves back. Freddie's eyes are shut, but he's smiling too.

'Goggles,' he says, when his head emerges from the surface.

He's nearer to the side this time and manages to clamber out by himself, his toes spread wide, like Carl's when he walks barefooted. Freddie's shoulder blades are curved and pink as he fumbles through the bag.

The older boys are motionless on sun-beds now. The eldest one, Phoenix, has a panama hat propped over his face. Luca's bent knees are open, a comic propped between them. Both boys are tanned and healthy, unlike Freddie who is almost translucent apart from those rapidly reddening shoulders.

Annie would bet her life on it that Tess hasn't put any sunscreen on the boy. There she is with a hand pressed to her svelte belly and – yes, Annie's almost sure of it – Tess is staring at Willow again. Annie strides over to Freddie, grabbing the sunblock from the paving along the way.

'Let's put some of this on,' she says.

'No!'

'You'd be lucky!' calls Tess. 'He never lets me.'

Freddie allows Annie to apply the cream, her hands working up and around his neck, his shoulders, his back. This frail little boy who doesn't seem all that loved. Her fingers mould over his right arm, the blond hairs on it glistening.

'It tickles,' he says.

'Don't you have a rash vest?'

Freddie shakes his head.

'Almost done,' she says.

He pulls the goggles on, squashing down his nose. They push his small ears out, so they sit almost at right angles to his head. He smiles at her and she thinks that his face is just about the cutest thing she's ever seen. She rubs the cream into his legs, the zipwire of the scar. How on earth did that happen? She smoothes her fingers over his wide feet with their fat, stubby toes and thin ankles, the high in-step. His feet, hers. The cicadas grow loud.

The children climb into a plastic sandpit and their legs crust with sand. They dig and pat and start building sandcastles. Tess goes over to them then, the loose buckles on her espadrilles chinking. She kneels and holds out her phone in front of the children, flicking her fingers on the screen.

'Smile!' she says. Both children look up at her and she snaps them. Willow puts a hand over her own face.

Tess takes off her espadrilles and sits on the edge of the sandpit, burrowing her toes in the sand. Annie looks down at her own breasts barely supported by the sagging fabric of her swimsuit. She folds her arms.

'I guess Freddie doesn't eat all that much,' she says.

'He eats quite a lot to be honest. He's just naturally thin.'

Annie unfolds her arms, crosses them in front of her stomach. 'His thigh looks sore.'

'Oh, that.' Tess smudges her lips together as if spreading gloss. 'We were involved in a car crash.'

'When?'

'A few months ago now. That's how we first came to realise that Freddie wasn't ours.'

'And his wrist . . .'

Tess turns to her quizzically and Annie pushes on with her question. 'That bruise on it, was that from the crash?'

'No, he was . . . well, he was doing something he shouldn't have been doing. He got into a cupboard and I had to help him out. His skin is like a peach; it bruises so easily.'

'Three boys, I bet you have to be big on discipline . . .' says Annie.

'The other two, they're easy.'

Freddie slams his spade on the top of an upturned bucket of sand.

'My mama used to make me bite into a bar of soap if I acted out,' offers Annie.

'I'd never do anything like that. I couldn't bear to hurt my children.'

Does that statement cover Freddie though? And why would Freddie lie about the bruise, the bite? Willow glares at Tess and moves further away from her. Can she sense something wrong about this woman? Freddie is deep in concentration as he digs.

'What day was Freddie actually born on?' asks Annie.

'24th February.'

'Willow's birthday is February 10th.'

Tess folds her arms and takes a noisy breath.

'What?' asks Annie.

'It's just that that was . . .' Tess scratches off the scabs of lipstick that have collected in the corners of her mouth. 'That was my due date. Freddie was two weeks late.'

Phoenix mushroom-jumps back into the pool. Willow's sand-castle collapses.

'Oh, no, darling, not like that,' says Tess, closing in on Willow. Tess kneels, scooping and loading and patting the castle-shaped bucket. She pulls it off. The sandcastle sits whole and impressive with turrets and arched windows. Willow gets up, pokes her toe into the castle then presses her foot down in a tumble of collapsing sand.

Annie's cell starts to ring, belting out U2's 'Pride (*In the Name of Love*)'. She rushes over to her bag and gets to it as her phone cuts out.

'Do you like U2?' asks Tess.

'Bono has such power to his voice, don't you think?' Annie whizzes through the music on her phone, lets another song blast out, and gives a little sway.

Tess' cardboard smile transforms into a grimace, her shoulders rising towards her chin. Annie punches a hand in the air, and slams her feet down, spraying sand.

'Come on!' she says, grabbing Tess' hand. 'I bet you're a good dancer.'

'Oh, no, really, I'm not.'

'Dance, Mummy!' Freddie claps his hands.

Tess doesn't move.

'So what kind of music do you like?' asks Annie.

'Classical mainly,' says Tess.

'Music for old people you mean.'

Tess frowns and pulls her hand away from Annie's. 'Actually, I really do love classical music. I used to play the cello.'

'Used to? Why not now?'

Freddie takes Tess' hand, wiggling his non-existent hips to the tinny tune still echoing out of the phone.

'Hey, you're a good dancer too!' Annie says to him.

She notices Matteo watching them from the stairs, a smile breaking on his face. She turns back to look at Tess who's swaying slightly now, her shackles of stiffness a little looser.

When the track ends, Annie puts on another and they dance to it, Tess, still reluctantly, and Annie, Willow and Freddie. Phoenix shakes his head and covers his eyes with a hand. Matteo has gone inside again – he doesn't seem all that interested in getting to know Willow.

'I need to sit down,' says Tess and spreads herself over a lounger, Annie following, taking the upright chair beside her.

'Didn't you say something about working in art?' asks Tess.

'I make pictures, but no one ever gets to see them. I do this thing called quilling, twirling pieces of paper into shapes, faces, you name it really.'

'I wish I was arty.'

Arty. Annie left that description of herself back at the university she dropped out of.

'Can I see some of your work one day?' asks Tess.

'Well, I've got some pictures on my phone.' Annie shows her the heart, and the face and neck of a woman wearing spangly necklaces.

'They're good.'

'They're okay, I guess.'

'Have you ever tried to show any of them? There are loads of art galleries around here.'

'No.'

'Maybe you should.'

All the reasons why Annie can't bombard her then. They're not good enough, what if a gallery accepted them and nobody bought them; she's got far too much going on in her life at the moment without throwing this pipe dream into the mix. Her phone pings. Annie presses a button on it and tuts when the screen doesn't respond.

'Oh, it's out of battery,' says Tess. 'I'll pop it on charge for you. Would you like an ice lolly, children?'

Freddie nods his head vigorously, Willow doesn't reply. Tess takes the phone from Annie and heads towards the stairs.

Phoenix climbs into the sandpit and lends his helping hands to the castle empire. Annie lies on a lounger, the sun drying her swimsuit. Time stretches, and the children continue to dig, slapping and grinding the sand.

Luca, lying on a sun-lounger, examines his fingernails. Phoenix swims lengths of the pool, gliding along and tumble turning at each end, and still Tess doesn't appear. A mosquito lands on Annie's arm and she slaps it away too late, her skin itching. What's keeping Tess? Water cascades from Phoenix's body as he pulls himself up the pool ladder and settles himself at the side, skin glistening.

'Would you mind watching them?' Annie calls to him, pointing to Willow and Freddie.

Phoenix looks up and nods.

'It'll only be for a second.'

Annie sidles up the stairs, her stubby toes pressing the rough teak. She goes inside and sees some shadow to her left. It's Tess on her knees in that swanky bedroom with Annie's cell phone in her hand. Her shoulders are rounded and a mascara-laden tear is meandering down her face, her eyes threaded with red veins.

Annie takes two steps backwards out of sight. She should go in there and snatch the phone out of her hand. She evens out her fast breath. *Think long term. Think Freddie.* Freddie who Tess doesn't seem to like all that much; it's clear she favours the two older boys. Annie takes another step backwards. She needs to find out more about Tess; she needs to peel back her layers, not for Willow's sake, but for Freddie's.

Squeak. Annie's stepped on a fish-shaped pool toy, water

spraying from its pin-holed mouth. There's fumbling and foot-steps, then Tess is standing in front of Annie.

'Just freshening up,' says Tess, her blotchy face dry now, her back restored to its poker-straight state.

Her hand shakes as she pulls open a freezer drawer and scoops a handful of ice lollies. She goes through the French doors, but Annie hangs back. She waits until she hears Tess speaking to the children downstairs then takes her phone from the bedroom and heads into the bathroom. The phone, partially charged now, is open on photographs, almost every one of them of Willow apart from the artwork she snapped for her website. She clicks off the photographs and sees that there are two missed calls from Tom. He's left a message too.

She dials and listens. Tom clears his throat. 'Oh, it's not you! Hell, I hate speaking to machines, but well . . . Look, Annie, please, don't shut me out. Maybe you're right, maybe I should have told you. But you know, I didn't want to see you hurt, I still don't. Come, visit. Please. All the best, Tom.'

She clicks off the phone and clutches it to her chest for two seconds then pulls her dress over her now dry bathing suit. She bounds back outside and looks over the edge of the balcony. Tess is standing too close to Willow who is sitting at the side of the pool licking an ice lolly. She has lifted a strand of Willow's hair and is smoothing it between her fingers. Freddie is sitting beside Willow fidgeting. Phoenix is back on the sun-lounger, his eyes hidden behind sunglasses. The bottom of Luca's lolly is dripping; he licks at it, looks up, sees Annie and waves. Willow turns to see who he's waving at.

'Mama!' she calls, scrambling up. Her hair falls away from Tess' fingers. Willow's red ice lolly breaks off the stick as she runs; it smashes apart on the ground.

'Bug in der,' shouts Willow, her footsteps thumping the stairs.

Every six minutes a child in the US falls down the stairs and has to be rushed to hospital, thinks Annie. But here Willow is now; she's made it up without the aid of a crash helmet or shin pads, and Tess is right behind her. Annie picks Willow up and goes inside.

Tess pushes her sunglasses on top of her hair, her brown eyes intense. 'You're not going, are you?'

Freddie arrives beside Annie and hugs himself to her legs.

'I wish you were my mummy,' he says. *Oh, Lord.*

Tess pouts her mouth in and out.

'Well, we have to go. Carl'll be back from work soon and—'

'Bug Bear!' says Willow, pulling at Annie's chin, directing it towards the door of Freddie's bedroom.

'Hush now, honey.'

'But you can't go yet,' says Tess, looking towards the stairs. 'Matteo hasn't even . . . Matteo!'

Annie hears a door opening overhead, footsteps on the stairs. Matteo appears, pale, the scab broken on his lip and seeping God knows what.

'Oh, I'm sorry.' A fleck of sleep in his eye. 'I got a bit bogged down with things up there.'

'But they're going now,' says Tess.

'Well, we'll keep in touch.' His forehead is scored with lines as he musses Willow's hair.

'You could have done whatever it is tomorrow; you're going back to it anyway.'

He chews at his bottom lip.

'Say thank you to Miss Tess,' Annie says to Willow.

'Miss?' says Tess. 'That seems rather formal given I'm her mother.'

Not again. 'Not mine, no,' says Willow, hugging her arms around Annie's neck.

Annie turns on her heel and heads towards the front door; Tess keeps pace beside. Freddie starts to cry. He's a confection of colours, his nose bright red, that purple bruise on his wrist, his red bathing shorts. Annie bends down and kisses his forehead.

'Don't go,' he says.

'I'll see you real soon,' says Annie, forcing herself through the open front door.

'My bear.' Willow's breath is warm on Annie's ear as they go down the stairs, and Freddie's cries grow louder.

Chapter 27

The room is dim from the weak bare bulb hanging from the ceiling. Annie heavy-foots it past the couch where Carl is squinting over his book, mouthing silent words. She switches on the lopsided lamp, which throws shadows over the room making it look even more cramped than usual, furniture butting up against each other, and every available space covered in dishes, keys and pieces of paper. She sighs and folds her arms.

Slowly, Carl puts his novel face down and looks up at her. 'Go on, get it off your chest.'

Even though she's talked about what happened at the villa earlier, clips of it keep playing in her head on a loop.

'You'd think Matteo would have made an effort to come and speak to Willow. I mean, he was the reason we made a visit.'

'Maybe he didn't want to crowd you.'

'He looked kind of stressed.'

'Who wouldn't be stressed by what's going on? I know I am.'

She sits beside him, her butt hitting the floor through the broken couch springs, sending him ceiling-wards.

'And those bruises . . .' she says.

'There's probably some reason for them. People like that, they don't hurt kids.'

'People like what?' She glares at the roll of opal-coloured flesh hanging over the waist of his pants. 'Rich people, you mean. Just because she dresses head to foot in Armani doesn't mean she's Michelle Obama.'

'I just meant she's more likely to palm Freddie off on some

nanny if he's getting on her nerves rather than hurting him.' He plunges his hands into his pockets. 'We can't exactly go around accusing these people of abusing their own kid. You say you want to build bridges, well that isn't going to happen if you call up Child Protection Services.'

'Our child is being looked after by those people and they could be hurting him.'

'But he's not our child.'

'Oh, you know what I mean.' She bats a hand through the air.

'We should mention it to Broo.'

'And then there's the way Tess keeps going on about how she's Willow's mom. "I'm her mother," in that snooty voice of hers.'

'The whole thing's pretty mixed up. It's hard to know what we are to Freddie, and she must feel the same about Willow.'

He struggles forward, hoists himself out of the couch then combs his hand backwards through his greasy hair, which holds the lines of his fingers. 'Poor little Freddie.'

'Oh, Carl.' She starts to cry. He clambers onto his knees in front of her and takes her head in his hands.

'I love him,' she says.

'But you don't even know him.'

'It doesn't matter,' she says.

He touches his forehead to hers and sighs.

Chapter 28

Tess is kneeling on the bedroom floor, her laptop propped on the double bed in front of her. Freddie is singing in the room next door. She finishes updating the Twitter feed for one of her clients and heads into the living room where Matteo's case is propped in a corner ready for his flight home tomorrow.

Someone is tapping on a keyboard. Her quiet feet press the carpet. Matteo is sitting at the desk with his back to her, his spine curved, the screen of his laptop aglow with words.

A croaky moan leaks from his mouth, his posture crumpling further. She steps closer and squints at the black text on the screen. The air conditioning kicks in then and he turns to look in its direction, flinching when he sees her. He fiddles with his touchpad, transforming the laptop screen into the beaming faces of the boys.

'What's going on?' she asks.

'I thought you were sleeping,' he says, reducing in size in front of her. 'I'm doing a bit of work.'

She reaches towards the touchpad, tries to double click on the document he's just closed, but he grabs her hand and shoves it away.

'We're in real trouble, aren't we?' she says.

He swivels around on the chair to face her, dark smudges under his eyes. He tries to form an answer, and she wants to lay her hand over the mess of his mouth, so that he won't tell her after all.

'Yes,' he says.

She turns away, takes his next words as a blow to the side of her face.

'I've tried to shore things up, but . . .'

'How can this have happened?' Her voice is a reedy thing.

'I told you before, the bookings have been dire. I've had to take money out of the mortgage to pay people. I couldn't tell you, not with Freddie, not with this.'

But she didn't need to be told. She's been using the IVF blunder as a cover to bury the way Matteo's been acting. She's been pretending, not asking questions on purpose.

'I borrowed so much money, and now the bank is demanding I repay the rest of the loan.'

'When?'

'They wrote to me a few weeks ago, but I can't keep up with the repayments, and now I've got a bloody enormous tax bill to pay as well.'

She steps back, leans against the wall, setting one of the ubiquitous beach signs at an angle.

'I thought I could make things work,' he says, fingernails scraping chin.

He presses his lips together, so that they turn white. She stares up at the ceiling, a swatted mosquito stuck to the paintwork.

'Surely there's a way we can save the hotel?'

He looks at the floor.

'At least we have the house,' she says.

'The house is collateral.'

She thinks of the rented flat that she'd moved to as a child after her father had lost his job, the brass horseshoes that her mother hung on nails on the wall. That time she left her games kit on the bus and they couldn't afford to buy her a new one. The two-sizes-too-small leotard pilfered from lost property, the charity plimsolls that smelled of somebody else's feet. She worked hard at university, and then she met Matteo and they'd worked hard together to build their hotel business up. She'd walked into another life, and now she's about to walk out of it again.

'Coming here wasn't just about finding out how the clinic had screwed up, or meeting Willow, was it?' she asks.

'It was about putting things right, making them pay for what they've done.'

'You need the compensation,' she says. 'That's why you've been driving it forward the way you have.'

'No.'

'All I want is to get my daughter back,' she says. 'And all you want is money.'

'I'm thinking about this family, our family.'

'You were thinking about yourself.' The words come out as spits.

'I was thinking about you. What you went through . . .'

She shakes her head.

'What you went through with Ava,' he says. 'And now this, I wanted to make things right.'

'You can never make things right,' she says, the volume of her voice rising. 'Not after you killed her. Because it was you. It was just that I was stupid enough to go along with what you wanted, and now she's dead.'

His body ricochets. 'It wasn't anybody's fault, not yours, not mine.'

'You took her away from me then you destroyed everything I had left of her.'

He covers his face with his ample hands. That white gold ring on his little finger has twisted round so she can't see its insignia. Something smashes in Freddie's bedroom and Matteo gets up and goes towards it.

'How did you manage to break that?' he snaps.

She walks out of the front door in her bare feet and heads through the semi-darkness towards the beach. She treads along an alley between two villas, past a bin overflowing with polystyrene takeaway boxes and orange peel.

Her feet take on tiny shells as she walks. Sitting near the water, she picks up a piece of driftwood and writes her name into the wet sand. *Tess Rossi.*

The dying sun silvers the water. A wave laps at the grooves of the letters then retracts, hissing and spitting with spray. Another wave draws in, soaking the skirt of her new yellow dress, her knickers, and tugging at the sand beneath her toes.

She looks at her signature. Her name has gone, the grains saturated and speckled with tiny holes.

Carl is taking photographs of Willow with his phone as she scribbles in her puzzle book.

'No Dada!' She hides her face with her hands.

'Come on, kiddo, we like having pictures of you. Okay, okay.' He holds his hands up in surrender.

Overlapping photographs of Willow are stuck to the fridge with magnets; there's a felt-tipped self portrait there too, the hair two long brown lines. Carl took most of those pictures; not that he's gifted in the photography department like his father was. Heads are cut off at the neck, some shots are blurred. There's a photograph of Lina there too, in grey chiffon at Willow's christening. Carl ended up snapping the base of a sun umbrella that was behind Lina, making it look as if her underwear had burst its elastic and fallen around her ankles.

Annie sits at the table opposite Willow, the little girl's tongue jammed between her teeth as she draws a line through the paper maze. There's a copper-coloured circular mirror on the wall behind her, a halo around her head. Our angel, thinks Annie, and Freddie's face drops in front of her eyes, his sunburnt skin, that bruise, what he said about Tess biting him. But why is Annie compiling this evidence against Tess? Is it so she can rescue Freddie or to convince herself that she's the better mom?

Carl starts chopping capsicums, sets the pieces into a pan to fry.

'Fed got Bug,' says Willow.

'Bug's gone, honey,' says Annie.

'No!' says Willow.

'What's that, kiddo?' asks Carl, the pan spitting heat.

'He's der.' Willow points at the window.

'Where?' asks Carl.

'Der!'

'She thinks Freddie's taken Bug Bear,' says Annie. 'But I'm not sure that—'

'He's der!'

Willow picks up her puzzle book and flings it across the room. It clatters against the couch and falls to the dusty floor.

Carl lifts the pan off the hob and crouches beside her, more of his butt on show than not. 'What's this all about, kiddo? Where do you think Bug is?'

'Fed,' replies Willow.

'Freddie has your toy bear?' asks Carl.

Willow nods her head.

Pixels start to sharpen in Annie's head then. The clinic was the last place she remembers seeing the teddy bear. After they'd got the DNA results back, a kind woman had touched her arm in the elevator. Another woman had been there too, a tall woman, but that couldn't have been Tess. Annie tries to grasp at the details.

'You saw the teddy in Tess' house?' asks Carl.

'Yes, Dada.' Willow nods fiercely.

'In Freddie's room?' asks Annie.

Willow continues to nod. She points to the ceiling. 'Up der. I want Bug!' She scampers into her bedroom.

Tess couldn't have known who Annie was back then because

Annie and Carl had only just got the results of the test themselves. A more alert part of Annie's brain takes over now. She'd only seen the tall woman in her peripheral version, but she remembers the stiff armour of her skin, the way she carried herself. And it couldn't have been coincidence that they bumped into Tess at the grocery store. She thinks of the person rooting around in the back of her car that day – Tess must have been following her.

Annie goes to the window, looks through the blind, but the stretch of asphalt is empty, a leaf hip-hopping in the breeze. A man in a polo shirt is pushing a lawnmower over the grass in the floodlit front yard of a three-storey villa across the way.

'I think Tess might have been at the clinic the day we got the results of the tests,' says Annie.

'You think she took Bug?' asks Carl, his mouth hanging open.

'I think it's a possibility.'

'What? Why?'

'Because she wanted to keep something that belonged to Willow.' Her sentence rises in pitch like a question.

'But she didn't even know who we were back then,' says Carl.

'You haven't met the eldest son, he's a carbon copy of Willow. Maybe Tess put two and two together, maybe she recognised Willow.'

He blinks so slowly that his eyes stay shut for a full three seconds. It's bad enough knowing her child is being looked after by someone else, like some essential part of her has been ripped away, but if Freddie is being looked after by a woman who doesn't really care about him, by a woman obsessed by somebody else's child . . . Oh, dear Lord, what can Annie do about that?

Willow comes back into the room, clutching a doll. 'I want Bug!'

'Don't worry, honey, I'm going to rescue him,' says Annie.

But it isn't the bear's bedraggled face that spools through Annie's head; it's Freddie's.

Chapter 29

Annie parks beside Tess' car, red like the one in the car park at Tom's place. Her rage thickens; it must have been Tess who broke into her car that day. And if she's capable of that, perhaps she really is capable of worse things, like stealing, and biting her son. Willow is asleep in the back, the window nearest to her open two centimetres, so Annie won't need to disturb her. It's probably best she doesn't witness what's about to unfold anyway.

Annie lets her anger take her over the handbrake, and towards the passenger door. It clinks against the metal of Tess' car when she opens it. She forces her way out into the tight space, humidity blowtorching her skin. Through the scrubby mounds of grass a hundred metres away, the sea is mirror still.

'I didn't think it would come to this!' a man shouts.

Annie registers the accent as Italian. Was that Matteo? Her eyes dart about, searching. All the windows running the length of the second floor are open, blocked by slatted blinds. A voice answers, too quiet to hear.

'But I've tried everything,' replies the man.

There's a splash of water from behind the high white fence set around the back yard, bubbling, thrashing. Someone wheezes. One of the boys must be swimming. Annie stands on tiptoes to see, but the fence is a whole head taller than she is. Someone gulps at the air.

'You're in denial, Tess, like you are about so many things!'

She finds a gap, peers through and sees a soaked, unrecognisable head plunging beneath the surface, a small arm chopping at the water.

Permanent brain damage begins after only four minutes without oxygen. She knows this, but how many minutes have already passed?

'Oh, my Lord! Help!' Annie shouts. 'There's a kid in the water!'

She tries the door in the fence, shaking it, but it doesn't give. She puts all her weight into it, ramming her shoulder against the wood, but it remains shut, so she climbs onto the bonnet of the red car, the suspension creaking in complaint. She can see a little more of the child from up here, the pale limbs magnified beneath the water, the bubbles rising.

'Somebody help!' Annie bellows, scraping her throat dry.

She looks up at the winding stairs to the front door, all twenty-five of them; the doorbell that doesn't work.

'You need to face it!' Matteo shouts.

By the time she's banged on that front door and somebody's come to answer it, that kid will be dead. She steps across the car, the metal buckling, groaning, the heels of her sandals making dents. She pushes her thigh over the fence and teeters; it cuts her nether regions like an unbridled, skeletal horse.

'Mama?' Willow's voice escapes through the open car window.

'Hold on now, I'm coming!' shouts Annie. She can see the child beneath the stillness of the water.

Don't think, just do. Thoughts hurtle through her head anyway. She could break her neck doing this, but that kid needs her help. It's Freddie, it must be him. His name starts to pulse through her head, her boy whose life she started; she won't let him lose it.

She pushes herself over the side of the fence, her arms flailing, the concrete careering towards her. She aims her feet first, but tips forwards and lands with a crack on her knees, pain bursting across them. The blood is boiling in her ears, and rolling down her legs as she sprints towards the water and jumps in.

The water slaps her stomach, the cold sliding over her and suckering her dress to her skin, her heart slamming, her blurry eyes searching, stinging. Then there he is, the fully clothed boy, face down in a red T-shirt, submerged, all his fight gone. She lunges towards him; her sandals trying to pull her feet backwards. One of them slips off. She grabs the boy by the hand, squishes her arms around his torso, and raises him up and out of the water.

He's limp, drooping; did she get to him in time? She hauls him higher, squeezing him harder, her toe en pointe on the pool floor. She can't stop coughing.

'Help us!' she splutters, chlorine up her nose, in her throat.

His hanging mop of hair has been darkened by the water, his eyes closed. This really is Freddie, an unmoving, heavyweight in her arms.

'Come on, Freddie!' She holds him tight and shakes him. 'Come on now, Freddie, just breathe.'

He remains still. Her legs cut through the water. She lays him on the side of the pool, steps back, cocooning the back of his head with her hands. She jumps out and sits, swinging her legs over him. With her bloody knees on the concrete now, she pulls him completely clear of the pool.

It's been minutes, just minutes, hasn't it? There's still a chance. Agony spikes her kneecaps as she leans her head towards his and listens, laying her hand on his chest – nothing. She touches his cold forehead, tips his head back and places her fingers into his mouth, which is clear.

His hair is like seaweed over his eyes, his lifeless nose streaming water. She puts the heel of one hand on his breastbone, her other hand on his forehead, and pushes down his breastbone hard and fast.

'One, two . . .'

'Mama!'

Annie can hear Willow's panicked shouts from the car, but on she presses to thirty.

'Help us!' she shouts again.

Willow starts to sob. Jesus, where are those negligent pair of fools? She can't leave Freddie to call an ambulance, not yet, not until she's done CPR for two whole minutes. She bends to his mouth and listens again, watching him and willing him to move.

'Come on, Freddie lamb, come on!'

He's stone still. She pinches his nose, presses her lips around his, her boy, her baby. She breathes in deeply then empties herself of air, feeling his chest rise and fall beneath her hand. She breathes into him again, and the same thing happens, but still he doesn't start to breathe on his own.

She starts the compressions again. What was she thinking? Why didn't she grab her phone before she jumped over the wall? She panicked, just like they told her not to do in the classes she took at the church hall.

'Help us now!' she roars.

She hears the slide of a door, then quick footsteps on the stairs.

'What's going on?' It's Tess' urgent voice, her shadow falling over Annie now. 'Oh my God, Freddie! What's happened?'

'You need to phone an ambulance,' Annie screeches. 'He fell into the water, I jumped over the fence!'

Annie returns to pumping the boy's chest and looks up at Tess squinting towards her son and stepping backwards. She turns around, runs back towards the steps and collides with Matteo.

'Freddie fell into the pool, he's drowning!'

Discoloured with shock and staring at Freddie, Matteo pulls a cell phone from his pocket. 'We need the paramedics. My boy, my son he's fallen into the swimming pool. He's not moving.'

Annie presses her mouth to Freddie's again.

'310 Sunshine Drive,' says Matteo.

Fifteen, sixteen, seventeen . . .

'He's going to be alright, isn't he?' asks Tess, kneeling now beside Annie hovering a hand over Freddie. 'Oh my God!'

'He's not responding. I don't know. Come on, Freddie, come back to us.'

Matteo continues to talk into the phone.

'They want to speak to you,' he says to Annie, tears brimming in his blinking eyes.

Twenty-nine, thirty.

'I know what I'm doing,' snaps Annie.

All those hospital drama boxsets, all those medical dictionaries. 'The most important thing you could ever learn is CPR,' Nancy had told her once. Nancy and her kindness, Nancy who ran away. Jesus, the boy's still not breathing.

Matteo, weeping openly now, clambers to his knees, water climbing up his chinos. 'Freddie, Freddie, my boy.'

Annie breathes into Freddie again, watches his chest rise and fall, but still he doesn't start breathing on his own. Four minutes must have passed by now. The time seems syrupy slow, delineated only by Annie pressing on Freddie's chest.

She becomes aware of some other person standing beside them then, Phoenix, his dark eyes fixed on his beached, defeated brother. He is shivering despite the glare of the sun, which is burning into the backs of Annie's shoulders.

'Mama!' shouts Willow from over the fence.

'Open the gate, Phoenix!' yells Matteo.

Phoenix doesn't move.

'For the paramedics!' shouts Matteo in a voice so high it's as if he never hit puberty. Phoenix rushes towards the gate and unbolts the door.

Luca is running towards them now. He reaches Tess and puts both his arms around her, leaning his head against her upper arm. Annie starts to shiver. Matteo's breath is laboured and loud.

'Oh, God,' whispers Tess. 'Please, no.'

And still they go on waiting, Annie readying herself to start the compressions again. Then it comes, a fountain of water from Freddie's mouth and he's vomiting, coughing.

'Oh, thank God,' says Tess.

'Is he going to be alright?' asks Luca.

'You're okay, Freddie. It's going to be okay,' says Annie.

Matteo's sobs are noisy, a fat tear rolling down. Freddie keeps coughing, white spew clinging to his chin. Annie lifts and presses him into the recovery position, rubbing circles on his back. A siren starts to wail in the distance.

'He knows not to go into the water without an adult,' says Tess. 'I don't understand this.' She's looking from Freddie to Annie and back again. 'If he dies . . .'

'Keep breathing, Freddie,' says Annie. 'That's it, you're doing great.'

The sound of the siren is on top of them now, there's the creak of vehicle doors opening, then footsteps crunching across the shell-covered ground.

'Mamaaaaaaaa!'

A paramedic, her cheeks scattered with concentrated freckles, puts a stuffed bag and a long red board onto the ground. 'Ma'am, I need to see the boy,' she says to Tess.

There's a poppy-like insignia on her chest.

'Ma'am, please step back,' the paramedic says to Tess who hasn't moved out of the way.

Tess, suddenly aware, climbs to her feet.

'Has he been responsive at all?' asks the paramedic.

'He threw up, he hasn't spoken,' says Annie. 'He's just started to breathe on his own.'

'You administered CPR?'

'Yeah, for about three minutes. I heard him fall into the pool; I jumped over the fence.'

'It was you who got him out of the water?'

'Yes.' Annie looks at the blood-spattered concrete where she fell.

'How long was he under the water for?' asks the paramedic.

'I'm not sure,' says Annie.

'What's his name?'

'Freddie,' says Tess at the same time as Annie. The paramedic starts to rub vigorously at Freddie's chest.

'What are you doing?' asks Matteo in a wobbly voice.

'I'm giving him a sternal rub,' says the woman, 'seeing if he responds to painful stimuli.'

Another paramedic, a man with sweat-lashed curly black hair holding an oxygen canister, bends down and presses a breathing mask over Freddie's face. Freddie starts to moan.

'Freddie,' the female paramedic says. 'My name's Amy and I'm going to be looking after you, okay? We're going on a little journey to the hospital. This is Jack; Jack's going to come with us.'

'How old is Freddie?' asks Jack.

'Three,' says Tess, through tears.

'Who are the parents?' asks Amy.

'Me,' says Matteo, his arms locked around his body.

'And you're the mother?' Amy asks Annie.

'No, she is,' says Annie, flicking her head towards Tess.

'No obvious abrasions,' says Jack.

Amy pushes a stethoscope into her ears. 'He's bradycardic and hypotensive. BP's 80/50.'

'Does he have any conditions that we should know about?' asks Jack. 'Allergies? Epilepsy?'

'He doesn't have anything, apart from . . .' Tess' voice tails off.

'There's nothing wrong with him at all,' says Matteo. 'Well, there wasn't until this happened.'

'Mama!' Willow calls.

'We'll need to use the back board,' Amy says to Jack.

The details of the next unfolding moments punch Annie: the red straps buckled around Freddie, the sensation of the blood trickling down her knees, Tess's eyes like those of a netted animal.

'Why would he get into the pool when he can't even swim?' asks Tess, starting to pace. She looks at Annie. 'When you were here yesterday, he must have got it into his head that he could swim.'

Annie leans down and plucks off her remaining sandal. Egg-shaped bruises are blooming on both of her shredded knees. Her other sandal is a blur of green on the bottom of the pool.

'He's going to be okay, isn't he?' asks Matteo, sniffing.

Jack goes to the ambulance, a lorry-like white van with blue and pink flashing along the sides. He comes back with a stretcher, and he and Amy lift Freddie onto it.

'Despatch, this is Eagle 31,' Jack says into his walkie talkie. 'We have a male, three years old, suffering from near drowning. The victim is conscious and breathing, possible spinal injury. ETA twenty minutes.'

'Spinal injury?' says Tess, her voice breaking.

'I need you to come with us, okay,' says Jack, helping to carry Freddie towards the ambulance now, the oxygen canister propped between the boy's legs.

'All of us?' asks Tess following.

'Just the parents,' says Amy.

Annie follows them out, shivering in her drenched clothes despite the heat. She can see Willow from here, her crying filtering through the air and closing around Annie.

'You left me!' shouts Willow.

Annie moves towards her, pushes her hand through the half-open window and smoothes her fingers along Willow's sweaty forehead. The paramedics load Freddie into the back of the ambulance.

'He is going to be alright, isn't he?' asks Tess.

'We need to monitor him, ensure he's not at risk from secondary drowning,' says Jack.

'Secondary drowning?' says Tess.

'He'll be monitored carefully,' says Amy.

Jack gets into the driver's seat of the ambulance and slams the door.

'I'll go with him,' says Matteo.

'Me too,' says Tess. The pair of them bolt towards the open back doors of the ambulance as if they're in a race.

'I really want to go too. Please, Mum,' says Phoenix.

'No!' snaps Matteo.

Amy clicks the final buckles into place to make Freddie secure.

'Your mother should be by Freddie's side,' says Matteo.

'Please,' says Phoenix.

'I can take you in my car,' Annie calls to Phoenix, but it's Tess who answers.

'Yes, you go with Daddy, Phoenix, and I'll follow on with Annie. Hurry!'

What is wrong with the woman? Her son has nearly drowned, could still drown, and she's not going in the ambulance with him. For a split second, Annie thinks she should climb into the back of the ambulance instead.

'We've got to go!' says Amy.

'I'm coming too!' yells Luca who has started to cry; he bundles his way through the doors as they start to close. Annie catches sight of Matteo staring at Tess from inside the ambulance, anger etched into the crimps across his forehead. The doors slam and the ambulance screams away, the siren shrilling.

'He didn't stop talking about you last night, then he goes and does this,' says Tess, her face awash with confusion.

The sound of the siren grows more distant. Annie opens the back door of her car and Willow stretches out her arms, her eyelashes wet triangles.

'I want out!' Willow wriggles against the seatbelt.

'Honey, you're going to have to stay in the car for a bit longer. We have to take Miss Tess somewhere.'

'Where's Bug?'

'Not now, honey.'

'I want Bug.'

Annie is shivering in her soaking wet clothes. Tess climbs into the front passenger seat, the suspension sinking to one side.

Willow's water bottle has fallen onto the floor and Annie picks it up. 'I'm sorry I left you here.'

Willow pushes her two fingers into her mouth and sucks as Annie shuts the back door, shivering, her nipples standing to attention like studs.

She opens Tess' door. 'You have to get out.'

'I beg your pardon?' asks Tess.

'My door's stuck on that side. I have to get in through here.'

Tess sits there staring at Annie.

'Unless you want me to climb over you,' says Annie.

Tess pulls herself out and Annie climbs, hyper-aware of her backside in the air, the wobble of her body as she manoeuvres herself through the obstacle course that's her little car. She sits behind the wheel, listening to her own fast breath as Tess gets back in and arranges herself. A swatch of Annie's torn dress is caught on the fence like orange bunting.

Annie drives with her face so close to the windscreen that her nose almost presses against the glass. Her foot takes its cue from her soaring stress levels and presses down hard, the speedometer rising, Tess wedging a manicured hand on the door.

If Annie hadn't arrived at that moment, Freddie would have stayed beneath the water, he'd be dead. The thought pours into the place where all her feelings for Willow are stored, sending tears into her eyes. Why weren't they watching him more closely? She takes her eyes off the road and follows Tess' gaze to the side mirror; she must be watching Willow in it. Her son is being rushed to hospital with God knows what injuries and Tess is still obsessing over somebody else's kid.

The car undulates over the road, and Annie sees that she's twenty kilometres over the speed limit. She applies the brakes a little too violently, throwing everyone forward. In her rearview mirror, she sees that Willow is asleep.

'He was breathing, so why did they attach all that equipment to him?' Tess asks.

'Nobody saw Freddie go into the water, so they can't assume anything. They're being careful.'

'They said he might have a spinal injury.'

Quadriplegic. Paraplegic. 'They're just covering all the bases,' says Annie.

'How did you know what to do?'

'My mom was a nurse; I used to patch up my dolls with band-aids all the time.'

Tess takes a noisy breath through her nostrils. 'She taught you resuscitation?'

'I did a course years ago.'

Someone beeps and overtakes Annie; another car replaces that one and sits on her rear end. She picks up speed again.

'He could have drowned,' says Tess.

She is making all manner of expressions without really moving her face, the slight flicker to her left nostril, her eyes swilling with fear. God, why does it smell so strongly of sweat in here? Fat lot of good that tree-shaped car freshener is doing dangling from the rearview mirror.

'It's like it's happening all over again,' says Tess. There's an expression on her face like she's about to sneeze.

'What do you mean?' asks Annie.

A tear forms in Tess' eye then falls, drawing a pale line through her foundation.

'My daughter died,' says Tess. Her eyes have found their way back to that side mirror and are staring.

'She died, and it was Matteo and I that killed her.' Tess lays her head back against the chair and closes her eyes. The next time she speaks, Annie can see what it costs her.

Chapter 30

London, England

▮

Tess had bought the pregnancy test on the way to work. Once there, she'd ducked into the ladies, urine pelting her hand as she held the stick beneath her. She stood inside the cubicle and watched as two faint pink lines had started to appear. Cells were expanding inside her and would reach critical mass, pushing up against her organs and filling her with fifty per cent more blood.

Her mother, Sheila, had pecked at her, 'I'm not sure how you'll be with a kid, the nappies, and oh, God, the breastfeeding.' Not like Tess' older sister Angela, who already had two children, together with a burgeoning career as a hand surgeon. 'The clever one,' that's how their father Keith referred to Angela. Keith who'd been laid off by the vacuum cleaner factory when the girls were teenagers. Tess had studied marketing at university, and she loved her job at the drinks company. She'd go back to work when the baby was six months old, she thought, a job-share or four days a week. She bought a hynotherapy CD and a book about spiritual birth. She tried to silence other people's stories about labour. 'Waves of pain? More like a fucking tsunami.' That was her colleague, Molly.

Tess invited Sheila to the twenty-week scan where they found out it was a girl. 'A girl is for life, not like a boy,' Sheila had said, and she started crocheting pink blankets.

Matteo had documented each month of Tess' pregnancy with a photograph, a slight swell in the first one, Tess' slim fingers on the veiny stomach fit to burst in the last. Tess' fingers were lithe and smooth; she twirled them around when she talked. 'You could get hand jobs,' Sheila had said and Keith had held his newspaper higher. 'Hand modelling, I mean. If the career doesn't work out,' Sheila had added.

The due date arrived and passed, the cot and the soft toys awaiting the new arrival. Tess peeled the plastic off the pram, ate fresh pineapple slices and drank raspberry tea. She ticked off all the things that would encourage the labour to start. She and Matteo had ungainly sex as the breasts she'd never known before bounced on her chest, but still the baby didn't show any signs of appearing.

A late scan showed the baby sucking her thumb, her legs bent, silvery lines decorating her face, her heartbeat watery loud. The hospital wanted to induce ten days from then.

'Wouldn't it be something if we shared the same birthday,' said Matteo as he and Tess sat in a cafe afterwards.

She hadn't considered how close the baby's birthday would be to Matteo's.

'If you had the induction 13 days from now, there might be a chance,' said Matteo.

'I want this baby out of me.'

Matteo looked like a little boy sitting there, his chocolate brownie laid on a serviette in front of him, his face scrunched with excitement. She wanted to extend that excitement. She wanted to make the connection between him and his first born even stronger than she knew it would be. Had she wanted to make up for the injured relationship he had with his father? Perhaps. His father had gone berserk when Matteo had talked of going into the hotel business. Matteo had got a first in his economics and management degree. 'What do you want to wait tables for?' Bruno had bellowed at him. But Matteo had stood firm; he landed a job as the assistant manager of a hotel after leaving university, and moved in with Tess. And so as she stared at him that day in the cafe, she came to a decision. 'Let's wait,' she said.

She's turned that moment over in her mind a thousand times, smoothing out its rough edges like an ocean transforming a shard of broken bottle into sea glass. Few of the details are left. She can't remember what Matteo was wearing, what it felt like to be looking forward to meeting their first child.

Delaying the induction had seemed like a joyous thing; it filled her chest with warmth. It would be something to make them smile in years to come, their first born sharing her father's birthday.

So they put the induction off. The midwife had been furious, but Matteo had said, 'Just a couple of extra days.' Matteo, the rower, the Oxford don, 'The man who was going places,' as Sheila had said. 'Landed on your feet when you met that one.'

Tess did a good job of convincing herself that it was okay to delay the birth. *The baby isn't ready to come yet. Maybe it would start naturally if she waited just a little longer.*

She arrived at the hospital. Her midwife's hair was pulled back with a black bulldog clip; her name was Claire.

Tess' stomach was slippery with gel as Claire frowned at the screen. 'I can't seem to locate the heartbeat.' Tess' pulse galloped; she felt dizzy and sick. Claire came back into the room with a stocky Northern Irish midwife called Joyce. 'Right, let's take a look,' Joyce said. Tess' stomach was prodded and pressed while her heart pumped marathon-hard. There was something about Joyce's face – a studied blankness to it. She turned the scanner screen away from Tess. Tess wanted to stay in that moment with the white noise rising in her ears, but Joyce pressed Tess' arm and her pitiful face said the words even before she'd opened her mouth. 'I'm sorry.'

The baby was dead. The cotton nightdress itched Tess' skin like wire wool. She curled into a ball, pressed her hand to the stomach that was a tomb now.

'Cut her out of me, just revive her,' she'd said.

Joyce levered Tess up and took her to a room with faux leather armchairs and a mural of a horse painted onto the wall. Matteo sat beside her with his lips tinged blue. Joyce went through the options: a caesarean or a vaginal delivery. Tess opted for the latter.

Late the next day, an epidural was plugged into Tess' back; she picked out shapes in the shadows on the ceiling. A baby's face side-on, the delicate nose, the pursed lips. And something else beside it, a monster's jaw, a circle of sharp teeth. The room smelt of eucalyptus, and Tess pushed and sobbed while Joyce spoke gently to her. Matteo clasped Tess' hand; she pulled it back again.

The baby flopped out of Tess at a quarter to three in the morning. 'Please, don't,' Tess said when Joyce started to rub the baby down with a towel. Matteo turned away, faced the wall, crying.

They stared at each other then, she and Joyce, the knowledge of what had been lost gathering in the space between them. All those firsts that had been snatched away. The knees that would never be scuffed by falling over, the hands that would never push their first seeds into soil, the girl who would not smile nor say 'Mummy'.

The silence swelled, and still the urgent cries of the newborn didn't come. Joyce put the quiet, still baby into Tess' arms as she was, bloody and vernixed and beautiful. Tess smoothed her hand over the baby's mottled cheek. Warmth hadn't left it yet.

'Ava.'

Living one, that's what it meant. Tess pushed a finger into Ava's still pliable fist and moved it up and down. Joyce sat on the edge of the bed, dabbed a tissue to Tess' wet face. A tear splashed down onto Ava's chin, square and smudged with blood.

Matteo's knees broke underneath him, but he caught hold of the lip of the sink to steady himself. The sob that came out of him put Tess in mind of sheet metal shaking. He looked down at his dead daughter, the colour leaching from his face.

Later, Joyce filled a basin with warm, soapy water and

unwrapped Ava. She passed a flannel to Tess who wet it and wiped her baby down, the baby's face splotched with purple, her legs cold. Tess paused over the pegged umbilical cord that had tied her and her daughter together. She'd been cut adrift from her life; she'd become her worst fear, someone whose child had died.

Joyce took fifty reportage-style photographs of Ava in Tess' arms, then in Matteo's as they sat together on the bed. Tess' face was bent low in each one. She touched her own puckered stomach.

She tried to memorise the baby's details, the tiny growth on her earlobe like a stud made of skin, the creases on her toes, the generous velvet brown hair that clung to her tiny skull. But the memories would fade, she knew that, so when Joyce gave her the data-stick with the photographs on it, Tess held it like a fragile thing.

The next day, Joyce brought in a small wooden box with a castle carved into the top. Joyce snipped off a kink of Ava's hair and put it inside. She pressed Ava's little foot into a square of plaster and once it was set, she put that into the box too.

They stayed at the hospital for three days while regret built a place inside of Tess, alongside the grief.

How could she say goodbye to Ava? Why did she even have to? She took one last look at her baby's face and whispered. 'I'll take you with me.' Then she handed the girl back to Joyce and forced herself to turn away, sobbing like someone was cutting out her heart.

At home, fear washed over Matteo's face when Tess cried. And oh, how she cried. On her knees in the bathroom, digging her nails into her cheeks. She knocked her head against a wall in the bedroom several times, trying to work up courage to smash her head harder. 'This won't do any good,' Matteo had entreated.

The coffin was tiny and white, a wooden heart carved into each side. Tess floated on valium. The crematorium gave Ava back to them in a tiny silver urn.

Tess was a dot to dot of pain, her head, her breasts, her vagina, but mostly that place in her chest where her heart was. She parcelled herself up, so that none of the grief would leak out. It was the only way she could stop herself from falling apart. People didn't know how to look at her with anything other than pity.

She went back to work at the drinks firm. She bought ready meals, which she ate from the microwaveable tubs. 'I saw a man carrying a baby in a papoose today,' she told Matteo one evening. 'The baby had a pink hat on.' Tess' curry tasted of nothing.

She framed the single photograph of Ava that she'd had printed and put the data stick into the memory box that Joyce had given them.

Ava became a thing Matteo wanted to move on from. The following year, he threw the handful of birthday cards that were mailed to him into the bin. He took Ava's photograph from the nail on the wall and shoved it into a kitchen drawer where the placemats were lined up neatly, alongside a box of keys, and a pack of new batteries.

He wanted his wife back, he said. Tess, who played her cello every evening for half an hour; Tess who had a habit of putting things away where he couldn't find them; Tess who used to thrash him at tennis – Ava had erased her.

Her face was a hollow thing. There were purple bags under her eyes. It was like she'd been programmed to conceal all emotion. 'There's this counsellor,' he'd said, showing her the details on the internet. But Tess only went to see her once. 'She sits there, doesn't say anything to me. Just nods her head every now and again,' Tess had said.

She and Matteo stopped really talking. They bought a kingsize bed, which meant they didn't have to touch. But he'd turned to her one night, kissing her urgently, putting his hands around her buttocks and squeezing, and she'd said, 'Don't.' She'd turned her back on him.

'For God's sake, Tess,' he'd said. 'I've had enough of this.'

The valium she was still taking put a fatigue into everything, so she managed to fall asleep. In the middle of the night, she woke, a light from downstairs bleeding through the darkness. She got up and went towards the light.

She opened the living room door, and Matteo was on his knees with the empty photograph frame and the wooden box, the plaster cast footprint in his hand, the door of the log burner open, the flames licking as if they had swallowed something significant. They cracked and hissed, and Tess leapt at him.

The plaster cast fell and broke, and her hand was in the fire, digging around, skinned by the heat, and the pain carving her up. The stink of burning flesh leapt into the air. Her pyjama top was on fire.

'Christ,' Matteo shouted, pulling her backwards and rolling her, so that her burning hand was stemmed. The pair of them lay there crying. It was the first time she'd shed a tear in months.

Tess felt her hand seething with pain and melting, and she stared at Matteo's horrified face. A question chiselled itself inside her head: *What have you done?*

Every piece of Ava was gone now, apart from her ashes, and a new layer of grief flexed its muscles and clamped itself around both of them.

Chapter 31

Florida, USA

Until now, Tess hadn't confided the details surrounding her daughter's death to anyone. She had explained away her burns as an accident. Her pyjama top had caught fire while she was throwing a log into the wood burner, she'd said. Everyone had accepted her explanation, no one had probed, not that she'd looked them in the eye when she'd lied. And she's never mentioned Ava to her sons because what would she have said when they asked why she died? They don't know that before them came a girl.

'Why did she die?' asks Annie.

Die. Annie hadn't tripped over the word, or faltered.

'The post mortem was inconclusive, but it was because of us.'

'What, because you waited an extra three days?'

'Yes,' says Tess.

Annie blows out air through her closed lips and brakes at a red light. *Why is it taking so long to get to the hospital?*

'There's no evidence the baby died because you waited,' says Annie. 'I mean, due dates are random, working back from your last period – who knows when that baby was conceived? Maybe you just carry babies longer than some other women.'

'All my boys were induced.'

'And what about you, how long did your mother carry you for?'

'Well over her time. I've had lots of blow-by-blow accounts.'

'So, there you are then.'

Tess holds her hand over the ineffective air-conditioning vent. 'The placenta had probably started to shut down.'

Annie shakes her head. 'That's a theory that's bandied about; it's bullshit.'

When Tess had returned to work after it happened, Molly had babbled to fill the spaces – conversation with Tess had been one big space. 'You never knew her though, wouldn't it be so much worse if you . . .' Molly's voice had trailed off, realising she was about to say something insensitive, but how could Molly know, that this was grief in reverse, mourning for what Ava would never be, not for what she was. If only Tess could have had an hour with her, a day; if only her hand had gripped Tess' little finger for one short moment.

The person Tess really talked to was Jenna, but she didn't tell her about the advice to induce. Tess didn't want to feel exposed, didn't want to risk devaluation. Tess flinches when she realises Annie is looking at her scarred hand.

'Surely the hospital were able to give you copies of the photographs?' asks Annie, shifting her gaze back to the road.

'It was more than a year after we'd lost her. There were no copies.'

'You have the urn at least?'

Tess takes a deep breath and sighs. 'I took the ashes out of it; I carry them around with me in a box now. That sounds weird, doesn't it?'

'It's not weird,' says Annie, turning a corner.

Slumped in the seat, Tess sees the hospital there in front of her. She presses her hand to the glass and holds it there. Freddie's inside one of those cream buildings. The vast box with smoked windows perhaps, or the hexagonal-shaped tower bracketed by shrubs.

Let him live. Thoughts billow through Tess' head like aerial messages. Annie is starting to shiver with such rabidity that Tess is starting to feel cold even though it's oven-hot in here.

'I'll get out here,' says Tess as Annie struggles to negotiate a parking space.

'Hold on!' says Annie. She turns her head backwards to look at Willow then lowers her voice. 'Have you ever spoken to anyone professional about what you've told me?'

Tess shakes her head. Annie takes a hand off the steering wheel and lays it on the back of Tess' shoulder. There's a beauty in the faces of kind people that has nothing to do with aquiline noses and porcelain skin. It's there in Annie's face, in the green eyes, the puffy cheeks. The woman who saved her son's life, the woman who gave life to him in the first place.

Tess climbs out of the car, slamming the door behind her. She starts to run, through the automatic glass doors, into a waiting room packed with people. She turns back to see the car almost colliding with the front bumper of another car.

What on earth was Tess thinking getting into Annie's car instead of the ambulance? She should have been with Freddie, her Freddie who is fighting for his life, her Freddie who'd been under the water drowning. Why is she so caught up in the past that she can't be fully in the present?

But he'll be alright surely. Four minutes, Annie said. Four minutes and he still has a good chance.

❚

Two hours later, the hospital room is a web of wires and bleeping machines. There's an oxygen mask over Freddie's face and Tess can't stop looking at him, his eyes shut. Luca is asleep in a wipe-down easy chair, his head thrown back, his mouth open, dribble flowing in a line down the side of his chin. Matteo has taken Phoenix to the cafe. The room smells of pine and antiseptic.

She can't remember a time when she stopped what she was doing and watched Freddie like this, without switching on her computer or scrolling through her phone.

Annie is waiting outside with Willow. 'Only family are allowed in,' a nurse had said. It made Tess think of her cousin Joely who she hasn't seen since they were little. Joely who's one of Tess' Facebook friends even though they probably have nothing in common apart from their bloodline.

A doctor comes into the room then, a stethoscope coiled around her neck, her netted bun.

'The chest x-rays are clear, and Freddie's oxygen saturation levels are good, but we'll carry on monitoring him,' she says. 'The results from the EEG should be back later this evening.'

There's the sound of crinkling. Annie is standing in the doorway in that paper gown the nurse gave her because of her wet clothes, the skin purpled around her plastered, padded knees.

'Why exactly have you done an EEG?' asks Tess.

'We want to examine all possibilities, encephalitis, head injury, epilepsy.'

Tess' heart is heavy with tenderness, her hand warm on Freddie's. The doctor presses a button on the ventilator then leaves.

'Carl's here,' says Annie. 'He's going to take Willow home.'

'You should go too.'

'I'll stay. I'm going to change into this though.' She lifts a yellow piece of fabric into the air, which releases the scent of patchouli then heads away. The urge to see Willow again pulls Tess up and out of her seat. She looks at Freddie lying there, pale and sickly, the monitors on his chest and head, the cup of the oxygen mask, the screen beside him beeping. She'll only be a moment.

She steps out into the corridor. Annie is standing at the end of it where the chairs are, the strings of the cloth gown tied together across her back. Willow is floppy in Carl's arms, her legs hanging. Annie rubs at Willow's back and talks to Carl.

'Really? Oh . . .,' drawls Carl. He spots Tess then, his eyes widening.

Tess about-turns and goes back into Freddie's room. The

kindness of strangers is abundant when something terrible happens, cabbies running people home for free, people putting their arms around victims, but isn't all that a blip? Afterwards, don't people go on as before and stop really looking at one another? Is Annie's kindness temporary? They're polar opposites grafted together by chance after all.

Annie comes back into the room in her dress, and Luca opens his eyes briefly.

'There could be something wrong with him,' Tess says to Annie. 'You heard what that doctor said.'

'They're checking him out, making sure he's alright.'

Tess looks at Luca, drops the volume of her voice. 'I'm sorry about going on earlier.'

'You never really get over losing someone like that, not entirely,' says Annie, sitting.

'Some days I'm fine, others, I'm . . .' She feels naked about all that she told Annie in the car, and if she keeps wittering on, she might let slip more of the things she wants to stay hidden, like the way she's been following Annie around.

'What a thing to have to come through, and then fate goes and does this,' says Annie.

'This is happening to you too.'

'I haven't lost a child though,' Annie whispers.

'Haven't you?' Tess' eyes settle on Freddie. 'When you're expecting a baby, you make a place for it in your heart. It never gets filled up by anybody else. I could have had seven children, and still Ava would be gone. You love them all differently.'

'I've got one child, so . . .'

'Two,' says Tess.

Annie swallows, looking ill at ease and probably not just because of that garish dress that's cutting into her every bulge and hinge.

'You're still a mother,' says Annie, sitting more upright in her seat. 'Despite this bullshit situation, despite everything.'

Tess looks at Freddie, but still he hasn't moved. When are those doctors going to arrive with the results of the tests? But then maybe it's a good sign that they're not rushing the tests, maybe there's no urgency.

'IVF,' says Annie. 'Were they all IVF?'

'The first three children came easily to us. I know we lost Ava, but . . .'

She can't tell Annie about the gender selection IVF. She folds her arms. Her son is lying in that bed having almost drowned, and still she's sitting here clinging to the artifice of herself.

'I had three miscarriages after Luca and then . . . We did everything in our power to have a little girl. We had gender selective IVF.'

It looks as if Annie's peeling her tongue off the roof of her dry mouth. She seems unable to speak.

'It wasn't something I undertook lightly,' says Tess. 'Time was running out for us.'

Annie crosses her leg away from Tess. They sit there for some time, without exchanging a word. When Tess glances at Annie, she sees that the kindness that was there in the woman's face earlier has been fractured, and she is now staring earnestly at her own fidgety hands.

Eventually, there's the squeak of shoes along the corridor and Tess straightens, anticipating the doctor's return, but it's Phoenix.

He dumps himself into the other easy chair. A dishevelled Matteo comes into the room. 'Any news?'

'They're checking him out for a head injury, epilepsy,' says Tess.

'What?' asks Matteo.

'Possibilities, the doctor said, but God, Matteo, he could be really ill.'

Annie picks up her handbag from the floor and clutches it to her chest. 'If that nurse spots me in here, me not being family and all, well . . .'

'You're going?,' says Matteo, his head snapping round as if he's only just realised she's there.

'I think maybe I should leave you guys to it,' says Annie.

'Will you be alright to drive?' asks Matteo.

'Well, some people might disagree, but yeah, I guess so.' Her smile peaks and fades, and the monitor goes on beeping.

'I can't thank you enough for what you did for Freddie today,' says Matteo.

'I just did what anyone else would have done,' says Annie.

Matteo holds out his arms and she walks into them, the back of her dress caught in her knicker elastic. This might have sent a jolt of mirth through Tess once, but she can't see anything funny about it now. Even so, she doesn't want anyone else laughing at Annie's expense. When Annie turns to look at her, Tess suggests she pulls down her dress at the back.

'Oops! Anyway text me when you know more,' says Annie.

And then she walks out, and a thought beats through Tess' head – his brain, Freddie's brain, what's wrong with Freddie's brain?

Chapter 32

Annie pulls out onto the highway and realises she hasn't got her headlights on. *Click.* A marsupial skitters across the road, and she swerves. She should have waited to find out whether Freddie's going to be okay, but then it could be hours before the results come back. Her sandalled foot presses down harder on the accelerator.

The road's empty ahead, and she's speeding, but so what? She races past a hotel with a flag drooping on a pebble-dashed wall.

Tess' daughter died, and now the loss has duplicated because she's lost Willow too. Grief lingers – you build yourself around it, muscle and flesh surrounding a pinned joint. All of this must be splitting it open again though, exposing it. Pain like that could turn a person crazy, could make a person capable of all sorts of things.

Annie veers into the wrong lane and the blare of the car she almost collides with makes her quake. This whole thing's out of control, a bit like her driving. Her dress is too warm, too tight, clutching at her like a thanksgiving roast smothered in bacon. She turns off her car's excuse for air-conditioning and rolls the window down, the breeze in her hair.

Eventually she arrives at the apartment, and parks up, wrestling her way out of the car. Christy's lights are on, the curtains pulled back, so that Annie can see the front room stacked with cardboard boxes. How she wishes she could throw this whole thing off and escape too. She punches the wheel in the wrong place and the car lets out a burp of a beep.

Inside, Carl is standing in the living room, the sound of Willow's crying filtering in.

'I called my mom,' he says, his eyes desperate and darting.

'It's okay, *schnuckel*.' Lina's voice sails from the direction of Willow's bedroom.

'I want my bear!' Willow says then sobs.

'Jesus Christ, Carl,' hisses Annie. 'Just this once, couldn't you deal with Willow on your own?'

'She's upset, and . . .'

'What?'

'I'm worried about Freddie.'

'So you need your mom to hold your hand, make it all better.'

'That's unfair. I . . . look, this concerns her too.'

'Bug!' calls Willow.

Annie goes over to the sink. What happened back there? Did Freddie jump in because she made so much about him swimming the other day or did he fall? Willow's crying grows louder in her ears as she drinks a glass of water. Carl lays his flat hands on his head, shambling slowly up and down the living room, the elastic shot in his pyjama bottoms.

Inside Willow's bedroom, the little girl is cocooned in Lina's arms, the fluorescent plastic stars on the ceiling above them, the sickle moon, the stencilled tree on the wall. Willow is sniffing, her mouth wobbling, inconsolable and phlegmy.

'Oh, honey,' says Annie.

'Come, Annie,' says Lina, shuffling off the bed and urging Annie to sit.

Annie climbs onto the bed beside Willow and Lina leaves.

'There now, there,' says Annie, pulling the girl into the basket of her arms.

The owl clock, its eyes clicking side to side, tells her it's one in the morning.

'I want . . .' wails Willow.

She goes on saying the same thing over and over again. 'I want.

I want.' It's a long time before she's quiet. Strands of her hair are matted to her hot, sleeping face, her fingers in her mouth.

Annie gets up and goes into the living room where Carl and Lina are exchanging quiet, heated words. The air is scented with cleaning products.

'But you never even told me that before!' snaps Carl.

'The chances of passing it down are minimal,' replies Lina, misting the table with antiseptic spray and rubbing.

'What's going on?' asks Annie.

'Carl tells me they think the child is ill,' says Lina, staying stooped and observing the floor.

'He almost drowned,' says Annie. 'That's why he's ill.'

Lina straightens, her mouth an imperious flat line. 'Carl says the doctor mentioned the possibility of epilepsy.'

'Well, yeah.'

'It's just that that swine . . .'

'Tell her, Mom.'

Lina folds her arms, the spray sloshing. 'Diedrich had fits when he was a child,' says Lina. 'By twelve, nothing more.'

'They should know about this, Freddie's family,' says Annie, dropping onto a chair, defeated.

'That's why I'm telling you,' says Lina, laying a rubber-gloved hand on Annie's shoulder. Carl's mouth hangs open like a human mosquito catcher.

Annie's fingers are itching to pull the medical encyclopedia from the shelf and start finding answers for Freddie right now. It's rising up in her, a red, fiery rage; she has to let out the pressure. Alan jumps onto the counter beside that old camera of Diedrich's, the camera that's worth money, as if money could change any of this. Hell, it was money that got them here in the first place. Annie grabs the camera and opens the front door.

'What? Where are you going?' asks Carl in a panicked voice.

Fury is boiling in her head like an instant hot water dispenser. She stomps outside, hangs the camera over the side of the balcony and lets it go. It descends, disappearing into the darkness then clattering onto the ground in a delicious, relief-inducing shatter.

Lina arrives in the frame of the front door. 'But that was an antique!'

Annie's thoughts are bashing against one another and fighting for space. Back inside, she grabs Carl's van key from a hook and throws it at him, and unlikely though it is for Carl, he catches it.

'You're going to have to go back to that hospital,' she says. 'You're going to have to tell them about Diedrich.'

Annie turns away from him, an ache in her chest that's sinking her to the floor, her knees scabbed and her heart crushed.

Chapter 33

Tess follows the doctor down the corridor, turning back to look at Freddie asleep in the bed, the gluey fronds of his hair sticking up where they pulled away the sensors. Matteo takes her hand. If Annie hadn't jumped over the wall like a stunt woman, Freddie would be dead. But her saving him wasn't a licence for Tess to overshare. She doesn't know Annie all that well and she's told her everything, without sieving out any of the details. No wonder Annie went quiet before she left.

The doctor goes into a room with weighing scales on the floor, several shrink-wrapped syringes and a cardboard emesis bowl on the desk.

'Sit down, please.' She ushers out her hand, and they sit, Matteo's thigh bouncing.

The doctor looks at Matteo then at Tess, doesn't smile. 'Does anyone in the family suffer from epilepsy?'

'No,' says Matteo.

The doctor's pen pauses over her paper.

'He's not our child though,' says Tess. 'What I mean is, he's not our genetic child.' She sits on her hands.

The doctor nods. 'So is there any history of epilepsy in Freddie's genetic family that you know of?'

'I don't know,' says Tess.

She's been so fixated on finding out about Willow that she hasn't asked Annie all that much about Freddie's roots. The pen scratches the paper.

'Do you think he's had an epileptic fit?' asks Matteo.

'The EEG shows some minor changes in Freddie's brain waves, but this alone isn't enough to diagnose epilepsy.' There's no conciliatory expression on the doctor's face; she doesn't soften her words, or slow them down.

'He can't have that, surely,' says Tess.

'We want to run a number of tests, subject him to various stimuli, see if it brings on a fit.'

'Oh, God,' says Matteo.

'We'll be monitoring him closely, and once you get him home, you'll have to do the same. I note you're here on holiday.'

It's only now that Tess remembers that Matteo was meant to leave this evening.

'Well, we were here to . . .' Tess starts.

'We were here for a family matter,' says Matteo.

'And when are you leaving?'

'As soon as possible,' says Matteo.

'When you get back to the UK, you'll need to see a specialist,' says the doctor.

Tess combs her hands over her face.

'We'll run the tests first thing tomorrow morning,' says the doctor. She gets up. 'And I'll be around if you need to ask any more questions. Take as long as you want in here.' She looks at them and flattens her mouth into a straight line that isn't a smile.

Tess laces her fingers together under her chin, anxiety crow-barring its way into her. The door closes behind the doctor.

'You always thought there was something different about him,' says Matteo. 'I couldn't see it; perhaps I didn't want to.'

Trembling, she gets up, goes out into the corridor and drags her hand along the wall. At the ward door, she watches Luca still asleep in the easy chair beside Freddie.

'Erm, hello,' an uncertain voice comes from behind her.

She turns and there is that baggage of a man, Carl, crumpled and slow motion.

'Can I talk to you about something?' he asks, his eyes landing on her then darting away. There's an old woman behind him with badly cut hair.

'Now's not a good time,' says Tess.

Matteo emerges from the side room, his good posture cancelled out by slouching shoulders and a hunched back.

'Carl?' he says. 'What are you doing here?'

'I need to talk to you both about Freddie.'

The old woman lays a hand on Carl's back.

'My dad had epilepsy as a kid, he grew out of it, but . . .'

Tess tips into herself, folding over and over into sharp creases, and everything around her blurs. Matteo turns away from them all, looking up at the ceiling, hands on his hips.

Carl carries on droning glutinous words. *Shut up. Shut up.* Her heart bangs. Her daughter is dead, her other daughter has been snatched away from her, and now her son might have a disease she knows little about. She's too brittle for this, too inadequate, she's not strong enough. She wants it all to stop, but there are walls around her, walls and the smell of bleach, and she can't seem to breathe properly. She needs to think, she needs time to calm down. She starts speed walking away from Carl's slow slur and Matteo's quiet questions.

She can see from the grid at the top of the lift that it'll take a moment for it to rise up here to the sixth floor, so she opens the door to the stairs and starts going down, her hand grabbing the rail for balance. She would have been a good mother to that girl. She should have been a good mother. There's still a chance she can be, but time is running out.

Chapter 34

Tess pushes her thumb into the road as a red van passes, but it doesn't slow down. Her son is in hospital and she's vacated the building, left all her boys back there. She's unfettered, out here with the backdraught of cars buffeting her, the four lanes of the highway lined by cube-like buildings, the smell of petrol in the air. It would be madness to climb into a stranger's car, but then she feels mad, her head too full and fast, and the need to get further away. She starts to walk, stretching her arm into the road, turning back to look in the direction she's just come from, but no one's following her.

Her son is ill and she's left him, but what kind of support can she be to him when she's breaking apart? A grey car is approaching and slowing, and she allows herself to be tugged in its direction, the window of the passenger seat winding down.

'I'm not going far, just over the bridge,' the driver says, cigarettes in the corners of her voice, in the lines scoring her top lip.

'That's where I'm headed.' Tess pulls open the door and gets in.

The woman is conducting the air with a toothpick pegged between her chapped lips. The wind bats Tess' hair through the open windows.

'How are you doing over there?' the woman asks, pulling the pick from her teeth and putting it into the slot on her door.

'Fine,' says Tess, heat burning through her and misting her with sweat.

'It's just that you out here, hitchhiking when it's dark like this . . .' The woman tuts, shakes her head.

'I know.'

'You're English.'

'Yes.'

'So what brings you here?'

An immense wave of guilt crashes over Tess. 'I was trying to find someone I'd lost.'

A row of palm trees dances beside the tarmac, the road sloping upwards, street lamps throwing out their glow.

'You'd think with the internet and everything, it'd be easy to stay in touch with people, but all this technology, it pushes us further apart,' says the woman. 'People don't know how to talk any more, hardly anyone picks up the phone, it's all texting and social media.' The woman clears her throat. 'Did you find the person you were looking for?'

'She's not who I need her to be.'

'Well, God, I need to be married to George Clooney, but I got Brian instead. Moody at the best of times, and so damn concerned about his bald patch that he went and had a weave.' She blows air from her mouth. 'But when I'm down he's the one that makes me see things differently.'

The woman's fingers on the wheel are festooned with scratched sovereign rings. 'So what are you going to do?'

'I can't walk away from her,' says Tess.

'You've come a long way to find her, so maybe you need to try a bit harder.'

Tess needs to put things right. She needs to take that rancid teddy bear round to the Amstels and leave it outside their apartment. She's been hanging onto it like a parent whose child has been snatched. She'll go round there, that's what she'll do.

She finds Matteo's painkillers in her bag, and swallows three of them dry. She turns to look at the woman who's resting her arm on the windowsill, her ringed fingers loose on the wheel. Tess expects her to carry on dispensing advice like some agony aunt, but she just drives.

Eventually, Tess sees a landmark she recognises – an inflatable red tube man filled with air and dancing.

'Just here's fine,' says Tess.

The woman rolls the car into the side of the road.

Tess' legs wobble as she climbs out. 'Thank you.'

She starts to walk away, her head swimming. Just because things haven't gone well with Willow, she can't give up on her. Her heart pounds. *I'm going to get her back,* she thinks.

Chapter 35

In the small hours, Annie wakes to the sound of the too-loud air-conditioning in Willow's room. The sheet is wrinkled and empty beside her. She touches her hand to it and it's cold. She switches on the spinning bedside light, and shadowy gymnasts cartwheel across the ceiling.

'Carl!' she calls.

Annie kicks the comforter to the side, tumbles out of the bed and switches off the air-conditioning.

'Carl!'

Something starts to thud. Annie goes out into the living room, her pyjamas creating static across her thighs. The front door is open, creaking and thudding in the breeze, the hanging heart clanking against the wood. There must be a storm coming. The scanty light from the road threads its way in.

'Willow?'

Annie flicks the light switch, scours the empty living room. Where can she be, and why isn't Carl back from the hospital? She looks at the clock – it's four o'clock in the morning.

'Willow?'

She goes into the bathroom with its dirt-encrusted white boards – nothing, back into the bedroom with the havoc of clothes spilling out of the wardrobe. Where is she?

Pacing the living room, she sees that Willow's pink jelly shoes have gone from the side of the front door. Annie goes out onto the balcony. Rolling back and forth along the boards is Willow's bottle, droplets of water on the wood. Annie rushes over to the play house, but it's empty. The wind pulls through the hedges.

She steps towards the balustrade, her eyes reluctant and slow. She doesn't want to see, but down she looks. There's nothing but shells, and fragments of the camera – shards of glass and black plastic. Panic spirals through her. She goes back inside and searches all the rooms again.

'Willow!'

She checks under the beds.

The car? Maybe she went downstairs and climbed in? Annie rushes down, the shells of the driveway pressing into her bare feet as she tries to sort through the jumbled thoughts in her head. Willow's not in the car.

'Willow!' she shouts. She wanders to the edge of the road. 'Willow!'

A green truck with the back uncovered hurtles past, buffeting Annie in its draught. She staggers backwards as sand blasts her arms and face.

'Willow!' she screams, stepping into the road.

She turns and there's a white van hurtling towards her, its lights on full beam. It judders to a stop, and she rushes to the driver's door and opens it, music belting out. The passenger seat is empty.

'What's going on?' asks Carl, turning off the engine and killing the song.

And still she stares at the crumb-speckled passenger seat. A map widens in her head, distant motorways and stretches of water, her daughter a dot in the vast landscape.

'Willow's gone.' She swallows hard, her mouth dry. 'I woke up, and the front door was open. Someone must have taken her.'

'What do you mean?'

The back of her neck prickles with fear. 'She wouldn't have wandered off. She's a baby for Christ's sake. Tess must have come in the night. She must have taken her away.'

'Tess left the hospital hours ago, and Matteo can't find her. That's why I've been so long.' His rushed words tumble over one another.

The wind is rising, the water, the waves. Is Tess driving away with Willow or is their little girl out there alone, and which is worse? But Tess wouldn't hurt her, would she?

Carl pulls his cell phone from his pocket and dials 911, his fingers trembling. He climbs out of the van, leaving the door ajar behind him.

'Get me the police,' he says, his voice booming through her like a fire alarm.

'Our daughter Willow; she's three. My wife woke up and found her gone.'

Carl paces. Annie breathes, drawing spit into her throat and coughing.

'About fifteen minutes ago,' says Carl. 'But maybe she's been gone for longer.'

A car zooms past.

'No, no medical conditions.'

She meets Carl's eyes, he looks away.

'Kidnap? Well, yeah . . .,' says Carl, nodding his head. 'There's one possibility. Her name's Tess Rossi.'

Annie closes her eyes. Time is precious, and she wants it to stop; she wants Willow to walk back through it into her arms.

'The thing is there was a mix-up at the clinic,' says Carl. 'We had IVF, and well, the embryos got swapped. This Tess person, she's Willow's real mom. And, she's kind of, well, she's gone missing too, and nobody can find her. She ran off.'

Noises in the street seem absurdly loud. The buzz of an air-conditioning motor on the outside of the house opposite, a car passing. And her daughter is out there alone. Annie moves away from Carl, and retches, spitting watery bile.

'Somewhere in Sunshine Drive,' says Carl.

'310!' hisses Annie, wiping her mouth with the back of her hand.

Carl repeats the number, clicks off the call and they stand there like a couple of buoys in water, wobbling, spinning, yet pegged to the same spot.

Tess really was trying to snatch Willow back in the supermarket. She'd admitted she'd never got over the death of her daughter, that she'd never had any psychological help, and all that business with Matteo burning their daughter's things. Anybody would lose it under that kind of pressure, and this.

A siren approaches, growing louder. She looks up and down the street, the alleyways, the trash cans, the parked cars.

'Willow!' she shouts.

And the light in Christy's living room comes on, just as the police car draws up and parks over the driveway, the siren giving a final squeal before it dies.

Chapter 36

Tess wakes in the semi-darkness on the beach, her cheek in the sand, granules of it between her teeth. She sits up. She'd walked back to the villa after the woman had dropped her off; she'd picked up the hire car and driven to this beach on the other side of the island, her vision blurry, the wheels swerving on the tarmac.

She stares at her crumpled dress, the swathes of it gathering above her knees. Rubbing at the spikes of her unshaven legs, she notices three boys in the distance, laughing and throwing sand at each other, the grains of it hazing in the frenetic beam of a torch.

She feels the tickle and itch of a mosquito on her foot and she kicks it away. Her arms are covered in welts and she scratches at them.

'Get it!' one of the boys shouts.

They seem to be playing catch with something. When the torchlight falls across it, she sees that it's the size of a purse. Their laughter bubbles through the darkness.

Tess should slope away now, get back to the car where her girl is. She left her there on the back seat. She should go back and get her, then cover up the mess of herself with foundation, pretend that these last ugly hours didn't happen. She should go back to her son. Her stiff back is in need of a stretch and she gets up and does a series of waist bends side to side.

'I'm taking it home!' someone shouts.

Then the torchlight lands and stills on the small object which one of the boys is holding in his hand – a baby turtle. Something quickens in her chest. She grinds her teeth. She starts to walk towards the boys, the sand churning through her toes. The tiny flipper-like legs of the turtle are swishing. She passes a roped-off square of sand and squints at the sign in the centre of it that says *Do Not Disturb – Sea Turtle Nest.*

'Excuse me!' says Tess, but the boys don't hear.

They continue to laugh. When she gets even closer, she sees that they are almost men and as tall as her, but it's too late to turn back.

'Holy crap, it's the Walking Dead!' one of them shouts.

Anger is stoking inside her. She calls out: 'Don't do that!'

'What?' yells the boy holding the turtle.

She walks closer to them and stops. 'You heard what I said, put that turtle down!'

She is shaking; and they are staring at her and laughing even harder, but she doesn't care; she feels unleashed.

Two of the boys spring away, sand flying about their bare feet. The last boy drops the turtle, spits, then saunters away. She arrives in the place he was standing and looks at the gooey globule that he's left there in the sand, alongside the upside down turtle, its legs flailing.

Tess picks the turtle up and lays it in the centre of the roped-off square like an offering.

Chapter 37

People are packed into the driveway and every house along the street is lit up.

'She's got on a floral nightdress,' says Carl from three steps below Annie on the staircase, his voice unsteady. 'Let's try and find her. Please God, let's find her.'

Annie looks down at Tanzy, a usually made-up woman in her thirties, a tissue sticking out of the pocket of her jeans. She's staring straight at Annie, her forehead knotted with pity. Annie sees then that lots of other people in the crowd are staring at her with similar expressions.

The people start to walk away then, in twos and threes, heads switching side to side, someone marching on ahead, arms pumping.

'Are you coming, or what?' she hears someone shout, a man pushing a buggy.

'Of course, I'm coming,' snaps Christy, her feet in brown walking boots, a walking pole jammed into her hand. 'We're going to find that little girl.'

Chapter 38

Something moves at Tess' side. A turtle's head emerges from the messy sand, its legs shifting. Another turtle bursts out. Three turtles, four, then more, all of them moonlit and scooping their way towards the sea.

She thought the first one was dead, killed by being dropped by that boy, but it's putting distance between itself and the others now, heading for the water.

The nest is seething with sand-encrusted shells, legs flapping like flightless wings. They jerk, and rise. A leg brushes against her calf.

The first of them pushes into the water and is taken by the tide. Another one is swept up and out. There is a twisting line of determined turtles.

How many of them will make it? How many will be eaten by gulls? She stares out at the roiling sea, letting herself imagine that all is as it should be, her daughter beside her, the Amstels making breakfast for their son. The last few turtles wind their way towards the surf.

She feels the press of sand against her heels, the smell of seaweed, the rush of the waves. She wants to go on sitting here; she doesn't want to face the impossible situation that lies ahead, but some need, some sense of what is right, makes her stand up.

She turns away from the scuffed lines that the turtles have made, and starts to walk back to the car where she left her.

Chapter 39

Annie is on the balcony, looking up the stretch of empty, dusty road. It's been four hours since she discovered Willow gone and the sun has come up. A police officer, Nicole, arrives at her side, curling her fingers around the parapet.

'Would you like a coffee?' she asks, a seed jammed between her front teeth. Why do people always offer hot drinks in times of crisis? *Your mother just fell off a cliff? Milo, hot chocolate, herbal tea?*

'I don't want anything,' says Annie. *Except my little girl.*

The police have already checked out the playground, the pier, the ice cream shop. Where could Tess have taken her? Because it's a sum of parts that Tess has taken her. Genetic mother + dubious grip on reality = kidnapper in Jimmy Choo sandals. Perhaps she made for the airport.

Willow's passport. Annie scrambles in the kitchen junk drawer. Recipes and leaflets go flying. She lifts placemats, attempts to tidy the fan of them into a pile. It's not in here. She slams the drawer shut but it's so full it rebounds. She can't stand this disorganisation, this mess. Where the hell is Willow's passport? She looks on the bookshelves amid the medical encyclopaedias and DIY tomes, and spots all their passports then. She opens one of them and looks down at the photograph of Carl, his shoulders raised towards his chin looking like a neckless drugs baron. She snaps it shut and opens another one. This one is Willow's, her photographed face holding back a smile. 'Don't smile,' Annie had said as the man in the photography shop had clicked the camera in her direction. Three snaps then the girl was laughing, and oh, the sound of that laugh. Even when she's asleep there's a faint smile on her face.

Annie should be out there with Carl and the others, looking, beating a stick through the growth. Jesus, no.

'Have they checked Tess' place?' she blurts.

'There's no one there.'

'Tess has got her, I just know it.'

'We haven't been able to track Mrs Rossi down.'

Annie takes her phone out of her pocket and dials Tess' number. She's lost count of the number of times she's done this.

She leaves another message. 'I know you're desperate, that you've lost so much, that Freddie might be ill, but please, you can't run off with Willow, you can't take her. You'll go to jail.' No that's wrong, that'll scare her, make her do something even crazier than this act of a woman who's on the edge. 'Well, maybe not jail, not if you bring her back.' The answer service cuts out and Annie swallows down the rest of her words. She pushes the phone into the pocket of her pyjama bottoms containing a mound of tissues the size of a tennis ball.

Why in God's name has she still got her pyjamas on anyway? Her daughter is out there, who knows where, and she's standing here in winceyette.

She goes into the bedroom and pulls a dress off the hanger, a clingy nylon thing with cats over the royal blue cotton. She gets entangled in it.

'Stupid thing,' she shouts to the sound of ripping.

She pulls it off, tries again. In the bathroom, she brushes her teeth through quiet sobs then goes back into the kitchen. Leaning her backside against the kitchen counter she looks at the flecks of light the bare bulb is casting on the floorboards. They'll find her soon, an hour from now, two at most. She starts making deals with herself. No more than three; that's how old Willow is, and there's a pattern to everything, a link, a connection. It has to be

Tess, it can't be anyone else. And if it's Tess, there's still hope.

She rubs a teardrop of oil on the counter, smearing it. The tap drips. The smell of garbage curdles the air.

How she hates this apartment, damp-riddled, in need of a good stripping down and repaint. And that front door, that stupid, spindly, dilapidated piece of wood that should have been locked.

The police officer's walkie talkie fizzes with sound, words Annie can't make out, and then: 'We've got eyes on Willow Amstel.'

More words crackle, and Annie hurls out a question: 'Is she alright?'

'Yes,' says Nicole. 'Let's go.'

'Where is she?'

'She's at Mrs Rossi's rental property.'

Annie is pounding down the stairs, like a runner trying to throw their chest over the line first. She stumbles and catches hold of the handrail to right herself. At the car, she jumps in, then they are pelting along the road, seconds feeling impossibly long, and the adrenalin pumping through her body and clearing her muffled head. Whatever hopes she had of navigating this embryo fiasco are over. She can't have Tess in her life, and because of that she won't have Freddie either.

The police car pulls up at the front of Tess' villa, Annie in the passenger seat, that swatch of her orange dress still there billowing in the fence. Nicole gets out of the car and runs up the stairs, Annie in lukewarm pursuit, wobbling and slightly breathless. She passes a male officer at the bottom with a pastrami face.

Willow is above her on the top step, her slender hands hanging over her pressed-together knees. A female officer, with beautiful eyes and terrible skin, is sitting beside her, speaking soft words, Nicole digging into a bag behind them both.

Annie staggers up the stairs, drops to her knees in front of Willow. The girl starts blinking fast and Annie pulls her in, hugs her hard, the boulder gone from her throat now and replaced by whispered thank yous. Maybe Nancy was right, maybe there is a God after all because for the past hours, Annie has been muttering prayers.

'You've got ouchies,' says Willow, looking at the plasters on Annie's knees.

'We've been so worried about you.'

'Sowee.'

Willow's arms are goose bumped and Annie keeps rubbing at them.

'Are you cold?' asks Annie.

'No.'

Even so, Nicole puts a blanket around the girl's shoulders.

'Did someone bring you here?' asks Annie.

'He did,' says Willow, thumbing backwards towards the shut front door. *Matteo? A stranger? Someone in handcuffs behind the wood?*

'Did Tess hurt you?'

Willow shakes her head, her chubby, flawless cheeks, her bunched mouth.

'I was posted here in case she turned up,' says the police officer with beautiful eyes. 'I don't know how anyone missed her on the road. She keeps saying something about a bug.'

The walkie talkie crackles with words and Nicole speaks into it.

'You came here to find Bug?' Annie asks Willow.

Willow nods.

'But you couldn't have got here on your own,' says Annie.

Everything seems paltry compared to this. A woman on a bike rides by, a trailer attached to the back of it, containing two small children. The wheels squeak. Birds chitter.

'Has anyone phoned Carl?' asks Annie.

'Yes,' says Nicole.

Annie forces herself to let go of Willow's hand and climbs the remaining stairs. She expects one of the police officers there to tell her she can't go inside, but when she pushes down the handle of the door, nobody says a thing.

The vertical blinds at the other end of the open-plan kitchen are chinking, the French doors are open. An apple core is lying on the kitchen counter, frenzied flies buzzing around it.

She shoves open the door to Freddie's bedroom. It smells of talcum powder. A Nerf gun is on the floor along with an inside out pair of socks. Through the front door, which she left ajar, there's the sound of wheels crunching over the shells in the yard, the creak of a car door opening.

There's a shelf near the ceiling. On it, there are cardboard boxes, ornaments and a plastic Troll with a quiff of colourful hair. Annie sees a furry paw flopping over the side. She climbs onto the bed, stretches and gropes her hand along the painted wood, unleashing particles of dust into the air. Then the toy is in her hand, with its left ear missing, its matted grey fur.

Annie gets down from the bed and goes outside carrying the teddy bear. She puts it into Willow's arms, and the little girl kisses it, buries her face in it and smells. Phew – that kid has a strong constitution.

'I want to take Willow home,' Annie says to Nicole.

She wants to be far away from Tess – wherever she is – and her holiday home. She wants to go back to the apartment and push the bolts across. She takes Willow's hand and they start to walk down the stairs.

They reach the bottom and turn towards the police car. And there is Tess, her hair practically dreadlocked into grizzled sandy ropes, red welts over her chest and arms, like she's method acting for a bit part in a castaway film. Tess looks at the teddy bear in Willow's hand then back at Annie, her head sinking into her chest.

'I kept meaning to give it back,' says Tess.

'You took something that didn't belong to you,' says Annie.

Tess' hire car is parked at a clumsy angle behind the police car that brought Annie here, half on, half off the grassy verge.

'We need to ask you a few questions, Mrs Rossi,' says the male police officer.

'Me? Why?' says Tess, her voice edged with trepidation. He opens the back door of her car and looks inside.

'Why did you bring Willow here?' asks Annie.

'I didn't.'

'She couldn't have got here on her own,' says Annie. 'It was you. You must have come in and taken her in the night.'

'Mrs Amstel, really—'

'It *was* you,' says Annie.

'How could you think I'd do such a thing?' asks Tess. 'Who is it that you think I am?'

'He told me things about you,' says Annie.

'Who did?'

'Freddie. He said you hurt him.'

There's the sound of wheels on asphalt, a vehicle drawing to a stop nearby.

'Mama, come!' says Willow.

'I didn't.' Tess' face starts to shake.

'He said you bit him, and there was that bruise on his wrist.'

'I told you, I pulled him a little too vigorously maybe, but—'

'Annie, leave this to us.' Nicole is beside her now, laying a hand on her arm.

'You must have taken the teddy at the clinic. You've been following us ever since. That's why you hired this place, you knew where we lived.'

'No, it's not like that.'

'You tried to take Willow from the grocery store.'

'I didn't.' Tess' face is contorting as if she's in pain.

Carl barrels towards them, his cargo pants in free fall.

'Dada!'

Willow runs towards him, Bug falling to the ground, and Carl lifts her and twirls her, then hugs his arms in a criss cross over her back.

'Why did you go, kiddo?'

Willow kicks to be put down. He sets her on the ground and clocks Tess.

'Where have you been?' he asks Tess.

Their voices fade as Annie focuses on Tess' deranged appearance, her ragged breaths. It's only Tess who's in her field of vision now, and in this moment, she seems to be everything that Annie suspected of her. The downturned arc of her mouth quivers as she stares at Annie.

'The way you keep calling yourself her mother, but I'm her mother, me.' Annie gouges her forefinger into her own chest, then points at Tess. 'And you, you're nothing to her.' The volume of her voice must measure ten on the Richter scale.

The colour drains from Tess' already wan face, her knee gives way. She's a snoop and a phoney and she's been acting like a crazy person, but her daughter is dead and her son is lying in a hospital bed. Annie shuts her mouth, her rage deflating, guilt pouring into its place.

Tess pulls her gaze away, her eyes fixing and squinting at something in disbelief.

'No!' She sways, flexing the fingers on both of her hands.

'No!' she screams.

Annie's head snaps sideways to see what it is that Tess is getting so worked up about.

Willow is standing beside the open back door of Tess' car. There is a small plastic bag of something in her hand. Tess creeps towards Willow, laying one quiet foot down, then the other.

Willow turns the bag upside down, releasing a cloud of ash. It puffs up and out, hazing the air with a dusty cloud. A thin layer of ash settles on Tess' desperate hands. She stops and looks at her own fingers then the breeze brushes her skin clean. Tess stares at the ground, a moan sliding across her vocal chords.

'What?' Carl asks. 'What just happened?'

Ava is more than ash, Annie wants to say. She's spirit and love and she's right there locked inside your heart forever, but she keeps her mouth shut, rushes towards the place where the ash must have settled and clambers onto her sore knees. She lays shells and specks of sand onto the skirt of her dress.

'We'll get a dish or a bucket or something and put them all in.' Her voice sounds forced and feeble, with no real conviction behind it.

The empty memory box is on the ground, the lid beside it.

'I'm sowee,' says Willow.

And Tess stands there, sagging and dazed and staring out into the middle distance. She turns to look at Willow and instead of obsessive devotion, her face is livid.

Chapter 40

Freddie is sitting up in the hospital bed, eating a biscuit, when Tess walks into the ward. She falters towards him while Matteo glowers at her.

'How are you feeling?' she asks Freddie.

She sits on the edge of the bed, lowers her face to his, feeling his heat, his breath mixing with hers.

'I'm sorry that I left.' She cups his elbow and his eyes stay locked on hers. 'I'm sorry. I'm so sorry.'

He takes her hand then and lifts it to his face, leans into it.

Her eyes fill. 'You're going to be alright,' she says to him. He puts the remaining segment of the biscuit onto the plate and closes his eyes.

'Where are the boys?' Tess asks Matteo.

The sun, pushing its way through the window, lights up the web of lines around his eyes. 'Having lunch in the canteen. You just left. I've been so worried.'

'I went back to the villa, got the car and drove around.' She lowers her voice to a whisper. 'I was coming apart.'

His hand is flat on her upper back then. 'I know,' he says.

They sit there in silence, the smell of cooked food wafting in, the clanking of distant trolley wheels. 'Yeah, okay, sure,' someone says. Freddie's breathing evens out; he must be asleep.

She feels her handbag in the crook of her arm, the mobile phone inside with the message that Annie left on it, her upbeat voice transformed into an accusation.

After the police had finished questioning her, Tess stood under the shower at the villa and washed her hair. She hadn't wiped a space into the fogged-up mirror, hadn't wanted to see her own face. Her hair is still wet, the smell of almond shampoo filling her nose.

She traces her finger over the sickly skin of Freddie's face, his cheek bones. If she had taken him to the doctor before, if she hadn't been so cowardly . . .

'Have the doctors said anything else?' she asks.

Matteo's eyes skim Freddie's face. 'They put him through those tests to see whether he'd fit again, but nothing happened. Maybe the doctors are wrong.'

'We could have lost him.'

'But we didn't,' he says.

'But what if he does have epilepsy?'

'We'll deal with it.'

She shakes her head. 'When our baby died, I thought this is it, the worst thing that we'll ever have to go through, but it doesn't work like that.'

'No, but there is a way back from this.'

'Is there?'

'We'll help Freddie, whatever's wrong with him. And Willow, you can still have her in your life in some way.'

'I'm not sure that I can. They think I took her.'

'Carl phoned me – he was panic-stricken.'

'They thought I took her, Annie and Carl, that I came in the night and took her away.'

He frowns. 'They were desperate, that's all. They don't know you.'

Shame like this should stay hidden, but it's pushing its way up and out of her, a blocked drain spewing effluent. She moves away from Freddie's bed and Matteo follows.

'I saw Willow and Annie and Carl before the official meeting,' she says. She doesn't want him to hear this, but she's powerless to stop her mouth from forming the words. 'That day I went back to the clinic for my phone, they were all in the lift. I knew it was her – she's like Phoenix's double. She dropped her teddy and I took it.'

'What? But why?'

Heat unfurls itself inside her.

'I don't know, I followed them in the car.'

Matteo fingers a painted-over blemish on the wall.

'I picked the villa because it was around the corner from where they lived,' she says.

All the tiny hairs on the back of her neck have stood up, every part of her alert so that she sees the stubble scratching through Matteo's skin, hears the hiss of breath pulling through his nostrils, the rasp of his fingers on the wall.

'But you didn't know who they were,' he says.

'She looked like she should.' She thinks of athletes and their rituals before a high jump or a serve, wiggling fingers into the air, blessing themselves. She was holding onto that teddy for protection. She feels undone; she brings her hands to her face, so she can cover up some small part of herself. 'I meant to give it back,' she says through her fingers.

She can feel him near her, he hasn't moved away.

'I followed them into a supermarket one day. Willow got lost and I took hold of her hand, and . . . But I wasn't trying to take her, I wouldn't.'

The supermarket office, where Tess had been made to wait for the manager, drifts into her head. The security guard had stood in front of the door with his arms folded until the manager had arrived. Then Tess had stumbled out her excuse about leaving the shop without paying because she'd been distracted. The manager hadn't called the police.

'Surely the police don't believe you kidnapped Willow last night.'

'They asked me so many questions.' She folds her arms, her head lowered. 'God, I just can't see the Amstels again.'

He leans his back against the wall, stares at the ceiling. 'You won't always feel this way.'

'I thought we could put this right, that we'd walk away from this with a neat ending, but we're not going to.'

'It doesn't mean you just bury it. You tried to do that with Ava. And look at you, you're still destroying yourself.' His clumsy hand takes hers, bobs it up and down.

'No wonder you threw all of Ava's things into the fire. Even that didn't make me start talking about her though.'

'I'm not having that.' He squeezes her hand. 'What I did was terrible. You didn't push me to it. I did it, not you.'

She looks over at Freddie lying on the hospital bed. As messy as last night was, being away from here for a few hours has built a space inside her and she can breathe again. She thinks back to the long summer holidays before Freddie was born. If she was cranky, the boys' moods followed suit. If she was tired, they reflected that back at her, and sat around watching television, lethargic, yawning. Perhaps Freddie's behaviour has been mirroring hers. She could be better; she could make Freddie better. She takes Matteo's other hand.

'I really do love him,' she says.

'And what about Willow? How do you feel about her now?'

She can feel her forehead crinkling, and he stares at her. Pressure builds in her throat. 'She's a stranger to us really. She doesn't even like me.' She gives a half-hearted laugh. 'Even if we wanted to have contact with her, however that would work, there's the distance; there's what it would do to us all.'

'I don't think I can walk away from her, Tess.'

'But we have to, we have to go home.'

He pulls her to him and the whole of her body gives, her tense neck, her tight jaw. And she stands there, letting him take the weight of her, rocking her gently, and fighting the urge to fall asleep on her feet.

Chapter 41

Annie pushes her way into the shop, wind chimes sounding, her pictures wrapped in a garbage sack stuffed beneath her arm. Christy's behind the counter, filing a nail.

'Hi there, Annie,' she says, her breath sending the smoke from the incense stick on the counter sideways.

Annie tries to smile. 'I thought Judy was in today.'

'She had to take off. Her mother's in that care home. Cody was around to look after Tiger, so I thought why not take another shift?'

The space is a jungle of knick-knacks – tie-dye sarongs on hangers dangle from the ceiling, crystals on chains. Every available space is packed with soap dishes, picture frames, and necklaces made from shells. Classical music floats in from the archway leading through to the gallery space.

Christy puts down her nail file. 'I still can't get over it, that Willow walked out in the middle of the night. It must have taken years off your life.'

'Thanks for helping.'

'That's what friends are for, darlin'. Anyhow, what have you got there?'

She comes out from behind the counter, teetering on stilettos.

'They're not very good,' says Annie and laughs raucously, nervously.

'Are you planning on exhibiting?' Bulging, interested eyes.

The only thing Annie's ever exhibited is her left breast when a particularly strong wave dislodged it from her bathing suit last year.

'It's probably not good enough, it's probably—'

'Come on, let me see.' Christy is pressing her hand around the perimeter of the pictures now. 'Don't be shy. I like a nice watercolour.'

Annie lets Christy take the bag, and she is there on the floor then, uncovering both of the pictures: the Native American with the pipe, and the kingfisher.

'Oh,' says Christy. 'They're abstracts, right?'

'I guess you could call them that.'

'Woo.' Christy stretches out the word, shakes her head. 'I can't quite figure them out.'

'I'll bring them back when Judy's in.' Annie tries to snatch up the pictures.

'No, wait!' says Christy. 'I think . . . yeah, I can see it now, the bird, the person. These are really different, Annie. How did you even make them?'

'With little pieces of paper.'

'You never mentioned you did stuff like this.'

'It's a pastime is all; nothing important.'

Christy pushes herself to standing, the canvases in her hands. 'Why are you even wasting time at that publishing company, when you can do this?'

'It's the money . . .'

'Yeah, I know, especially when you've got little ones. One.' She swallows. 'Well, you leave these right here with me. I'm going to show them to Judy as soon as she's back.'

The bell over the door chimes and a group of shoppers descend, a jostle of bum bags and coloured visors.

'I'll leave you to it then,' says Annie. 'And thanks.'

She walks through the arch to the gallery – gold frames, splotchy watercolours of flowers, a pencil drawing of a wood stork, portraits, nothing remotely ground-breaking about any of them, but maybe Christy will be able to talk Judy round. Annie weaves her way back through to the shop.

'That is your work?' says a woman in a velour tracksuit, pointing at the quilled Native American.

'Yeah,' says Annie, regarding the forest of trainered feet.

'Well, that is just so good.'

'Thanks,' says Annie. The temperature dial on her cheeks turns up to full.

'You want to buy it?' asks Christy.

'Oh, honey, that wouldn't fit in my suitcase,' says the velour woman.

Annie pushes her way out of the shop, looking back through the window, but the sun is glancing off the glass, and she can't see in. Someone buying those pictures is fantasy. It's going to be impossible for Annie to step out of her money-tight life into one where she can see Freddie regularly, not until the compensation comes through anyway. But after what happened the other day, Tess might not be so eager to build a connection now.

Half an hour later, Annie climbs the steps to the office, cigarette smoke enveloping her as she opens the inner door and shuffles between the columns of books. A cigarette is burning in an over-flowing ashtray, the desk strewn with pens and ring-bound notebooks. There's a mug of coffee with a skin on top.

'That you Bob?' The door to the ladies' room is ajar.

Roz rushes out of it, the buttons of her beige jumpsuit in the wrong holes, so that the collar doesn't quite meet, the crotch of the fabric carving her nether regions in two.

'Frida Kahlo returns.'

Roz clearly hasn't noticed Annie's unibrow is gone. 'Here I am.'

Roz sidles over to her desk, starts lifting papers and dumping them down.

'I want you to work on the cover for that book. The synopsis is here, and I've written a brief. It's an autobiography about what it was like to drive a Greyhound bus for twenty years.'

Annie walks over to the desk as Roz tokes on her cigarette, smoke gushing from her mouth. Annie fans the air with the synopsis. In an office chair as large as a throne, Roz presses her nose up against the computer screen, muttering.

Annie opens a window and sits at the desk furthest away from Roz. She brings up Pinterest and types the word 'bus'. A pink Winnebago appears then a picture of two kids sitting in an outdoor play bus, both in duffle coats.

Tess isn't replying to Annie's texts. She called at the villa, but no one answered. They must have been in since the car was outside. She knocked faintly at first, then thundered her fist on the door, but still no one came.

She needs to know how Freddie is doing, but they might leave without telling her. She Googles the name Tess Rossi and several links come up. She clicks onto one of them, but it's not Tess. She tries another, but still no luck. She opens a Facebook link.

It's her. *Happiness is . . . Florida.* A photograph of the family on the pier, Tess smiling into the camera, Matteo's arm draped around her. Annie scrolls down, more pictures. *Family Adventures.* A photograph of Matteo paddle boarding with an arm-banded Freddie kneeling on the back. There's a picture of Willow and Freddie too, that one Tess took of them that day at the pool, captioned *My Water Babies.* Oh, please. Annie scrolls down. Bright white smiles, and poses, exclamation marks. It should be called Facebook fiction.

'Er, earth to Frida. Come in, Frida.'

'What?'

'I'm not paying you to stare into space.' Roz starts to cough.

Annie clicks back onto Pinterest and tries to focus. Scrolling through the pictures, she settles on the interior of a battle-worn bus, the windows missing. She finds a picture of the back of an elderly man's head, and tries to blend them somehow.

Roz opens a letter, tuts then stuffs her hand into the Marlboro Light packet, but it's empty. She gets up, the chair spinning backwards on its wheels, colliding with a stack of books, and almost toppling sideways.

'I'm going to lunch,' says Roz.

She heaves her handbag onto her shoulder, and the door with the safety glass slams behind her. Annie glances at the time in the corner of her computer. 11.30 a.m.

A short while later, a delivery man bustles through the door, grunting, a cardboard box in his hands, sweat dripping down his forehead. He drops the box to the floor, pulls a folded square of paper out of his back pocket. 'Is there a Miss Rosalind Shields here?'

'I'll sign for it,' says Annie, clambering out of her seat and dragging the pen across the signature line of his electronic terminal.

The man leaves. Through a rip in the box, she can see the spines of books. She strips the tape off the top, and pulls one out. *It's a Funny Old Life* by *Tom Pearson*. She winces at the colours and thinks of what it could have been. She turns a page.

For my family . . .

Even though Annie has opened the windows to their full capacity, the place is still thick with the stench of smoke. She sniffs her clothes; the mothball smell of her turquoise dress has been replaced by eau du cigarette.

She thinks of the hike in their rent, of Carl's sullen face whenever he opens his payslip, of Susan telling them it could take years for the clinic to pay out. Then she thinks of Tom's weathered, silvery face and him saying, 'I'm on borrowed time now.'

She rushes copies of the book into a carrier bag, a corner of one of them poking through the torn plastic. Picking up a pen, she scribbles on the first piece of paper that comes to hand. 'I'm not coming back.' She signs her name, props it in front of Roz's computer and marches down the stairs, the books thwacking against her leg as she goes.

Annie drives over to Tom's place. There are more cars than usual in the carpark, and as she clips towards the pink-pillared porch, she sees a van with a flashing rectangular light across the front, an ambulance.

She fights her way out of the car, and breaks into a run, the handle of the bag containing the books yawning wider. She reaches the ambulance doors and looks at the man strapped onto a gurney in the back with an oxygen mask over his face. The hair is white not grey, the face short rather than long.

A paramedic in a grey uniform is standing beside the man. 'It's alright, Herb. We're going to look after you,' he says, slamming the doors.

The handle of the plastic bag breaks and two of the books slap onto the concrete. The ambulance careers away, the light on top of it spinning and flashing.

What if Tom had died and things between them had paused on that moment when the flimsy version of her and her mother had disintegrated? He and Marie had looked after her, but instead of thanking him she'd marched away. If they hadn't looked after her, she would have been taken into care, adopted maybe. Her life would have followed different twists and turns, and none of them would have led to Willow.

She pushes the books back into the bag, puts it under her arm and makes her way inside. Looking at the diamond grates of the half-open elevator door, an image of herself stuck inside it refuses to be sidelined. She opens the doors anyway and steps in, putting deep breaths between herself and the panic. Rising up and up, the metal juddering, her neck is clenched and the motion is pulling at her insides. She climbs out and click-clacks towards Tom's front door.

'Hello there, stranger,' he calls as she pushes open the door.

She peeps in, and he's sitting there in the lounge, his feet in brown slippers. 'How did you know it was me?'

'Recognised those footsteps.' His face looks drawn.

'They took Herb away in an ambulance,' she says.

'Herb's like the Bionic Man – they'll just put another piece of metal inside him, keep him going for a bit longer.'

She sits on the arm of his chair, puts her arm around him and lays her head on top of his.

'You're still here then,' she says.

'Parts of me are disappearing every day, my teeth, my memory, my goddamn reading glasses, but I'm still here.'

'I brought you these,' she says, unleashing a book from the bag and sitting on the pouffe.

'It would have looked a whole lot better with that cover of yours,' he says.

She follows his gaze to the marble mantel where her more ambitious cover is propped next to the photographs, and the prints she did as a kid.

'You smell like smoke,' he says. 'You've got to get out of that place before she makes you ill.'

'Yeah, well, I just quit.'

He takes in her set jaw, and smiles. 'I'm glad.'

'I'm sorry I haven't been to see you.'

His fingers tap-tap the arm of the chair. 'You went back to that clinic, didn't you?'

She averts her gaze and nods. 'The test showed that Willow isn't our biological child.'

'Well, to hell with biology. Willow's yours – it doesn't matter what any test says.'

Guilt pushes against her chest. 'I shouldn't have gone off at you like that.'

He puffs out air. 'We should have told you before; I should have told you.'

She looks at his baggy jowls trembling. 'We thought about it often enough. Course, Nancy asked us not to tell you, but in the end we didn't keep quiet because of her; we thought it would hurt you if you knew. And then Nancy died, and what would have been the point in telling you then? It seemed like it was too late.'

'I've been trying to create this perfect family to make up for me and Mom, and now . . . Lord, it's all such a mess.' She gives a thin smile.

He keeps his eyes trained on her and shifts in his seat.

'There's a boy,' she says. 'His name is Freddie, and he's ours, well, my egg, Carl's . . .' *She will not say that word again in front of Tom.* 'He looks like Carl, a little bit like me.' She lets out a breath.

'You don't want to give up on him, right?'

'No.'

'So don't.'

'But the boy's mother – well she's Willow's mother really – she's been acting like a crazy person, and I said some terrible things to her.'

'You can come back from this.'

'I'm not sure I can.' She laces her fingers together.

'This kid, and Willow, they're both going to want to know eventually, hell they need to know. Think about the way you felt when you found out Nancy had left you. This is no secret any of you can keep.' He clasps the arm of the chair.

'But they live so far away, in *England*; it's going to be impossible to see them very often, if she wants to see me at all after what I said.'

'Well, even if she doesn't, you keep knocking. You've got to keep the lines of communication open.'

She takes out her cell phone and looks at it, but there's no new text messages, no new missed calls.

'Feel like a walk in the grounds?' she asks.

'I'll take the elevator,' he says, smiling and trying to push himself out of the seat. 'See you at the bottom.'

'Who said I was taking the stairs?' She winks at him, puts one arm around him, a hand beneath his shoulder blade and helps him to his feet.

Chapter 42

Annie knocks on the front door of the villa, and waits. She can hear them splashing around in the swimming pool, one of the boys laughing.

'That's not fair!' shouts Matteo.

How can they go anywhere near that swimming pool after what happened? She looks down at her knees, dry and tight beneath the plasters that are lifting in places, a corner curling. She should have put a longer dress on.

She knocks again. 'Hello!' she calls.

Nothing. She breathes in, forces her shoulders back and down, and tries the handle. The door gives. The air is thick as if someone is standing inside the room, some faint agitation on the hairs of her arms. Her sunshine-filled eyes adjust to the shade of the inside and she starts as she notices Tess standing there in a yellow dress, her hair lank and greasy, one of her arms held horizontal across her belly.

'Oh, I'm sorry, I . . .'

Tess bunches a clump of her dress in her hand. 'We can't see each other anymore,' she blurts.

'Look, I know I went overboard,' says Annie. 'I shouldn't have said those things.'

'But they were true, apart from me taking Willow.' The words come quietly.

'I was pulled apart by worry; I hadn't slept, and after the way you'd been following me around, I jumped to conclusions.'

'You think I'm someone who'd take a child.'

'No. I know that you had nothing to do with it, that Willow found her way here on her own.'

'You don't know me at all.' Tess' nostril is flickering. She's staring at the floor. There's a shout and laughter from outside. She gathers some more fabric in her hand and wrings it. 'We shouldn't have come. I thought that by coming over here we could resolve this quicker. Clearly we can't resolve it at all.'

A breeze sets the blinds on the French doors in motion.

'Yes, we can,' says Annie. 'I want to work this out. For Freddie's sake, for all our sakes. I want to be part of his life.'

'You were right what you said,' says Tess. 'I am nothing to Willow, just as you are nothing to Freddie. I'd been deluding myself that there was some hidden meaning to all of this when it causes nothing but pain for everyone involved.'

Annie steps towards Tess. She can feel the blood descending from her face to her chest and down into her toes. 'It doesn't have to be like that.'

'Anything could have happened to Willow last night,' says Tess, folding her arms. 'She could have been hit by a car, been snatched by some stranger, and that would have been my fault. I was the one that took that teddy bear.'

Annie stretches out her hand then drops it back by her side.

'All of this, it's just hurting everyone,' continues Tess. 'Seeing each other is a constant reminder of what we've all lost. I've got to focus on Freddie from now on. I need to put my head back together for his sake. Staying in contact will chip away at all of us.'

'Please don't do this.' Annie touches the tips of her fingers together.

'Willow belongs to you,' says Tess. 'And Freddie is ours. To think anything else would be delusional. And God knows I've been deluding myself for long enough.'

'We can work this out, we have to. Please. I mean you said you were here for a few weeks, we can see each other again.'

'We're leaving in the next couple of days. Together.' Tess is breathing hard, her non-existent bosom heaving.

Annie could go on begging Tess, she could take hold of her hands and squeeze them into a prayer, but she doesn't. 'We'll push for a contact order. We'll demand to see him.'

Tess takes a step backwards.

'I want to see him, I want to keep seeing him.' Annie's eyes start to fill.

Tess turns her head away.

'We have rights,' says Annie, putting a hand on her hip and lifting her chin. A tear splashes off the end of her nose.

'What rights do any of us have in this situation?' asks Tess, her voice trembling. 'What is the right thing to do?'

'Not this, not cutting contact altogether. We'll have to tell the kids eventually, and what if Freddie wants to see me when he's older? You won't be able to stop him. I won't be able to stop Willow either. Don't we owe it to them both to have some kind of contact? You can't pretend this didn't happen. Jesus, I know I can't.'

Tess bangs a fist to the flat line of her determined mouth.

Annie wants to be able to twirl Freddie around, and kiss his tiny nose. She wants to be able to laugh at some of the funny things he'll say. She wants to be the one to bury his milk teeth beneath his pillow for the fairy to spirit away; to teach him to write his name, but those things were never hers to do. At least she would have been in the fringes though. Sending him gifts, talking to him via Skype. Because it's not clear cut that Willow is Annie's and Freddie belongs to Tess. It's much more slippery than that.

'Is Freddie alright? Have the doctors said anything more?' asks Annie.

'They still suspect epilepsy, but they haven't diagnosed anything yet.'

'Please let me see him,' says Annie.

'Look at you, you're upset,' says Tess. 'I don't want him upset too.'

Annie can feel the tears rivering down her face. A sound like a creak escapes from her throat. She goes back through the still-open front door, down all twenty five of the steps, dropping her car key then bending to reclaim it with her shaking hands.

'Come on, my boy, there's nothing to be afraid of!' Matteo shouts.

And then Annie is up at the fence, positioning her eye over a gap. The water is sloshing and there is Freddie dipping a tentative toe into the pool, Matteo's hand around his ankle.

Any fool would know it's too soon for that, thinks Annie. 'Huh!' The sound shoots out of her like a sneeze. She looks up at the villa and sees that the slats of a blind are parted, slender fingers slotted through. The fingers snatch away then, and the slats fall back into place.

Chapter 43

Tess watches Matteo's moccasin on the accelerator and leans her head against the glass. His hands are white-tight on the wheel, his upper lip almost entirely covered in cold sores now. A hotelier. How she'd orated that word at dinner parties she'd thrown. The lace tablecloths, the good wine, the guests surrounded by all those family pictures - no one suspecting the fissures. It feels a long time ago that she was that person, dedicating so much time to place settings and painting herself with make-up.

The sat nav counts up the kilometres. They'll be gone from here soon. The spaced-apart wooden houses roll by, a wooden anchor fixed to one, a criss cross of oars on another. An orange towel dotted with dolphins hangs across the parapet of a second floor balcony, lifting and flapping in the breeze. One of the boys burps.

'Luca!' snaps Matteo. The hunch in his back is a shelf she could lay a cup on.

She looks down at her fingernails, the shiny pink polish ragged around the edges; she picks a fleck off. There's a line hooked to her heart and it's pulling her back; she's being fished out of herself, but this is the only way. Maybe she should write a note to Willow, send it to Annie's lawyer. *To be opened when you're sixteen. You started off as my child, and how we'd planned for you. And even though you've been far away, I have loved you. I love you still.*

The tarmac is a fat black line with ocean at either side of it. Power lines skewer the sky. She closes her eyes and feels the rise and fall of the road. The journey passes, and eventually they are in the grounds of the airport.

'Car Rental Returns, which way?' asks Matteo.

Phoenix leans forward, his hand brushing the back of Tess' neck. 'Go right, Dad!'

The wheels nick the grass verge as Matteo negotiates the fork in the road. Then they are under the darkness of the concrete-covered car park and Matteo is heaving the suitcases from the boot. A man comes out of a prefabricated hut and starts walking around the car, examining it for damage. That's when Tess notices a dent in the bonnet as well as a thin scratch. The man's eyes don't linger on it though. He ticks his clipboard and walks back into the hut, Matteo following. Phoenix has a single earphone jammed into his ear, the wire of the other earphone dangling. He taps his foot. Freddie is crouching, his fingers reaching towards a forgotten purple hairband on the concrete. Around them, people wheel cases, the cars navigate their way into bays. Freddie squeezes the hairband between his fingers.

'Leave that, Freddie,' she says, her voice soft. He carries on examining it.

'Dirty,' she says and unlocks his fingers. The hairband falls to the ground. She goes into the hut where Matteo is leaning against a counter looking at forms.

'That's fine, Mr Rossi. If you could sign here,' says the man, behind a counter now.

Then they are walking through glass doors and rising up in a lift. They step out into the bustle and noise of the terminal. Tess checks her tickets. There are snaking queues and it's impossible to pick up speed because of all the milling people.

Freddie is straddling his blue Trunki case. 'Look!' he says pointing.

There, walking towards them, are Annie and Willow, Annie a lolloping thing, her swollen leopard-print bag on her shoulder, a black bin liner in her other hand. When Willow sees Freddie she waves. Tess doesn't want any more images of Willow to add to the ones already embossed in her head. She looks at Matteo who pushes a tiny, flattened tube of coldsore cream into his pocket.

'How did you know we were here?' he asks.

'I went back to the villa again – all your stuff was gone from outside,' says Annie. 'It was a long shot that I'd catch you, but I need to know how Freddie is doing?'

Matteo inches forward, stands in front of Tess. 'He's . . . well, we just have to be vigilant.'

The flight. What if he fits in the air?

'I'm sorry about the ash,' says Annie.

'It doesn't matter,' says Tess. And yet it does, the last specks of Ava sunk into a place where she least wanted her to be. Her real baby, not this little girl standing here in a grubby pink dress, her hair plaited into two ropes. Perhaps it's a good thing that Willow let that ash go since it's given Tess a reason to feel differently about her.

'We better get to the desk,' says Tess.

'We can't leave things like this,' says Annie, keeping pace with Tess, her head craning to its furthest reach as she looks up at her.

'This isn't really the place,' says Matteo, looping his arm around Tess' waist.

'But what about them?' asks Annie, pointing to the children. Willow is doing her best to pull Freddie's case along, with him on top of it. 'And us?'

'We don't know what's ahead of us, what's ahead of Freddie,' says Tess. 'I told you, I want to focus on him.'

'Let me help.'

'You're going to be five thousand miles away,' says Tess.

Matteo clears his throat. 'Look, I'm sure we can work something out. Just not right now.'

'Let's get in the queue,' says Phoenix.

'Here,' says Annie, thrusting a wrinkled piece of paper into Matteo's hand.

'It's my email address, my cell phone number. Please, I can't deal with not seeing Freddie again, not knowing how he's doing. And Willow – she should know you too.'

Tess hears Willow choo-choo-ing and turns to look at the child, who is still trying to pull Freddie along on his suitcase, her face animated by a smile. Luca gets behind Freddie and gives the suitcase a shove. Matteo whips something from his wallet. It slaps to the floor, face-up and redundant – *The Rossi-Perry: Kensington.*

He bends, the pouch of his stomach filling his shirt. 'Oh, Christ,' he says, hand flat to the small of his back.

'Come on, we have to get to the desk,' says Tess.

'Pass me one of my painkillers, will you?' asks Matteo.

Tess riffles in her bag, her fingers brushing the empty blister pack. 'I can't seem to find them, darling.'

He tuts.

'This is for you,' says Annie, pushing the black carrier bag towards Tess.

Tess doesn't want to take whatever it is, but she does. She pulls the plastic off. There's a canvas in front of her, coiled ribbons of paper stuck to it – a face with brown eyes, teardrop-shaped nostrils, a cascade of hair made from papery loops and circles and lines. Willow's face.

I don't want this, she thinks. 'I can't take this,' she says.

'Yes you can.' Annie delves into her handbag and brings out a pair of scissors and a roll of parcel tape. She takes the picture from Tess, clambers to the floor and kneels.

'Oh my God,' shrieks a woman in high heels as she trips over Annie's calves.

'Sorry,' says Annie, putting up an apologetic hand.

She covers the picture with the bin liner again and winds the tape around.

'We can't take that on board,' says Matteo, counting the passports yet again. 'It won't survive the hold.'

'The amount of PVA I put on that thing, it better,' says Annie.

'We should go,' says Tess. 'Come on Freddie, we need to check in.'

Freddie turns then, a twisted expression on his face. He moves towards Annie and she crouches and puts her hands on his shoulders and says something to him that Tess can't hear.

'I'm sowee for the dust,' a little voice says.

Tess turns to Willow. 'You don't need to be sorry. I'm the one that's sorry. I should have given you your bear back.'

She bends and looks at the girl closely, the dash of pink felt-tip pen on her cheek, the gap between her incisors, then Tess remembers the hair slide still in a pocket of her bag. She finds it, and secures it in Willow's hair, and it's like someone is lancing her heart. She straightens her back and stands. She pats Willow's head, the hair soft beneath her fingers, and takes in the little toes sticking out of her battered sandals. 'Goodbye now,' she says.

Annie's eyes are wet, her chin wobbling as she releases Freddie from a hug.

Tess shuts the feel of Willow's hair into her hand to keep it there. Annie hugs Tess, her arms clamped around her so tight it's as if this barrel-shaped woman is trying to lift her right off the floor. Tess tries to break her folded arms free and fails. Eventually Annie lets Tess go, and taps both her hands against Tess' arms as if she's trying to rearrange her.

Tess is aware of Annie and Willow moving away now. Freddie lifts his hand up to wave and leaves it there, and Tess keeps her eyes fixed on him, trying not to see the shapes of the woman and the girl growing blurry and more distant in her peripheral vision.

Part Three

Chapter 44

Six months later

i

Surrey, England

Matteo slaps through the living room in a pair of tartan slippers as Tess pulls another handful of books from a cardboard box. Jenna is on her knees, unwrapping tissue paper from packages.

'Do you want a cup of tea?' asks Matteo, his chin peppered with stubble.

'Please,' says Jenna.

'Me too,' says Tess.

He disappears into the lean-to kitchen with the mouldy bathroom beyond. Freddie, on the sofa, turns another page of his book, a bruise on his head where he fell on the tiles of their old house while suffering a seizure last month. A goose egg had risen on his forehead. He'd suffered three days of drop seizures, falling to the floor without warning, one seizure after another. There was no jerking, no movement at all after the sudden loss of consciousness, only the fluttering of eyelashes then he woke, exhausted every time. There was nothing for a week then they started again. The doctors think he has a rare syndrome called Doose, but they haven't made a formal diagnosis yet. They're slowly withdrawing one of the drugs he is taking, and introducing another. He has been seizure free for a week, but then he's been seizure free before. After falling into the swimming pool, Freddie didn't have another episode for two months.

'Are you alright, love?' Tess asks Freddie, planting herself beside him, and kissing the top of his head, his delicate head.

'When can I go back to nursery?'

'We need to make sure you're better first.'

She finger combs his glossy curls. She looks about the room, piled high with cardboard boxes, some of them unpacked, swathes of tissue paper here and there. The room smells of boiled cauli-flower.

Matteo comes back into the room and lifts Freddie. 'Do you want to help me make a smoothie?'

'Okay,' says Freddie. And they disappear through the narrow doorway into the kitchen.

'Is he still drinking?' asks Jenna in a lowered voice.

'Not as much.'

'It probably didn't help that I went on at him about what he did to Ava's things,' says Jenna. 'I can't believe you didn't tell me.'

'If I didn't tell you, I could almost pretend it didn't happen.'

'But you could have told *me*.'

'It was bad enough everyone not knowing how to treat me because my baby had died. Imagine if I'd thrown Matteo's pyro-technics into the mix.'

Jenna's forehead pleats. Tess looks away. She wants to move on; God knows, she's had enough of wallowing, and speaking about it once a week for an hour to Natasha at her psychotherapy practice is more than enough time spent on the past. 'Can we talk about Willow?' Natasha had asked. 'Not yet,' Tess had replied.

'Anyway what do you make of our new pad?' Tess asks Jenna. Jenna pulls a face.

'Come on, you need vision,' says Tess.

'That's what she said to me!' calls Matteo from the kitchen. 'We need a bloody bulldozer more like.'

Tess laughs. The kettle starts to boil. Tess unpacks some more books and piles them on top of a wonky shelf. The memory box is already there gathering dust. Beyond the rotten sash window, the broken-up driveway is partially covered by a skip, weeds splintering around it.

'Admittedly it's a mess,' says Tess. 'But we can change that. Well, eventually.'

'And how's the job?'

'I'm not doing as much.'

'But Matteo's around now,' says Jenna. 'He can look after the kids.'

'Actually I've taken on a new assistant.'

Matteo comes in, mugs of tea slopping in his hands.

'Equal partner,' he says.

'You two are working together?' says Jenna, screwing up her face as if this is one of the most disgusting things she's ever heard.

'Well, yes, Matteo's doing some of the campaigns; that way we're able to share looking after the children and working.'

'But you said you'd end up killing Matteo if you had to spend all day with him.'

'Thanks for that,' says Matteo, passing over the tea.

'Turns out it's not that bad,' says Tess.

'What about the hotel?'

'We've found a buyer,' says Matteo. 'So that'll pay off some of the debts. I've got a plan to repay the others, but it's going to take ages.'

Tess unloads the rest of the packages from the box and starts breaking it down with a trainered foot. Matteo goes back into the kitchen.

Jenna opens another box and digs in, clutching something rectangular and covered in plastic. 'What's this?'

'Oh, leave that. It's for the loft.'

There's the sound of slicing from the kitchen, of lids being pulled off and set down. Jenna unwraps the parcel and looks at the picture inside. A thin sliver of paper falls off it and curls onto the carpet. Recognition settles into her face.

'This is Willow, isn't it?' says Jenna. 'That picture you posted on Facebook ages ago, it's like her.'

Tess doesn't want to look at it; she doesn't want to touch it. She snatches up the plastic and gives it back to Jenna, hoping she'll cover the picture up again.

'You should put it up,' says Jenna.

'God, no.'

'Did the mum do it?'

Tess gets up and whips the picture out of Jenna's hands. She pulls open the front door and steps out over the concrete. All the junk that they found in the loft is piled in the skip, broken chairs and saucepans, and a folded carpet damp and stippled with dust. There's a tabby cat on it, clawing and purring.

A man is keying the lock next door while vaping.

'Alright, love?' A gush of smoke.

'Hello there.'

She looks at the picture. She isn't ruthless when it comes to the children's art, stacking it under furniture, pressing it into boxes, but she doesn't want a picture of this.

'Poor old Madge; she had a terrible time at the end,' says the man, his scalp shiny beneath his sparse pale hair.

'I beg your pardon?'

'Madge, pegged it in the living room. Was there for days before anybody found her.'

'Oh.'

'I don't believe in ghosts. I hope you don't neither.'

She takes a deep breath, and drops the picture into the skip with a clatter. The cat jumps onto the side of the skip, the fur on its tail standing on end, then it's gone.

'No, I don't believe in ghosts,' says Tess.

She goes back inside and shuts the front door behind her with a click.

'What did you do?' asks Jenna, still on her knees.

Tess folds her arms.

'You can't shut that child out,' says Jenna. 'She could track you down in the future; she's bound to want to meet you. And what are you going to do when she turns up – say that you just gave up on her, that you moved on?'

'I'm focusing on Freddie.'

'But this other family, they could take you to court over this. You could really piss them off, they could push for custody, or some kind of contact at least.'

'They're not like that.'

'Well, from what you've told me, you don't know all that much about them. They could do anything.'

'I know enough.'

Tess opens another box, this one full of her old clothes, slippery black trousers, a checked grey shirt. Stuffed down the side is a sheaf of papers. She pulls them out and sees that it's old sheet music for her cello. The weighty, sonorous strings start up in her head. She smoothes out a ripple in one of the pieces of paper. You take parts of yourself with you, she thinks, and leave others behind. She shuts the box containing the clothes and puts the sheet music onto the carpet, her multi-coloured bangle swivelling back down towards her wrist.

'So you haven't heard from them, the other couple?'

'They've been in touch with our lawyer, asking questions about Freddie. We sent a recent photograph, a few other details, told them about the possible diagnosis.'

'Surely they'll want more than that?'

'We're thousands of miles away. They can't afford to fly over here, and obviously we can't go there, not now.'

'You'll be able to once the clinic settles though.'

'Our lawyer's rejected their initial offer.'

'They should shut the bloody place down,' calls Matteo.

Jenna's mobile phone alerts her to a text message. She pulls it out of her back pocket and reads. 'Oh, shit, I completely forgot. I was meant to pick up Ruby from a playdate half an hour ago.'

She leaps to her feet, and Tess follows her to the front door.

'No, no,' Jenna sweeps a hand through the air. 'Don't bother to see me out. You're busy.' She plants kisses on both of Tess' cheeks, slamming the front door behind her.

Chapter 45

Florida, USA

Annie slices the letter open with her finger and reads: *On this occasion, your application has been unsuccessful.*

She sits on the rickety staircase, the breeze lifting her hair then dumping it down. That's the third rejection in the space of two weeks. A mosquito does a loop the loop of her head; she flaps her hand to no avail, rips the letter in half then makes confetti from the two sides. *Has been.*

She feels flattened out by staying at home, lonely. When Judy said her artwork wasn't the right fit for the gallery, Annie went to seven other spaces, but not one of them invited her to show her work. She asked at Crystal's Cake Shop, saying she could create some pictures of cupcakes, a Victoria sponge perhaps, but Tanzy who works behind the counter said. 'It's not like there's any room.' And there wasn't, every available space on the wall packed with ornamental plates. If they could just move away from here, her chances of employment might multiply, but then Carl wouldn't have his swimming pool job anymore. Tom's offered to help, but there's no way she's going to let him. He's done enough for her already.

Their apartment is up for sale now, a board poked into the ground outside like it was before Christy moved away. They're going to have to find a new place to rent. 'We could always move in with Lina for a while,' suggested Carl, and Annie laughed, then said, 'No.'

She stands, and her skirt drifts down to her hips. She's lost weight even though she's been putting away more chocolate than a kid at Christmas. Forget the thin-thong diet, she's been following the maxi-stress, melt-away-fat one.

She goes inside, puts the fragments of paper onto the table. A princess clip-clops towards her, nylon curls cascading over her shoulders, a satin pink dress and tiny toes sticking out of Annie's platforms.

'Hello der!' says Willow.

'Great outfit.'

Willow stomps over to the basket of toys and starts unloading the wooden fruit.

Annie switches on her computer, and opens her emails. Nothing new from Tess and Matteo. She's only had two emails delivered via their attorney and they haven't asked about Willow, even though Annie's sent several photographs. Tess seems to have deleted her Facebook page – either that or she's using privacy settings now. Annie's thought about telling Susan to push for a contact order, but she keeps waiting and hoping. She doesn't want to alienate the Rossis even more. And what is Freddie to her anyway – a son, a relative, a person who she hopes one day might be able to sit with her without ceremony and just be? A person who might come into wherever she's living and feel as if it's a second home? Even if the Rossis wanted a form of contact, how much of it could there really be with all the distance between them? And so Annie will go on missing her son, the warmth of his breath, the sound of his voice.

A settlement from the clinic might go some way to reuniting her with him, but Susan has turned down an initial offer, and time is passing, sucking away her son's childhood with it. If the clinic doesn't settle by the end of the year, Susan will initiate court proceedings to sue, but that could take years.

If that embryologist had confessed earlier when Annie was pregnant, would she have had a termination? Would she have carried on to the end and swapped Willow back? Could she have brought herself to do any of those things?

Annie stares at the computer screen littered with folders, a lit-up picture of Willow in the background. There's still no word from that other company she interviewed for – designing brochures for holiday lets. Her inbox is empty. She looks at the three emails in her junk folder. *Sexy Brazilian Brides.* Delete. *You've Won a Prize.* Delete. This next one looks suspicious too, but her fingers click it open anyway. She reads the first paragraph and rolls her eyes. *As if I'd fall for that.* But she starts reading it again from the top, letting the words land.

This is Tom giving her a sympathy vote, it must be. Perhaps he got one of the care assistants to email on his behalf. She doesn't recognise the sender's name.

She clicks off the email and goes outside, sitting on the stoop again, her stubby red-nail-varnished toes shot out in front of her, the laptop on her thighs.

Motherhood has left her with holes; the guilt about wanting to work, and not being able to, her desperation to see Freddie. Being a mom is nothing like she envisioned: a little house, her brood playing in the garden. Two children, she'd always imagined two, and she thought they'd come easily to her. She looks out into the distance now, the wind lifting the sand on the road and hazing it, the sun making her squint.

She takes the sunglasses propped on top of her head and pushes them onto her nose. She reads the email again through the scratches, turning the brightness of the laptop up to full. It's fanciful and full of spelling mistakes, but maybe, just maybe, it could be the start of a life she thought was lost to her.

Chapter 46

Surrey, England

The rain is pummelling the skylight and gushing in through the edges of the frame. Tess pulls the sloshing bucket from underneath it and puts a basin there instead, pouring the bilge into the sink.

'Matteo!'

She carries on with this filling and swapping for five minutes more, but Matteo doesn't arrive.

'Matteo, the window's leaking!'

With the bucket underneath the leak, she makes for the stairs, rushing past Freddie, her purse open on his knee.

She goes up three stairs and shouts, 'There's water pouring through the roof down here!'

'Why don't we see her any more?' asks Freddie.

She goes back down. 'Who?'

'Willow.'

Footsteps scatter and Matteo falls with a thump, the tread of the stairs too narrow for his size tens. 'Ow!' He blunders into the kitchen, rubbing at his lower back.

His broad shoulders bash either side of the narrow door frame then there's the scrape of things being moved about, water gushing. 'Bloody hell!'

Freddie is holding a small photograph, softened with creases, and surprisingly vibrant for an iPhone picture that for once she's printed up. It was slotted beneath the picture of her boys that sits in the display envelope of her purse.

'I miss her,' he says. 'The lady too.'

She can feel her chin concertina, she who's written several emails to Annie then moved them to trash. All that they've sent the Amstels are officious emails – none of the small details that a parent would want to know about their child. Except that Annie is not Freddie's parent, so what on earth is she supposed to know?

'Tess!' calls Matteo.

There's the sloosh of water being poured into the sink, the laying down of another empty utensil. She stares at the photograph, the only one she took of Willow, Freddie's thumb pressing its centre. She wants to pluck it from his hand and stuff it back into her purse, but she doesn't. She goes on staring then the thought that she's tried so hard to close over is back inside her head and growing unwieldy. *I miss her.* It stays there repeating, so that even if she were to try all those tricks that her counsellor has suggested, no amount of deep breathing could let the words go. The words are not just for Willow, they're for Annie too – her clumsy, colourful self, her habit of speaking too loudly.

Tess has backed this photograph up, put it on a hard drive, emailed it to herself, though she hasn't looked at it again until today. But hasn't she been sequestering it away for later?

The photograph slips out of Freddie's hand then and lands on the couch, face down. His head has dropped forward, hands floppy – he's lost consciousness. He comes round then, and licks his gluey lips. She runs to the kitchen, past Matteo who is still battling with the window and the rain.

'He's fitting,' she says.

'Shit.' He pours a bucketful of water into the sink.

She takes a clean face flannel from the drawer, saturates it with cold tap water then rushes back out and presses the flannel to Freddie's mouth.

He loses consciousness again, the softness of the sofa plump around him. She puts more cushions beneath his head, then he's back and gone again and back and gone.

She sits there with her hand over his and stares at him. And then he's sitting up, his feet on the floor, and for now it seems that it's over.

She irons her fingers across her son's cheek.

'You're alright, it's okay,' she says softly.

He hasn't bitten anyone since his birthday party. She's had a couple of children over, her eyes trained on Freddie in case he had a fall or showed signs of hurting another child. The doctors don't think his erratic behaviour had anything to do with his condition, so she can only conclude that he's changed because she and Matteo have. They're not elsewhere any more, at least not all of the time; they're less consumed by the past.

Matteo comes into the room and stands over them.

'It's alright.' She breathes the words over her son.

Matteo sits beside him, pulling him into a hug, and stroking his hair. And the water throttles onto something hard in the kitchen, cascading, battering, ignored.

The skip is blurred through the rain-patterned glass. The picture that Annie gave her is out there, probably a sodden, spongy mess by now. She climbs to her feet, and opens the front door. The side of the skip is grazed with dirt, warning tape zigzagged across it. She heads towards it, takes a large, splintered wind chime out, and drops it to the concrete with a clack. She keeps taking things out, moving them aside, and the rain drips into her eyes.

When she can't reach any further in, she pulls herself up the metal side, throws a leg over, and tumbles, thudding into the debris. She stands, the detritus slithering beneath her lopsided feet. She sifts through nails and dust, bricks and paper, old telephone books, a rusty wheelbarrow missing a handle. *I'll find you,* she thinks. And she carries on searching, lifting and turning things over, her jumper powdered with dust.

Chapter 47

It's the unveiling today, but there won't be any ribbon cutting or speeches. The park gates will open, the children will come surging in; the first footsteps will fall on this project of Tess' – a play castle with arched windows, and slides. She raised the money for it through crowdfunding.

It didn't look much when the carpenters started, straight wooden rods stabbing the sky, a few horizontal boards slatted into place. The drawbridge slants up to the arching front door.

She spent a long time choosing the right grain for the stairs inside – swirls in one, lines in another, a single knotted eye for the one at the top. There are random letters carved into the wood in places, F and P and L and A. There's even a W – added at the eleventh hour, the carpenter's last day. Geese squall from the lake behind the bushes.

She sits on the grass and stretches her bare feet out in front of her. Freddie appears in one of the arches on the second floor then he's gone again.

'Be careful, love!' she calls.

He hasn't had a seizure for six weeks now, though a 24-hour EEG has shown abnormal activity in his brain during the night, which means he could be fitting when he's asleep. Another drug has been introduced to try to combat this.

She hears the rumble of engines turning over. Five more minutes until the park opens.

Jenna said she'd be here by now, but she hasn't texted. Perhaps she's busy with the event she's organised for tonight, not that

Tess is going. She doesn't want to stand out, doesn't want to rekindle any of the gossip that clung to her after their story hit the headlines. *Hotel Owner Loses Everything.* Tess had opened the front door in her nightdress – the tabloid photographer with the zoom lens camera in his hand. And there she was, the next day, plastered across page six, with her red face and her hair in disarray, the caption running along the bottom: *Wake-up call for wife of failed hotelier.*

She treads over the grass towards the castle, and as she does, two children pass by, one of them climbing up the chute of the slide. Another bends and goes through an opening at the bottom, then there are more children.

Tess feels someone watching her and looks up. Jenna has arrived out of breath.

'Don't be cross,' she says and hooks her thumbs into the belt loops of her jeans.

A woman in a green halterneck dress steps out from behind Jenna, her fingers tucked around the hand of a little girl, fear spread across the child's face. Tess glances at Willow then her eyes collide with Annie's. Annie's hair is trailing past her shoulders now.

'Mummy, look at this,' calls Freddie who comes out of the castle door and sees the new arrivals.

He stands still, his mouth a surprised O and when Willow smiles at him, her face relaxing, her cheeks dimpling, Freddie laughs. Willow lets go of her mother's hand and runs towards him, and together they disappear through the castle door.

Tess looks at Jenna. 'Was this Matteo's idea?'

'It was me who took that picture from the skip,' says Jenna. 'Annie's website was on the back.'

'I'm sorry,' says Annie. 'I shouldn't have turned up like this.'

'Why are you here?' There's a clip to Tess' voice. 'Why would you pay all that money to come over here?'

'Jenna sold some of my pictures.'

Tess feels her lip cinching. 'What?'

'There's no sign of this compensation coming through,' says Jenna. 'So I thought—'

'It was probably a sympathy vote, those people buying my work,' says Annie.

'I wanted to see if I could drum up some interest,' says Jenna. 'I wasn't sure I could, but it turns out people love what Annie's doing. I managed to sell four of her pictures for a decent price.'

You stuck your nose in. You interfered. Tess' thoughts rise and recede. She drags in air through her mouth, then blows out hard. 'It's *your* private view tonight, isn't it?' she asks Annie.

'I wish,' says Annie, and laughs.

'It might be one day though,' says Jenna. 'A dealer from the States is going to be there tonight.'

The wind rushes through the trees like waves hissing.

'The castle looks great,' offers Jenna.

'You built this?' asks Annie, catching Tess' eye again.

'I raised the money to build it.'

Tess' ears are alive with the stamp of small feet, childish voices shouting 'Come on!' and 'Up here!'

She walks over to Annie then and stands a metre away from her, her heart denting her chest, her head shaking.

'I'm glad you ignored what I said.'

'What was that?' asks Annie.

'To stay away from us.'

'Well, I've never been all that good with instruction,' says Annie, a lump of grey chewing gum inside her mouth.

Tess steps closer and hugs Annie. It's an awkward, fumbling embrace, Annie's hair in Tess' mouth, but Tess holds on, and slowly her limbs relax, and settle.

It's Annie who pulls away first. 'I've got to see this for myself,' she says, kicking off her platforms.

'Come on, Mama!' calls Willow from a window, beckoning with her hand.

Annie forces herself through the little door. A child gets stuck halfway down the slide. There's the pop and fizz of a can being opened on one of the picnic rugs cubing the grass. Jenna's phone is ringing, her voice becoming distant as she walks away.

And Tess goes on watching Willow through the window. It's easy to find the version of herself that wanted that little girl so much. The woman that flew thousands of miles for the chance of falling pregnant with her, the woman who stole things to try to get her back, because there's nothing she wouldn't do for her own child.

Tess has tried to give up on Willow, and in doing so, has only given steel to what she feels about her. This love will be painful, she thinks, but if she doesn't let some of it in, she'll destroy herself. She can't imagine ever feeling right about it, but her anger has dissipated and some kind of acceptance is making its slow arrival. She is looser, less private, and because of that, she's becoming more robust. She is not truly this girl's mother, but she wants to be something to her, whatever that is.

She tucks her skirt into her knicker elastic, bends and goes through the low, arched doorway. When she gets to the centre of the castle she grabs the rope dangling from a circular hole at the top.

The grooves of the rope press into her palms as she shimmies up. She closes her eyes, inhales the smell of cut grass, and lets the sound of Willow's claps and yeses pluck at her ears. She moves each of her hands up a notch, and she rises, slowly and painfully, she rises.

Halfway up, she hangs there and looks at the sky as the sun comes out again. She remembers the weight of Ava in her arms and how all those hours had been edited down to a single moment of gazing at a face empty of all possibility.

Freddie and Willow poke their faces over the side of the circular hole and look down at her, Willow's hair hanging, Freddie's bulging cheeks. Would they even be here if Ava had lived?

Everyone collects scars and losses along the way, but new things arrive because of them.

'Keep going!' shouts Willow.

And so Tess does, one hand at a time, but the pressure builds in her fingers. Looking down, she sees there are no children below her, so she lets go of the rope, then stumbles, clattering onto her backside, her hair all over her face.

Freddie stares at his mother, the lines dark around his deep blue irises, complication etched into the curves of his face.

'Are you okay, Mummy?' he asks. Willow moves away.

Tess looks up at her son, the afternoon bright blue behind him.

'Yes,' she says. 'I'll live.'

She stays there smiling for a few seconds more, then rolls onto her side and clambers to her feet.

Epilogue

The Chronicle
Women Receive Compensation for IVF Mix-up

Two women who had the wrong embryos implanted into their uteruses during IVF treatment at an American fertility clinic have agreed to compensation of undisclosed amounts.

The women, who cannot be named for legal reasons, had the IVF at the Pavilion St Michael Clinic in Florida. A British woman, then 41, was mistakenly implanted with the embryo of an American woman. The American woman unknowingly received the British woman's fertilised egg. The British woman's pregnancy resulted in the birth of a live baby boy and the American woman gave birth to a girl.

Mark Ripley, the embryologist responsible for the mix-up, was dismissed from the clinic last year.

Gill Cousins, an American lawyer acting for the British couple, said: 'This has been a harrowing ordeal for the families involved. Though initially devastated by the revelation, both families have shown incredible fortitude and decided not to pursue a lengthy custody battle through the courts.

'Both families intend to continue parenting the child that was born to them while maintaining contact with each other.'

Ripley and his former boss, clinic owner Doctor Philip Michael, are currently being investigated by the Florida Board of Medicine. Doctor Michael refused to comment.

A nurse at the Pavilion St Michael Clinic, who asked not to be named, said, 'It was so busy back then when the couples were treated, chaotic even. I often used to worry that something like this might happen. My heart goes out to the families. Science keeps striding forwards, but what about psychology – where are the guidelines on how to deal with something like this?'

Acknowledgements

I am enormously grateful to everyone who contributed to the creation of this book, particularly to my excellent editors: Kate Howard for taking this book on and steering it in the right direction, and Emma Herdman for being such a star. Thank you to Louise Swannell and Lily Cooper also. It's been a joy working with everyone at Hodder & Stoughton.

To my wonderful agent, Rowan Lawton, I am so grateful for your advice, wisdom and kindness. My appreciation goes to Rachel Mills for taking up the temporary reins with this book, and to Liane-Louise Smith and Lucy Steeds for all that you do for me.

I was lucky enough to talk to Doctor John Webster, one of the doctors who delivered Louise Brown, the first 'test-tube' baby – thank you so much, John, for your thoughts and advice on my story. Professor Judith Daar, Chair of the American Society for Reproductive Medicine Ethics Committee – thank you for so generously sharing your knowledge of reproductive technologies and law – your help was invaluable. Any errors are my own. Thanks to Epilepsy Action for taking the time to answer all my questions.

Love and gratitude to my mum and dad for your belief in me and for influencing this book in so many ways.

Thank you Sara Sarre – always my first reader – your talent in spotting what works and what doesn't is uncanny. You are a teacher as well as a friend.

Massive thanks to my dear friend Anna for reading excerpts of this book, and for your unfailing love and support – you are a continual source of inspiration.

Thanks to Gerry Vincent and Lucille Grant for reading early versions of this book; and to Sue Webster and Emma-Jane Beer for allowing me to pester you with medical questions.

Thank you to all my friends who have listened, cajoled, celebrated and commiserated with me. Particular thanks to Lindi Reynolds, Paola Marioni (I'm still marvelling over that painting), Ruth Hughes and Lizzy Leicester.
Special thanks to my writer friends Claire Douglas and Louise Jensen who understand just what a rollercoaster publishing a book can be.

It really is the most fantastic feeling when readers connect with my writing, so to all the people who have bought my books, left thoughtful reviews and helped spread the word – thank you so much. Many thanks to all the book reviewers and bloggers who have supported me too.

Finally, to my husband Mike and daughter Olivia, thank you for celebrating the highs, listening to the lows, and being there for all the bits in between. You mean the world to me.

Before I began writing this book, I read a great number of newspaper and magazine articles about IVF mix-ups, but I am particularly indebted to the following texts: ' "To Err is Human" – Art Mix-Ups: A Labor-Based Relational Proposal' by Leslie

Bender printed in the Iowa Journal of Race, Gender and Justice, Vol 9, No 3, Spring 2006; and *Inconceivable - A Medical Mistake, the Baby We Couldn't Keep, and Our Choice to Deliver the Ultimate Gift* by Carolyn and Sean Savage.